The Pink Cadillac

Austin Macauley Publishers

London * Cambridge * New York * Sharjah

Copyright © Rebecca Harlem 2024

The right of Rebecca Harlem to be identified as author of this work has been asserted by the author in accordance with sections 77 and 78 of the Copyright, Designs and Patents Act 1988.

All rights reserved. No part of this publication may be reproduced, stored in a retrieval system, or transmitted in any form or by any means, electronic, mechanical, photocopying, recording, or otherwise, without the prior permission of the publishers.

Any person who commits any unauthorised act in relation to this publication may be liable to criminal prosecution and civil claims for damages.

This is a work of fiction. Names, characters, businesses, places, events, locales, and incidents are either the products of the author's imagination or used in a fictitious manner. Any resemblance to actual persons, living or dead, or actual events is purely coincidental.

A CIP catalogue record for this title is available from the British Library.

ISBN 9781035864508 (Paperback)
ISBN 9781035864515 (Hardback)
ISBN 9781035864522 (ePub e-book)

www.austinmacauley.com

First Published 2024
Austin Macauley Publishers Ltd®
1 Canada Square
Canary Wharf
London
E14 5AA

Rebecca Harlem is a New York-based author who enjoys delving into the world of romance and erotica. She was born in 1984 in Rotterdam, Netherlands, to a Spanish mother and Dutch father. She loves to explore the complexities of human relationships and desires through her writing.

Drawing inspiration from her own experiences and the works of literary titans, Rebecca's writing is nothing short of intoxicating. With an unapologetic approach to exploring the darker side of human nature, she fearlessly delves into the taboo and the forbidden, leaving her readers breathless and craving more.

Her debut work *The Pink Cadillac* knows no bounds as she fearlessly explores the depths of human sensuality, leaving an indelible mark on the literary world with her spellbinding story of love, lust, and unbridled desire.

Table of Contents

Book One: The Pink Cadillac	7
Book Two: Su Boleto Al Cielo	25
Book Three: Sailors Without a Compass	63
Book Four: The Ballad of Lily	127
Epilogue	229

Book One
The Pink Cadillac

Chapter 1

It was a lazy Saturday afternoon at Edward A. Thomas building, Police headquarters, Houston, Texas, in the final week of March.

Officer Samuel Theodore, a tall black police officer assigned to the auto theft division, sat in his cabin, holding the most recent edition of Cosmopolitan. He couldn't take his gaze away from the bikini-clad chubby-bottomed cover girl. He was always drawn to fat-bottomed girls. He began to feel a sexual yearning rouse within him. He was not an aggressive person by nature, but rather a bashful one. He didn't chase after his fantasies. Rather, he understood from his own experience that everything he required came to him on its own. That stimulating yearning brought up some unpleasant recollections from his past and filled him with shame. He had had a bad experience with his girl a year ago. The girl simply vanished from his life, as well as from the town. He stuffed the magazine into the drawer and tried to forget about it by tilting his head back in his chair and closing his eyes.

A glamorous blue-eyed young lady in her late twenties, wearing a yellow satin bustier corset dress, stepped out of a cab outside the police headquarters and entered the building. She inquired at the front desk. She was told to go to the third floor by the girl at reception. She climbed to the third floor in the lift.

When the lady knocked on the door of Officer Theo's cabin, he was sitting with his eyes closed.

"Please come in," Officer Theo said aloud.

"Good afternoon, Officer," said the lady as she walked into the cabin.

"Good afternoon, ma'am. How may I assist you?" Officer Theo pointed his hand toward the chair in front of his desk, asking her to sit down. She sat down and informed the officer that she had come to file a complaint about the theft of her car about half an hour ago.

"I'm sorry for your loss, ma'am. Could you perhaps tell me where exactly it happened?"

"I was having lunch at the Lake Club, and when I came out, it was gone."

"Okay. I need your driver's license information, license plate number, and vehicle identification number to file the complaint. Please jot it down on paper." Officer Theo approached her with a small notepad and a pen. She took the pen and scribbled down all of the necessary information. Officer Theo took the paper from her and began entering the data into his computer. When he retrieved the driver's license information, the computer displayed the lady's picture as well as her name—Scarlett Garcia.

"All right, Miss Garcia, now please tell me the specifics of your vehicle."

"Please call me Scarlett. It's a 10th-generation Cadillac Eldorado convertible. The color is pink."

"It's an older model. How come you're still driving it?"

Scarlett was ready to respond when her phone began to ring inside her bag. She took the phone from her bag and disconnected the call.

"Actually, my late father owned this car. He used to tell me that he bought it soon after his marriage with my mother. He was in Florida at the time. Later, he relocated to Texas, where he grew his business. This was his first car. He bought several more vehicles after that, but this was his favorite. On my 25th birthday two years ago, he gave it to me as a gift."

"Okay. As far as I'm aware, that car's security features are fairly good. To pull this off, the thief must be extremely skilled."

"Officer, I've become exceedingly distracted and absent-minded these days, I believe I left the keys in the ignition."

Officer Theo inhaled deeply.

Scarlett's phone rang once more, and she disconnected it again.

She explained that his boyfriend had called because she had texted him about the theft. Officer Theo offered her coffee, but she refused.

After the formalities were completed, Officer Theo asked for her mobile number so that she could be kept up to date on the status of her pink Cadillac. Scarlett gave Theo her phone number. As she turned to leave, Officer Theo closed his eyes again; he opened them after Scarlett had left the cabin.

Chapter 2

Scarlett walked away from the police station building, pulled out her phone and dialed her Mexican boyfriend, Victor Burgos, while walking down the street. Victor was a partner in a major law firm in Houston. Scarlett had hired the law firm to settle property disputes with her step-siblings after her father, Alonso Barros Garcia, died unexpectedly a year ago without leaving a will. Scarlett began to like Victor after a few meetings with him, and they soon began dating.

"Honey, I was trying to call you," Victor said. "Did you file the complaint?"

"Yes, dear, I was sitting in front of the officer in charge when you called. I'm sorry I didn't answer your call."

"It's all right, honey. I'm on my way to pick you up. I'll be there right away."

A breeze-blue Bentley Mulliner Bacalar appeared out of nowhere and came to a halt close to Scarlett. Victor smiled at her from behind the windshield. Scarlett admired his smile and curly hair. Victor pressed the accelerator as she sat inside the car. He knew that Scarlett was upset because her car had been stolen. He intended to take Scarlett to his house that evening and make her happy by making love to her.

Scarlett and Victor were naked in Victor's bed around six o'clock in the evening. They were passionately kissing each other. Scarlett's eyes were filled with sadness that day. Victor was playing with her hair. Scarlett's left hand was clutching Victor's penis. And she was twisting it as if she were trying to shift gears in her Cadillac. Victor touched Scarlett's lips after pointing his finger to his penis, but she refused to give him a blowjob. He didn't force her because he knew she was upset. Then everything went exactly as Scarlett's wishes. Victor buried his desires in his heart and completely surrendered.

He did it the majority of the time when they made love. But he felt Scarlett was never happy after that. She became sadder than before. They had been together for a long time, but Victor was aware that there was some strange aspect of Scarlett's personality that was still undisclosed to him.

Around 9:00 p.m., Scarlett and Victor were having dinner. Victor himself had prepared Scarlett's favorite enchilada. He persuaded Scarlett to spend the night at his house. Scarlett refused because she wanted to return home. Victor drove Scarlett to her home in his Bentley.

While Victor and Scarlett were enjoying dinner together, Theo was watching TV and sipping beer in his apartment. He turned on MTV and saw some bikini-clad chicks dancing and wiggling their asses to loud dance music. Theo quickly changed the channel. He turned on the Discovery Channel. A documentary on the Museum of Classical Archaeology was being aired, where he saw some ancient Greek and Roman sculptures with naked bums. Then he changed to a news channel where a farmer was displaying a massive butt-shaped watermelon. "Damn," Theo murmured, "why are the asses haunting me these days?" He switched off the television.

***

The next Sunday, Scarlett's maid was cleaning a room that was rarely used. She discovered an antique wooden box containing pictures from Scarlett's school days. She handed it over to Scarlett. Those pictures were captured with a Polaroid camera. Scarlett sat on the couch and began going through the photos one by one. One shot in particular drew her eye. Scarlett couldn't take her gaze away from it. She stared at it for quite some time. Her heart sank with sadness and tears welled up in her eyes. In the background, a vinyl player was playing John Waite's classic song 'Missing You'.

Chapter 3

Five days later, at around 10:00 a.m., Scarlet walked into the city's premier sex shop 'Purple Desire' to purchase a dildo for herself. Officer Theo was patrolling on his bike almost three miles away in a remote area of the city at the same time. Scarlett's eyes were darting around the shelves when an Asian girl approached her.

"Good morning, ma'am. My name is Maria. I am the shop attendant. How can I assist you?"

Scarlett smiled and said that she was seeking an excellent sex toy. "Sure, ma'am," said the girl. "We have representational dildos here on the upper shelf and vibrating ones here on the lower shelf. But if you want double-ended or strap-on, you'll have to go to the other side of the store. Which one do you think you'll prefer, ma'am?" The girl locked her gaze on Scarlett.

Scarlett wasn't sure which one she preferred. She was also perplexed as to why she required one when she already had a boyfriend. She had been on her way to the market to get some groceries when she was drawn here by some strange desire.

Maria realized her customer required some time to make a decision, so she left Scarlett alone and went to the counter. Scarlett walked around the store, looking at various types of toys. Some were made of silicon, while others were made of glass. Scarlett examined the various shapes and sizes of the toys but couldn't decide which one to purchase. Her phone rang while she was in a state of confusion. She thought it was Victor. But it was Officer Theo.

***

Officer Theo was patrolling when he noticed a pink Cadillac parked on the side of the road. He came to a halt, took his diary from his pocket and matched the number. It was the stolen car. He immediately took out his phone and dialed

Scarlett's number. Scarlett picked up her phone. "Good morning, ma'am," Theo said. "This is Officer Theodore. I've got some very good news for you." Scarlett inquired as to what it was. "I've just found your stolen car outside the city," Theo said. "The thief must be close by. I'm confident I'll catch him soon."

Scarlett inquired about his location and stated that she would be there shortly. Scarlett noticed a change in herself after speaking with Officer Theo. That strange desire that compelled her to enter the sex shop vanished. She had lost all interest in the toys she was planning to purchase. She had no idea why this had happened. Was it because of the information Officer Theo shared with her? She quickly realized that it was not the news she had received. But it was the voice on the phone that sparked the change. Her steps were quick, and she was soon out of the shop.

***

Scarlett arrived at the location in a cab after ten minutes, and they both hid in the nearby bush while waiting for the thief. After a few moments, a lovely young black lady wearing blue denim jeans and a white top arrived and unlocked the car. But before she could sit in the car and drive away, Theo appeared from the bush, pulled out his revolver, and asked the lady to surrender. Scarlett emerged from the bush and took a position behind Theo. From behind, she noticed his broad shoulders and nice ass. Theo was surprised to see the thief because she was his ex-girlfriend, Paulina. The thief also recognized the cop and exclaimed, "So now you're going to shoot me. I've always suspected you didn't like me. You were always looking for reasons to end our relationship."

"No, babe, I still miss you a lot," Theo replied. "You were the one who abandoned me."

Scarlett was taken aback when she overheard their conversation. She was at a loss for words. The situation there quickly became tense.

"But why did you steal the car?" Theo inquired of Paulina. "It's a crime. And you have an excellent job."

"After the break-up, I was unable to concentrate on work, made numerous mistakes and was consequently fired," Paulina responded. "Now I have to steal things to make ends meet."

"But why did you break up with me if you were so much in love with me?" Theo inquired. "Then you changed your contact number and moved somewhere else, making it impossible for me to find you."

"It happened because of that filthy demand of yours," Paulina answered.

"But it wasn't a filthy demand," Theo clarified. "It was a fairly common request."

Scarlett wondered what the demand they were talking about was. Both of them kept blaming one another until Scarlett stepped in and said, "Excuse me. Will you please hand over the car keys to me? I'm sick of your drama. I have to leave."

Paulina tossed the car keys at Scarlett and shouted, "I'd rather be starved to death than fucked in the ass."

Scarlett snatched the keys and burst out laughing, "So that was the filthy demand. Oh my goodness. You people are insane. You two split up because of this minor squabble? I'm surprised."

"Listen, you got your car, now you must leave," Paulina said. "It's been a particularly bad day for me. Please don't make fun of me."

"I am not laughing at any of you," Scarlett remarked. "I'm just curious why you denied it when your man demanded anal sex from you. It's absolutely hilarious. Have you ever tried it? It's a lot of fun."

"I've read about it, and I know that unnatural sex is a sin," Paulina said. "And it's excruciatingly painful with that big cock of his. So I'll never do it. (Scarlett's eyes sparkled when she heard 'big cock'.) And I request you to stay away from this matter and mind your own business. I don't need your wise counsel."

"All right," Scarlett said. "I finally got my car. However, theft is theft. I want this girl to be held accountable for her actions. Are you going to detain her, Officer?"

Theo was now nervous because he didn't want his girlfriend to be detained. He attempted to resolve the situation by asking Scarlett to withdraw her complaint. Scarlett, on the other hand, stated that she would only do it on one condition. Theo inquired as to what it was. Scarlett stated that she would discuss it later. But first of all, they must both accept her invitation to dinner. They both saw no harm in accepting the invitation.

Scarlett sat in her car, about to put the keys in the ignition when she noticed Paulina had changed the keychain. It was a keychain bracelet. She assumed Paulina was inattentive and was concerned that she would misplace the keys. She recalled Paulina saying that after their break-up, she was unable to concentrate on her work. She smiled as she slipped the bracelet on her wrist.

***

Chapter 4

One Year Ago

Paulina worked in a publishing house. She was very fond of reading. That was one of the reasons she enjoyed her job. She rented a one-bedroom apartment a few yards from her office. She had a relationship with Theo. They went shopping together a lot, watched movies, took long trips together, and had a lot of fun. They were both emotionally attached to one another. They thoroughly enjoyed each other's company.

One night after the dinner, Theo dropped Paulina outside her apartment and she invited him inside for a cup of coffee. Theo agreed, and the two of them entered Paulina's apartment. They were seated on the couch together after finishing their coffee. Paulina's head was resting on Theo's thigh. Theo was moving his fingers in Paulina's hair. He then put his finger on Paulina's lips. Paulina opened her mouth. Theo put his finger inside her mouth. Paulina takes a bite off of his finger. Theo instantly pulled his finger out and Paulina laughed naughtily. They began kissing on the couch. They had been seeing each other for two months and were about to make love for the first time.

Theo didn't have any plans. Everything seemed to be happening on its own. He began pressing Paulina's boobs gently. Paulina became excited, and she took Theo's hand in hers and stuffed it into her panties. The wetness was felt by Theo's fingers. Paulina moaned with delight as he moved his fingers around her vagina. She began to unbutton Theo's shirt. Theo removed his shirt first, followed by Paulina's top. He then removed her bra, revealing her luscious chocolate breasts in front of him. Paulina smiled, put her right hand on the back of his head and drew it toward her. Theo buried his face in Paulina's breasts. He could feel Paulina's hot breath on his head. Both were in no condition to wait any longer. Paulina removed Theo's trousers and briefs. Paulina's panties were removed by Theo. Both of them were completely naked.

Paulina rose and motioned her finger upward asking Theo to stand. Theo sprang up from his seat. Paulina clutched his stiff cock in her left hand and walked into her bedroom. Theo trailed her in silence.

Paulina squatted on the ground after entering the bedroom and took Theo's cock into her mouth. She sucked it perfectly. Then she gently licked his balls. Theo laid her down on the bed and began licking her vagina. Paulina strewed her legs out in front of him. Theo's tongue brushed across her warm, wet vagina. After a few moments, Theo positioned himself on Paulina. They then exchanged passionate kisses. Paulina snatched his penis and stuffed it into her wet vagina. Theo began fucking her in the genital area. It went on for a while. Theo then requested Paulina to change her position. He intended to do it in doggie style.

Paulina shifted her position to doggie, and then Theo without her consent inserted his penis into her ass. Paulina screamed in agony and shoved Theo away from her.

Theo asked, "What's the matter with you?"

Paulina shouted, "What is the matter with you? What were you attempting to accomplish?"

Theo explained, "All I wanted to do was fuck you in the ass."

Paulina said, "You filthy scumbag. This is no way to treat your girl." Her voice was filled with rage and anguish. Theo asked, "But what's wrong with it?"

Paulina replied, "I've read that it's a sin. I can't do it. You spoiled the moment. This is something you should never do again. Okay."

Theo tried to calm her, "But we should be open to all kinds of fun."

Paulina disagreed, "This isn't going to be any fun. This is excruciating. You should have consulted with me first."

"But..."

Paulina stopped him from speaking with the gesture of her hand and said, "If you ever demand this of me again, I'm done with you."

Theo said: "Paulina, the world has changed dramatically. It's now accepted. And I am confident that if you allow me to do this, you will enjoy it as well."

Paulina stood up, picked up her clothes, saying, "That's enough, please leave. I'm not interested in seeing your face again."

Theo dressed himself and walked out of the room with his head down.

Chapter 5

All three of them were waiting for dinner to be served at a restaurant. Drinks had already been served. Scarlett was sipping an Aperol Spritz, while Theo and Paulina sipped Martinis. Dinner was soon on the table. After having a brief informal conversation, Theo asked Scarlett to inform them of the terms under which she would withdraw her complaint against Paulina. Scarlett was now ready to open up her heart and let her emotions out. She smiled and began to speak in a low voice, "When I was in high school, my boyfriend Jim fucked me in the ass numerous times. We both had a great time together." That scene of her having anal sex with his boyfriend began to play like a reel in front of her eyes. She kept saying, "But after the school was over, his family shifted to another location. We were no longer in touch anymore. But I yearned for anal sex because I was addicted to it. I had a tremendous desire for it. I made new boyfriends but none of them were as perfect as Jim. I was never satisfied by any other man."

She appeared to be conversing with herself in her thoughts. A tear dripped from the corner of her eye. And she continued to speak, "Some men don't like to fuck in the ass. Others don't have significantly larger dicks. Years passed, and I still hadn't had a good anal sex. Because of the lack of that, I felt like something was dying inside of me. Then I read somewhere that black men are ideal for anal sex. So I started looking for a black man and one day my car got stolen. After that, I met you. I figured if you were successful in finding my car, I'd thank you by making love to you. You found my car. Then Paulina informed me that you were interested in anal sex and also you had a large penis. All my wishes were granted. So that was an opportunity I couldn't afford to miss."

The face that was engulfed in sadness just a few moments ago was now having a diabolical glow.

"So here's the condition. If you agree to make love to me and fuck hard in my ass, I'll drop my complaint and your girl will roam free. Your girl's freedom is contingent on my satisfaction. Are you willing to go through with it?"

Theo looked into Paulina's eyes. Paulina nodded his head slightly downward in approval as she didn't want to go to prison. Scarlett smiled and said, "I can see you both still love each other. My advice is you should stick together and respect each other's viewpoints."

After thinking for a few moments, Theo declared that he was ready to make love to Scarlett. Scarlett cheered and said "Yesss…I've reserved a room at a nearby hotel. We should go there right now. And it would be fantastic if Paulina could join us." Theo looked toward Paulina. She hesitated. Scarlett said, "Oh, come on, dear, it'd be fun." Paulina agreed.

Chapter 6

The three of them checked into a hotel room on the first floor that Scarlet had reserved. Scarlett slammed the door shut with her foot and began kissing Theo as if she had been craving sex for a long time. Theo became excited as well, and they began undressing each other. They had completely forgotten about Paulina as they exchanged passionate kisses. Paulina, who was also feeling ignored, sat in a chair. She reached for a magazine on the side table. It was the same issue of Cosmopolitan that Theo was reading in the police station. She enjoyed reading books a lot but wasn't really interested in magazines etc. Still, she began turning the pages of that magazine. But moving her gaze away from what was going on in front of her and focusing on the magazine was not an easy task. She occasionally glanced away from the magazine to covertly stare at Theo and Scarlett.

Scarlett was still kissing Theo passionately and removing his shirt. Then she sat on the floor, unzipped Theo's pants, and pulled out his massive black penis. She was overjoyed when she saw the size of the penis. She put it in her mouth and began sucking. Her mouth was opened wide enough to welcome Theo's penis. If even half of it had been opened for Victor, that poor soul's lifelong wish would have been granted. Theo took his penis out from her mouth and whacked her on the cheek twice with it. She put it back in her mouth. Scarlett noticed Theo's penis growing larger in her mouth. After a while, Theo tossed Scarlett onto the bed and spread her legs. He began licking her vagina. Scarlett let out a joyful scream. She then raised her head and saw Paulina sitting on the chair. She called her name and invited her to join them. Paulina stood up and approached them. Scarlett sprang out of bed and began kissing Paulina on the lips while undressing her. They were all completely naked now.

Scarlett sat down next to Paulina, holding Theo's penis in her hand and pointing it at Paulina's mouth. Paulina opened her mouth and began sucking. Scarlett started licking Theo's ass. When she was done with the licking, she asked Theo to lick Paulina's vagina. Paulina lay on her back and Theo started licking it. Paulina enjoyed it a lot. Scarlett sat on Paulina's face and Paulina started licking her vagina. After a while, Scarlett rose from Paulina's face and said to Theo, "Come on, you naughty boy. Let's take the party up a notch." She then drew him across her body and inserted his penis into her vagina. Her hips began to jump upward. Paulina sat by the bedside, watching them. Theo began fucking Scarlett hard, and both of them again forgot about Paulina. Paulina felt ignored once more, so she got out of bed and sat naked in the chair. She took the same magazine from the side table once again and placed it on her lap. This time, her focus was drawn to the magazine's cover. Paulina's eyes widened with surprise when she saw that picture.

That fat-bottomed cover girl looked like Scarlett. She felt as if the girl from the cover of the magazine had stepped out of the picture and was making love to Theo. She smiled and shook her head as if to clear her mind of this weird thought. She was silently watching them both. She began to be envious of Scarlett. As she too was aroused, she placed the magazine back on the table and began fingering herself.

After a lot of fucking, Scarlett shifted her posture to doggy and stretched her asshole. She was essentially inviting Theo to fuck her in the ass. Theo grinned. He was also prepared to do so because it was his favorite sport. He rubbed his large black penis on her asshole before slowly inserting it into her ass. Scarlett let out a joyful scream. Slowly and gently, the penis entered and exited Scarlett's ass. Scarlett's face was filled with pure delight. Her shattered existence was reuniting again. Paulina noticed it as well. Both of them were enjoying anal sex a lot. Their moans and screams reverberated across the room. Paulina was thinking that she had never experienced such ecstasy with her man before. Maybe it's the magic of anal. Her jealousy grew stronger, and she rose from her chair, approached the couple, took Scarlett by the arm, and gently pushed her aside. Then she said to Theo, "My ass deserves your penis as well. Why should this woman have all the fun?"

She pushed him onto the bed, sat on him, grabbed his penis, and stuffed it into her asshole. Theo widened Paulina's buttocks with his hands and began fucking her in the ass, first gently and then hard. Paulina grabbed Theo's shoulders with her hands and screamed with delight. Scarlett stood off to the side, her hands on her hips and a surprised expression on her face. She couldn't believe what was going on. Then she also joined them. The three of them did a variety of naughty things together. Theo dropped the semen on Paulina's vagina and Scarlett licked it. She then sucked the sperm-smeared penis as well.

It was midnight. All three of them were lying together naked after having an amazing sex session. Scarlett rested her head on Theo's left shoulder, while Paulina rested hers on Theo's right one. Paulina was gently touching Theo's chest hair with her right hand's fingertips. With her left hand, Scarlett was massaging Theo's balls. "Will you drop your complaint now?" Theo asked Scarlett.

Scarlett responded, "Yes, of course. Why would anyone like to put this sweet girl in prison? I had a long-standing itch in a certain body part that urged me to do something like that. Otherwise, my heart is devoid of any form of animosity." They all burst out laughing.

Theo said to Paulina, "Listen, sweetie, if this incredible lady didn't withdraw her complaint, you'd almost certainly end up in prison for two years."

"Honey, I'd rather stay in lock-up where I can see you every day," Paulina replied.

Then Scarlett asked Paulina. "I believe your views about anal sex have changed by now."

"Of course," Paulina said with a smile. "I realized that if you avoid the sin, you will also avoid the fun." They all laughed again.

All of their eyes were heavy with sleep. Paulina began to speak softly, "I want to tell you something else that will sound very strange. I committed a few minor thefts following my break-up and job loss, but I never stole a car. Neither did I intend to do so. When I was passing by that day, I felt as if the car was calling as though it was urging me to take it with me. I had never felt like this before, so I was really startled. The car key was still in the ignition, as I could see. After that, I quietly got into that car and sped off. Then I realized I had made a serious mistake. I accelerated the car in a fit of terror. I was going to run over a girl who was crossing the street. But she was fortunate that her friend was able to save her. My jail term would have been inevitable if there had been an accident."

Paulina became silent after saying this. After getting no response from any of them, she raised her head and noticed that Theo and Scarlet had fallen asleep. Paulina also closed her eyes and fell asleep quietly.

***

Scarlett awoke the next morning, got out of bed, put her clothes on, grabbed her car keys, strolled out the door and descended the stairs while Paulina and Theo were still asleep. She got close to her car when an idea flashed across her mind. She smiled and gently caressed the car's hood as if it were the head of her beloved pet. Then she returned to the hotel room. Paulina was still sleeping, but Theo was not in the bed. She found him in the shower. Scarlett turned off the shower and kissed him on the lips. Theo's penis instantly got erect. Scarlett felt it on her thigh. She said to him, "I think the differences between you two are now settled. You are a perfect couple and both of you must stay together. I wish you both a happy life ahead. This is a small gift from me to both of you." Then she took out the car keys from her pocket, put the keychain bracelet on his erect penis, tapped his nose with her finger, and walked away.

***

Book Two
Su Boleto Al Cielo

Fiona Rios, a 26-year-old fat-bottomed Spanish supermodel, was walking naked on a foot trail, with a lot of confusion in her mind. What had brought her here? Where was she headed? What had happened to her clothes? Why was it so foggy here in the summer? Was she dreaming? Or was she under the influence of some drug? She was unable to see clearly anything around her. Just a few moments earlier, she felt like she was flying, and now she was walking. There was no trace of any human beings nearby. She had no idea how long she had been walking like this. She didn't seem to be controlling the movement of her legs. All she recalled was that she was having a photo shoot in a studio for a modelling agency when someone shouted her name. Then, all of a sudden, it was pitch-black everywhere. After a long walk, she observed that the fog wasn't as thick as it was earlier. Then she observed a large pearly gate not far away. She kept moving forward and eventually arrived at the gates.

"Hello, is anyone around?" She called while yet being fully aware that it would be quite embarrassing for her if someone saw her in the open while she was naked.

"Could you please give me your name?" A strong voice emerged from the other side of the gate. Fiona felt relieved knowing that she would eventually find out what was going on. She called out her name loudly. The voice on the other end remarked, "But I didn't find your name on the list."

Fiona was confused. She began to wonder what kind of list he was referring to. After a brief pause, the voice said, "All right now. I have received the updated list. And your name appears on it. Please come in."

Fiona countered, "But I'm naked."

"Don't worry," the voice said. "This is how everyone comes here." The massive gate opened and Fiona walked through it. Inside, everything was crystal-clear. There was no fog at all, and there were many colorful flowers and green trees. On the left side of the gate, she observed a small cabin. Perhaps it was the location where the voice came from.

She entered the cabin and saw a tall young man sitting in front of a computer wearing a white robe and oversized eyeglasses. When he saw Fiona walk in, he smiled and said. "Welcome to Elysian Fields."

"Thank you very much," Fiona said with a smile. "But I'm not in the condition to recall anything. How did I end up here? Am I here for a photoshoot?"

"No dear, this is the final resting place for noble people," the tall man replied with a smile. "This is heaven."

The shock hit Fiona. Her visage faded. "What?" she asked, her voice was trembling.

"That's right, dear. You died just a few moments ago," the tall man said. "You were in this studio when a heavy light fell from the ceiling and struck you in the head. You passed away on the spot. Look at this CCTV footage of the accident." When the man turned his desktop screen toward Fiona, she saw her lifeless body lying on the floor, surrounded by the entire crew.

"Oh my God!" shrieked Fiona, "How could this happen to me?"

"Could you please calm down, lady? I understand that this was not the right time for you to die. You got a very short life to live. But who can escape death?" The tall man removed his spectacles and placed them on the table. He then turned to Fiona and said, "After inspecting your file, I discovered that you began your modelling career at the age of 19. You've made a lot of money so far. You are overly generous and have a kind heart. You provided financial assistance to many people in your community. And you haven't committed a single sin in your 26 years of life."

Fiona was gradually regaining her composure. "Is this the reason I arrived in heaven so quickly?" she asked.

"It's not that simple. Noble individuals are automatically admitted to heaven. The souls of these people are as light as a feather. Hell is a downward spiral. After they die, sinners continue to descend into hell."

"Ooh."

"In order to enter, you must pass a final interview. Our terms and conditions have just been modified. We had to update because there were certain loopholes in our previous system that allowed some unauthorized people to gain access here. Your interview will be conducted by the Lord himself."

Fiona was taken aback. "So now I'm going to meet the Lord?"

"You'll only be able to hear his voice. He can't be seen by anyone."

"And what kind of questions will the Lord ask during the interview?"

"There will be no questions asked. It's basically a scanning process of the numerous levels of your personality."

"When will it begin?"

"It will begin soon. You can wait outside, and I'll call you when it's time to begin."

Fiona was now at ease because she was confident she would pass the interview. She expressed gratitude for the tall man's assistance and inquired about his name.

"We don't have names here," the man replied.

Fiona exited the room and took a seat on a bench outside. She became accustomed to the situation as time passed. She no longer felt awkward being naked in public. It appeared to her to be completely natural. The memories of her life were gradually fading.

She began to feel contented on the inside as she gazed at distant hills. A river was flowing down the mountain in the distance. Fiona kept watching it, and soon she noticed that the waterfall was getting closer and closer to her as if she were looking through a binocular. She could see it clearly as if she were sitting right next to it. She was taken aback by the fact that her eyes were zooming in on the objects. She became so engrossed in watching the waterfall that it appeared to her that she and the flowing water were one and the same. She was the flow of the river. She was totally absorbed in her surroundings when the tall man called her by name. She returned to the cabin, and the man said, "It is time for your interview. Continue straight and then turn left. There is a large hall that is painted white. There, the Lord will interact with you."

Fiona exited the cabin and began walking in the direction indicated by the unnamed tall man. She realized the flowers on the sideways were smiling at her as she walked. She began to believe that she was under the effect of some powerful drug and that everything she was witnessing was merely a figment of her imagination.

After a short walk, she noticed a white hall on the left. She made her way toward it and soon arrived at the main entrance. She entered the hall through the glass door. It was a massive space with a stage. There were only two chairs in the hall: a large one on the stage and a small one in the hall. Fiona sat in the chair that was facing the stage. Soon, the hall was completely dark, and an egg-shaped light appeared on the stage's giant chair. Fiona's heart was filled with a peculiar mixture of love and affection. Her heart seemed to be melting away and oozing out from her vaginal opening.

She also noticed tears welling up in her eyes for no apparent reason. She realized it was the result of the supreme power's presence.

"Welcome to the Elysian Fields." Fiona's ears were filled with a strange sound. "The purpose of this final test is to determine your eligibility to enter this place. I request you to remain motionless for a few moments."

Fiona felt as if her brain was melting and pouring into her vaginal area as she listened to the voice. She felt like she was a river pouring down the mountain while sitting immobile in her chair.

"You have a noble spirit. During your lifetime on this planet, you did a great job. You have fulfilled your obligation to serve humanity. As I can see into your soul, there is just one barrier that will prevent you from accessing this area."

Fiona wanted to inquire about the impediment, but when she opened her mouth and tried to speak, her tongue began to melt and drip down as well. She was unable to communicate.

"Throughout your entire life, you have never had a complete sexual orgasm. A single orgasm has the power to alter the entire scenario. You, on the other hand, were always having partial orgasms with your partner. And that thing disqualifies you from entering here."

Fiona never noticed this throughout her life. She was unhappy with her boyfriend's weird demands, but she also actually enjoyed having sex with him. And she had no idea that there was still something she wanted to accomplish.

"The reason behind this is that you had two boyfriends at the same time and you were cheating on them both," the voice continued.

Fiona was not surprised because she knew it was true.

"You were always afraid of being caught while having sex, and that fear never allowed you to completely surrender to any of your partners. That was why you had never achieved a full orgasm that was required to fulfil your soul."

Fiona had the impression that someone had already said this to her. She made an effort to remember, but she failed. The reason for this was that she was gradually losing her memory. She remembered everyone who had been a part of her life, but she had forgotten about the events that had occurred throughout her life.

"When a soul enters heaven, it should be in complete harmony with every object. And if I let you in without perfection, things will be uncomfortable for you."

"So, dear, I must send you back to Earth to complete that unfinished business. Only then will things go smoothly."

The light oval began to fade and eventually vanished. Fiona remained seated in her chair. The melting of her body organs came to an abrupt halt. She discovered herself in the same state as before. She sprung from her seat and dashed outdoors. When she approached the cabin door, she noticed the tall man sitting behind his computer. "The Lord never misses a thing," he remarked with a smile.

"So, what should I do now?"

"The Board of Directors is currently having a meeting to discuss your case. The decision will be communicated to you shortly."

Fiona sat down on the same bench as before. That location appeared to be considerably different from Earth. There was light in every direction, but there was no sun. Everything seemed to be glistening. And there was soothing, silent music playing in the background which could not be heard but may be felt.

"It has been decided to send you back to earth for five days to achieve your goal," the tall man remarked as he called her inside. "You will be welcomed here if you succeed. Otherwise, you'll have to reincarnate. They will also provide you with a personal assistant who will accompany you at all times and coach you through everything."

Fiona inhaled deeply and inquired about his assistant's name. "He, too, has no name," the tall man added with a smile. "He is, nonetheless, an extremely intelligent individual. He has extensive knowledge in a variety of fields. He'll be here in no time. Then he'll whisk you away to any corner of the globe you desire."

Suddenly, an elderly man with long grey hair and a neatly trimmed beard dressed in a white robe entered the cabin and smiled when he saw Fiona. Fiona returned the smile.

"So, young lady, where do you want to go?" he asked.

Fiona's decision had already been made. As a result, responding to him was quick.

"My hometown…New York City."

Because the trail was so narrow, they couldn't walk side by side. Fiona was following the elderly gentleman as he walked ahead. The fog thickened as they walked. Fiona was full of questions, but she remained silent since she didn't know where to begin. She continued to walk silently behind him, her head bowed. Fiona knew it was going to be a long walk, but she figured she might make it easier by engaging in some intriguing conversation.

"All right, young lady, now I'd like to pass along a set of instructions that will be useful to you over the next five days." The silence was broken by the elderly gentleman.

"Would you prefer calling me by my name, sir? It is Fiona," Fiona, who was anxious to communicate, swiftly responded.

"That was your name when you were alive. A soul has no name."

"But, sir, as we return to Earth, wouldn't it be more appropriate that we address each other by name?"

The elderly gentleman laughed. Then he raised his hands and said, "It is impossible to win an argument with a lady."

Fiona laughed as well. "Would you mind telling me your name when you were alive?" she asked.

"I just remember my name from my previous life," the gentleman replied. "Adam Mavros," he said.

Fiona was surprised when she heard his name because she had recruited a manager with the same name when she was alive, who she later fired because he was not managing anything effectively. "All right, Mr. Mavros, what instructions do you have to give?"

"First and foremost, you must understand that you will be invisible to everyone on Earth. In addition, the world is not colorful enough for a soul. It'll look black and white."

"Is that so? I've never heard about it," she said.

"It can only be heard from the dead. Also, I must add that if you are deeply shocked by something, you will become visible to others for a short period of time. At that point, you will notice the colors of the world. If you see the world as colorful, you should be aware that others can see you. Everything will return to normal as soon as your mind stabilizes. We do not want to cause panic among people, so please avoid crowded areas." She remained attentive as Adam continued, "Just like the students are given grace marks if they do not pass an exam, in the same way, you have been allowed an extra five days. Take advantage of your good fortune. Even if you don't have a body, you will experience the same sensations in all of your parts until you complete your work."

"You must also enter someone's body in order to achieve your goal. You'll need to discover a noblewoman who is similarly passionate about sex."

"It's a difficult job."

"You believe this because you are unaware of your unique abilities. A soul can see through the souls of others and read their thoughts. Souls aren't required to travel anywhere on the planet. You can simply vanish from one location and reappear in another in an instant. You can go back in time. You also have that amazing quality known as foreshadowing. If something is going to happen somewhere, you will know about it before it happens."

Fiona felt relieved when she heard this. "You should enter into someone's body just before having sex," Adam continued. "When the couple is kissing each other, they both are out of time at the moment. That is when the gate opens and a soul can enter the body. Additionally, the individual is least conscious that a spirit has entered his or her body. Your soul can enter into anyone's body through a specific point located on the backside of the person's head. You must remain in that woman's body throughout the entire act. And if she experienced that supreme state of orgasm during sex, you can as well, making you eligible to enter heaven. During your time in someone else's body, she may pick up some of your good or bad traits. She'll be transformed into someone she's never been before."

"Wow, that's fascinating."

"I should also state unequivocally that I will not remain with you during the sexual intercourse."

"I understand," Fiona laughed.

The trail came to an end, and they found themselves on the precipice of a cliff.

"Fiona, no more walking," Adam declared. "There are two more things you should be aware of. That is something I will tell you about later, as we are about to land on Earth. Please take my hand in yours and close your eyes." Fiona did exactly as she was told. "Do you wish to attend your funeral?" Adam's voice asked again.

"I passed away only a few hours ago. How can my funeral be completed so quickly?"

"You are now out of time, and it appears that you have just perished. Actually, it's the third day. Now, tell me if you want me to take you to St. John Cemetery, where it is currently taking place?"

Fiona thought for a moment and then said, "No."

Fiona had the impression that she was on a fast-moving elevator. She clutched Adam's hand fiercely. She noticed some dampness on her legs. Perhaps it was the clouds that were making her soggy. She wished to see, but then she changed her mind.

Adam asked her to open her eyes when they landed safely. Fiona perceived everything around her to be black and white. She had no trouble recognizing the location. Carnegie Hill, to be precise. Rick, her lover, owned a home in this area. She used to spend her nights with Rick at his residence while she was alive. It was getting dark, and it appeared like the city would soon be engulfed by the darkness.

Fiona asked the first question as soon as she set foot on the earth, "Both of us are similar to the wind. So, how do we make contact with matter?"

Adam smiled and said, "You've asked the right question at the right moment. Try to pick up this pebble that is lying on the ground."

Fiona knelt and attempted to pick up the pebble, but was unable to lift.

"The secret lies in the fingers of your left hand." Adam continued, "Join the tips of the ring finger and thumb of your left hand together and press firmly."

Fiona did exactly what she was told.

"Do you notice any changes in yourself?"

"Yes, it appears like I am clad in armor."

"Now try to lift it again."

This time, the pebble was easily lifted. She threw it away.

"You must have figured it out by now. Keep in mind that your finger and thumb should be firmly attached to each other whenever you need to make contact with matter. This rule, however, does not apply to trees. The trees, in both Earth and Heaven, exist in the same form. So always keep in mind that even in your natural state, you will collide with a tree. You will never be able to pass through it. We can't keep our fingers attached together while we're sleeping. As a result, whoever comes to visit the Earth is given the instruction that he should always sleep on a tree."

Fiona appeared to be impressed.

"How about the other thing you were going to tell me?" Fiona asked as they walked.

"But I think I've covered everything you needed to know," Adam said after a brief pause.

"You said you'd tell me two more things when we landed on Earth. However, you have only told me one. What about the other?"

"Is that so? It happens to me every time I visit the planet. I experienced temporary memory loss. Don't worry, I'll let you know as soon as I recall."

Fiona was feeling tired now. She yawned and said, "Well, that was a very useful information. And please tell me another one also when you recall it. For now, I need to find a tree."

Day 1

It was 7:00 in the morning when Fiona opened her eyes and looked around. She slept soundly at night and was no longer feeling tired. She jumped off the tree and started looking for Adam. He said that he would spend the night on some other tree. When she walked a short distance, she heard the sound of snoring. She looked up and saw Adam lying on a branch. Fiona joined her left hand's fingers, then lifted a pebble from the ground with her right hand and flung it upward. The pebble passed through his face without hitting him. Fiona realized her mistake. She then said in a loud voice "Come down, Mr. Mavros. We have to work hard all day."

"Good morning, young lady." Adam woke up and jumped off the tree and started walking behind her. "But where are you headed to?"

Fiona was moving fast in some direction. "My boyfriend's house is in this area. I just want to take a look at him."

Fiona stopped at an intersection, moved her right-hand index finger in a circle and tried to remember something. Then as soon as she was confirmed where Rick's house was, she started walking fast. Adam also started walking along with her.

"Considering the fact that we need to find an appropriate female right away, don't you think five days is too little time to do this task?" She asked Adam while walking.

"There are also five nights in addition to the five days. The search may last all day because the work must be done at night," Adam replied.

Soon the two reached near Rick's house. Outside, there were two cars parked. Fiona was well aware that one of the cars belonged to Rick. Others may be the property of a visitor. But who would have shown up so early in the morning? She was lost in thinking as the door to the house opened and a lovely young lady stepped out. Rick had also arrived with her. After a two-minute conversation, the girl wrapped her arms around Rick's neck and the two began kissing. The girl was clearly on her way back after spending the night with Rick. Fiona was shocked by what she witnessed. Things around her became colorful in the blink of an eye. She stood there frozen in awe. At that same moment, Adam grabbed her by the arm and dragged her behind a tree. She peeked surreptitiously from behind the tree. Rick was looking in the same direction, rubbing his eyes. Perhaps he had caught a glimpse of Fiona. Fiona began to wonder how Rick could be having fun with another girl when she had died only a few days before. There was also the possibility that they had been having an affair for quite some time. Just like she was cheating on Rick, he was also cheating on her. The second thought seemed more accurate to her. She said to Adam that she wanted to know everything about this girl. She would get into her car right now and see who she was and what she did. And if she found everything right, this young lady would be her first prey. Using her body, she would achieve her target as she knew that Rick was a fantastic lover. This girl would experience great orgasms while having sex with him and will also help her experience it.

"I believe I don't need to explain this to you, but please pay attention," Adam said. "When you enter the car by crossing the closed door, press your fingers before getting on the seat, otherwise the car may slide, leaving you standing on the road."

"I will take care. Please don't be concerned."

When the car passed near Fiona, she jumped and sat in the back seat. Adam also did the same. Everything went fine. Adam's expression showed a hint of relief. Then they both smiled at each other.

Fiona, after her death, spent her first day on Earth with that girl. By the end of the evening, she had learned practically everything there was to know about her. Her name was Liza Petrov. She was Russian. She was a struggling model in the fashion industry. She went to several modelling agencies during the day and met a lot of individuals and took a walk around the lake. She ate Golubtsy and Schi for lunch. Wherever she went and whatever she did, Fiona was always by her side like a shadow. And so was Adam, who was thoroughly bored with the entire day's job. At one point, when he couldn't take it any longer, he asked Fiona, "Don't you think you are wasting your time?"

"Why do you think so?"

"We don't know yet if this girl is going to have sex tonight or not?"

"She will for sure. I can smell the desire. And it is getting stronger as the time is passing."

Around 7:30 in the evening, Liza called someone on her phone, "How are you, honey? Are you free tonight? Can I have dinner with you at your place?"

Fiona nudged Adam and winked. Adam also smiled.

Liza disconnected the phone. Her blushing face told that her request was approved. She walked around the market for half an hour and then around 8:00 p.m., she sat in her car and started moving toward her destination. Fiona was doubtful that the man on the other side was not Rick. She was talking to some other person for sure. Fiona smiled and thought that Liza too was not getting entry into heaven after her death. The car was running on the busy roads of NYC. At one point Fiona saw her own picture on a billboard and sadness filled her heart. Liza turned her car toward Cranberry Street and Fiona started getting goosebumps. She had a sneaking suspicion that she was about to receive a tremendous shock. Her fear was justified. Liza stopped her car in front of a small house on the corner of the street. She got out of the car and rang the doorbell. Fiona's face turned pale and she ran toward the opposite direction as if she were searching for some place to hide. Adam also followed her.

"What happened?"

"I don't know why my whole fucking life is revolving in front of my eyes?"

"What are you trying to say?"

Meantime the door opened, a man came out and Liza hugged him.

"That bastard…" Fiona pointed toward the man, "is Chad Brown. And he is my other boyfriend."

Adam burst into laughter. Fiona kicked his butt and started moving. Adam laughed and shouted, "Won't you like to have dinner with them, baby?"

"I don't want to see that bastard's face again."

"But you are missing a chance to get your ticket to heaven. Soon they will be fucking."

"That girl is having the same state of mind as me. And that is of no use to me." She continued, "This incident had blown my mind. I don't know what to do now. You were right. I was wasting my time the whole day."

"Then what is your next plan?"

"We will think about the next plan tomorrow morning. Right now my brain needs rest. Please help me in finding a tree."

Day 2

"Dear, Mr. Mavros, can we attend my funeral?" This was the first question Fiona asked Adam after waking up on the second day. Adam was surprised when he heard that.

"Fiona, I asked you if you wanted to attend your funeral as we were about to land on Earth. And you said no."

"I understand. But things have become considerably more complicated. I'm curious to find out which of these two bastards was there and if they were grieved by my demise."

"When I asked you earlier, it was during the time that that thing was happening. But now we must go back in time. That is not something I would advise."

"Why? What's the harm in going back in time?"

"If we travel back in time and then return to the present, it will not be the same day. I mean to say that whether you stay in the past for a few minutes or several hours, we will return at the same time the next day. Another day will be lost, which is why I don't recommend it because your first day was also squandered."

Fiona paused for a moment. Adam was correct. She only had four days left on Earth. But who knew if she devoted all four remaining days to her work she would still achieve that state. But she was determined to solve the puzzle at any cost. So she stated emphatically, "Don't worry. Let's do it."

Adam took Fiona's left hand in his and instructed her to close her eyes. She did exactly what she was told. When she opened her eyes again, she was seated on a tree branch with Adam in St. John Cemetery. Her funeral was taking place. Her initial focus was on her parents, who were looking very sad. When she saw them, she was deeply depressed. Then she started looking around. She recognized a lot of people. Every eye was filled with tears. Her eyes began to look about for someone. She had no idea that she was about to experience another tremendous shock. Chad Brown was there, she noticed. Someone was soothing him by patting him on his shoulder while he was crying. Fiona cast a cautious glance in that direction. Rick was the other man. It was a mind-blowing event for her to witness. How did they become acquainted? Did they realize they were both banging the same girl? What were they up to with her? And what was the story with Liza? Was the same thing happening to Liza? She felt she was cheating on them, but they were both making fun of her. Fiona's mind was racing with all of these ideas. Darkness descended before her eyes, and the surroundings started to turn colorful again. Her legs began to tremble. She was in no condition to be there any longer. As a result, she informed Adam that she needed to leave immediately.

Day 3

When Fiona and Adam returned from the past, it was already the third day on Earth. Fiona's mind was about to explode as a result of an incident she witnessed at her funeral. She decided after much deliberation not to investigate the cause and instead focus on her mission. She used to spend a lot of time in the malls and shopping complexes when she was alive. She adored going shopping. She decided to go to the market and reminisce about her happier days. She had Adam with her as they roamed.

She noticed on TV while wandering an electronics store, a famous female porn star named Luna Fawx being interviewed by a press reporter. The interview was taking place on the set for a pornographic production. She stood in front of the television and began to listen to her. The interviewer inquired about her family history and qualifications. Luna provided detailed responses to each topic. Fiona was uninterested in any of this. So she searched around for something more exciting to do. The interviewer then inquired about the porn star's love and married life. Fiona's gaze was drawn to the television, as this was a matter of interest to her. She had only recently discovered that she had been cheated in love and was being mocked by those two bastards.

Interviewer: "Ms. Fawx, when a regular man returns home from a long day, he unwinds by having sex. However, if a porn star gets tired of having sex on set all day, how does she unwind at night?"

Luna: "Love is something we don't find on set. When I receive love from my partner at home, I feel at ease. My medicine is love, not sex."

Interviewer: "We'd like to learn more about your marital life."

Luna: "I've been happily married for six years. I'm not interested in having kids. My hubby respects my decision and is always there for me in any circumstance."

Interviewer: "Tell us a little more about your husband. Is it true that it was a love marriage?"

Luna: "You can say that. He worked as a cameraman on one of my films. He met me on the set and instantly fell in love with me. He revealed his feelings and offered marriage. I inquired as to why he wanted to marry me after I had just fucked three males in front of him."

Interviewer: "And what was his response?"

Luna: "What he said in return captivated my heart and I consented to his marriage proposal right away. He said that no one knows what his partner is up to behind his back. At the very least, I am aware of what you do. Your body can be shared with anyone, but your heart will always be mine."

Interviewer: "That's fantastic, Ms. Fawx. We consider you fortunate to have such a considerate companion. Now, tell us if you've ever cheated on him throughout the years. We're confident he won't mind if you cheat on him because of how you described him. As a result, you are free to express the truth in this situation."

Luna: "Because I am really successful and work on the sets throughout the day. I had sex with a variety of male models. If my spouse accepts all of this, he will be unconcerned if he discovers I cheated on him at some point in the future. That is how much he cares for me. Never in my wildest dreams did I consider defrauding him. When something becomes legal, it is common for people to lose interest in it."

Interviewer: "Okay, Ms. Fawx, What message do you want to give to the upcoming models?"

Fiona was unconcerned about the response to that question. She had already found the answer to her question. She hurried out of the store, frantically looking for Adam. She came across Adam in a neighboring ice cream parlor. Two sexy ladies were licking ice cream, and he was staring at them with eager eyes. Fiona put her palm in front of her face and remarked, "Hello, I didn't realize hot chicks were your weakness."

"Not chicks," said Adam, "ice cream is the weakness. I really wish I could eat it." No one knew if Fiona heard his response or not, but she took his hand and led him to the electronics store, where she stood in front of the TV that was showing Luna's interview.

"Who exactly is this?" Adam inquired.

"She's an adult entertainer," Fiona replied. "For the first time, I discovered someone who is devoted to her partner. Find out where she is right now. My intuition tells me that this woman could be useful to me. I've never seen anyone with such clarity of thought."

"Look, Fiona, these celebrities say whatever they want in interviews, etc.," Adam added. "In actual life, things aren't like that. You'd be better off looking for someone else."

By that moment, the reporter had finished the TV interview. He went on to announce, "You were watching Miss Luna Fawx's interview live from Houston's 'Wicked Queen Studio.' Now we'll take you to our studio for the weather forecast."

Fiona's face was filled with delight. In a cheerful tone, she said to Adam, "O my savior, please hurry up and take me to this fucking Wicked Queen Studio. I'm sick of wandering around on this planet. I need to get back to my home right now."

"I repeat, their comments aren't to be taken seriously. These folks say decent things in order to project a positive image in public. In reality, they have never practiced anything like that in their lives."

"Mr. Mavros, we have to spend the day looking for someone who can be useful to me. Why don't we take a trip to Houston? We'll find someone else there if we don't see anything promising in this woman."

Adam was well aware that he would not be able to win a debate with a woman. As a result, he agreed to take Fiona to Houston. The next thing they knew, they were in front of the Wicked Queen Studio. Fiona seemed to be in a good mood. She was confident that she would pass the test today. There wasn't much going on in the studio. The crew consisted of only a camera operator, a director, a makeup artist, and two assistants. Aside from that, there were two male models, Ricardo and Louis, who were accompanied by Luna Fawx.

Luna sat with both of the male models after conducting the interview. Looking at them, it was evident that Luna and Ricardo got along well. The set was being prepared for shooting. The director approached the three of them and began to describe the scene. They were all silently listening to him. It was clear that the director held Luna in high regard.

In roughly ten minutes, the shooting began. Fiona and Adam have never seen anything like this before. Both of them were undecided on whether they should stay or wait outside. Until now, all three models had been dressed fully and were kissing. Both stood motionless as they watched the shooting. But as soon as the clothes disappeared from the bodies of all three, Adam bolted outside.

Fiona locked her gaze on the three. She was unaware that Adam had left the room. Ricardo and Louis were standing naked in front of one another. Luna squatted on the ground between them, sucking both of their cocks alternately. Fiona noticed that she was devoting more time to Ricardo than to Louis. She began to notice that Luna and Ricardo shared a deep bond. Maybe they were having an affair. She suspected Adam was correct about Luna.

Then she reasoned that what difference did it make if the two were having an affair? Whatever both of them were doing would be seen by everyone sooner or later. As a result, Luna wasn't concerned about being exposed and so she could entirely surrender to her husband during sex. No amount of dread was going to deter her.

By that time, all three of them had shifted their positions. Luna moved her ass up and down while sitting on top of Louis, holding Ricardo's cock in her hand and sucking it. In the next thirty minutes, they fucked by changing various positions with complete devotion toward their work.

Finally, there was the double penetration scene. Luna was doing it very naturally. But for Fiona, it was very awkward. Despite her being so open-minded, she had never considered having anal intercourse.

Luna's groan reverberated across the room, as she had two cocks in each of her holes. Fiona wondered if Luna's moaning was genuine or staged. After a while, both studs alternately dropped the sperm on Luna's face. By then, the shot was over. The director applauded and congratulated everyone on a fantastic shot.

The makeup artist dashed over to Luna with a towel to clean her face. But she stopped him and requested him to bring her handbag. She took out her phone from the bag. Then she took a selfie of her semen-soaked face and two hanging dicks near her both ears and forwarded it to her spouse. Fiona had a feeling that tonight would be special for her. Luna was a very bold woman who was well-versed in all the tricks for making life more enjoyable. There could be no room in her mind for any kind of fear.

Louis left in his car after the shoot was finished, but Luna and Ricardo continued to chat for a long time, holding each other's hands. Fiona had already discovered that Adam had fled the scene. She was planning to go out and see him, but then she chose to stay there and listen to Luna and Ricardo instead.

Fiona obtained the following information after listening to both of them.

Luna currently resides in Miami.

Luna's husband's name is Karl Davis.

Luna had known Ricardo for a long time. They'd collaborated on a number of videos.

Ricardo was a Houston resident.

He frequently traveled to Miami for shooting.

He had some special gifts for Luna this time, so he asked Luna to schedule the shoot in Houston by contacting the director.

The director of the film she was working on had a lot of admiration for Luna. He had only agreed to shoot in Houston at Luna's request.

Ricardo was a motorcyclist. He disliked driving cars. He arrived on the set on his bike as well.

After obtaining all the information, Fiona came out and noticed Adam strolling around aimlessly.

"What is so upsetting about seeing people having sex that you rushed out here?" She asked.

"I had a hunch you'd try on that model's body. If you believe she is an ethical lady, you should not have passed up this opportunity."

"No. That would have been a fruitless endeavor. While in front of the camera, these guys pretend to have orgasms. Our job will be completed only when she'll make love to her husband."

"How certain are you that she will meet her husband tonight?"

"I overheard their conversation inside. Luna has been staying here for a week. Her husband arrived at Luna's hotel room shortly before noon today, having flown in from Miami. Luna is on her way to Ricardo's house because he has a surprise for her. She will then proceed directly to the hotel to meet her husband. Because today was the last day of shooting, both of them are leaving for a vacation tomorrow morning."

While they were talking, Luna and Ricardo came out. Luna hopped on the back of Ricardo's bike and he rode away to his house. Adam and Fiona remained motionless, kept their eyes on them as they faded from view. They couldn't ride with them on the bike, and they didn't know Ricardo's address. Both of them were staring at each other as if they were idiots. Nobody had a solution.

However, some invisible force wished to help them.

From inside the room, the director was saying to the assistant, "Look here, Harry, madam has forgotten her mobile. She will be at Ricardo's residence. I believe you and Ricardo both live in the same area. Will you be able to deliver this cell phone to her?"

Harry replied, "Okay, sir, I'll do it."

Before Harry got into his car, Fiona and Adam had already sat in the backseat.

Harry arrived outside Ricardo's house after a 15-minute drive. He stepped out of the car and rang the doorbell.

The door was opened by Luna. Harry gave her the phone back. Luna gave Harry a warm hug and expressed her gratitude. After that, Harry continued on his way.

Fiona and Adam were standing in front of Ricardo's home.

"Should we enter?" Adam inquired.

"I don't think it's necessary." Fiona quoted. "Ricardo has something special for Luna. And I'm not interested in finding out what it is."

Luna stayed at Ricardo's house for 30 minutes. Then she booked a taxi on her phone. As soon as the taxi arrived, the door opened and both of them came out. Luna boarded the taxi and Ricardo went back inside the house. Fiona and Adam boarded the same taxi as well. Fiona noticed a strange gleam in Luna's eyes.

The taxi took 20 minutes to arrive at Luna's hotel, after which Luna paid the fare and checked in. Adam indicated that he would not be coming with Fiona. Fiona grinned and walked alongside Luna. Luna took the elevator to the first floor and found her room. Fiona was almost there as well.

Karl possessed the demeanor of a college lecturer. He had a thick moustache and wore spectacles. "How was the journey?" Luna asked as she hugged him. The journey, according to Karl, was fantastic. There was no issue at all. Luna requested him to place the dinner order because she was in desperate need of a shower. She then proceeded to the washroom.

Karl took the phone and placed an order for dinner. Fiona sat in a chair off to the side. The sound of a running shower began to emanate from the washroom. Karl began checking his text messages. Then he addressed Luna, saying, "Darling, which is Ricardo's dick from the photo you sent me?"

Luna's voice came from the washroom, "The one on the left."

Fiona realized she wasn't in the shower when she heard Luna's voice. She wanted to inquire, so she went inside the washroom via the closed door. She noticed Luna standing naked in front of the mirror, head up, looking inside her nose. And she was moistening her finger and moving it inside her nostril. Fiona thought this was odd. Luna eventually stood beneath the shower.

Luna emerged from the shower with a towel wrapped around her body. Karl poured wine into two glasses, and they both sat on the bed and began to drink. Dinner arrived at the same time. They shared the meal. There appeared to be a lot of chemistry.

The two finished their meal, and then the moment Fiona had been anticipating arrived. Luna threw off her towel and began kissing Karl. Fiona didn't waste a second and quickly entered Luna's body.

Fiona took complete control of Luna's body in a matter of seconds. Fiona noticed that Luna's mind was not in a normal state. The waves of joy were surging inside her mind. Fiona discovered Luna had taken some drugs. This was the result of it. She was also cleaning her nostrils while in the washroom. She, on the other hand, had been with her since noon. When would she have taken the drug?

Fiona relaxed her mind and pondered what it meant to her when Luna took the drug. That was great news for her. The drug would assist her in having a satisfying orgasm.

Then she began to be afraid of something else. What if Karl was interested in anal intercourse? During the day, he noted Luna enjoyed anal intercourse very much. If Karl loved it, it would be awkward for Fiona. Karl, on the other hand, had a decent appearance. Looking at him, it did not appear that he would like unnatural sex.

Everything went off without a hitch. Both of them continued to have natural sex on the bed. Fiona was having a great time. But she couldn't reach the heights she desired. Fiona peered into Luna's heart in an attempt to find out the reason. There was a sense of fear present there. Fear of getting caught. Fiona was perplexed. What was the source of such a fearless woman's trepidation?

Fiona needed to know this secret urgently. She attempted to extract the memory from Luna's mind. All of the secrets were soon revealed. The most special asset Ricardo possessed, and for which Luna traveled from Miami to Houston, was high-quality cocaine ordered from Barcelona. While she was in Ricardo's place, Luna snorted that expensive cocaine. Fiona, who was outdoors, was completely ignorant of this. Luna used drugs on occasion without informing anyone, whereas Karl despised drugs and drug addicts. Luna was terrified that if Karl found out about her nasty habit, he would divorce her.

The intercourse was over in no time. That intercourse gave Karl a feeling of unprecedented pleasure. On the other hand, it failed to bring back Luna to reality, as she had been floating into another dimension. And it left Fiona with a deep hatred for Luna.

Fiona quickly exited Luna's body and sat in the same corner chair. Soon after, the couple fell asleep. Fiona was now very concerned. Another day had been squandered. She had a strong desire to murder Luna. She was such a scumbag. Drugs, not love, were her medicine.

Fiona was still in the room at nearly midnight. That night, she had no desire to sleep. She was down in the dumps. She felt something occurring in her head as she awoke from her depression. She began to get visions. Adam gave it the name foreshadowing. She wished to share her foreshadowing experience with Adam. Then she thought that Adam must have fallen asleep by now. She would see him in the morning tomorrow. She sat in the same chair as a statue with her left hand's finger and thumb joined for the rest of the night.

Day 4

Karl Davis awoke at around 7:00 a.m. He attempted to rouse Luna from her profound slumber. "Wake up, love," he urged. "Our flight is at 9:00 a.m., and we only have a short time to get to the airport." Karl decided to take a bath after waking Luna up. Luna began to pack her belongings. Both paid the bill at the hotel reception about an hour later. While Karl was using his credit card to pay the hotel bill, Luna was making some notes in the hotel's suggestion book. They both then checked out.

Fiona followed the two of them out of the hotel. She saw Adam as soon as she stepped out. Adam discovered that something went wrong last night. He consoled Fiona, telling her that she still had two more days. Fiona informed him of her visions from the previous night. Adam requested Fiona to show him the room. Fiona led Adam upstairs to the room where she'd spent the night before. Adam inhaled deeply before closing his eyes for a brief moment. "Yes," he exclaimed, "I can sense it as well. There will be some incredible sex in this room tonight. And that sex is going to satisfy someone's years-old thirst."

"So, in my opinion, we should return here at night." Fiona stated, "It's also a beautiful day outside. We could spend all day walking around this lovely city."

When they arrived at the reception area downstairs, the manager was on the phone with someone. He called the housekeeper after hanging up the phone and remarked, "Room no.107 which was recently vacated has been re-booked for tonight. She is also a highly affluent lady and a valued customer of ours. After you've cleaned the room, make sure to replace this latest issue of magazines with old ones."

Fiona spent the entire day with Adam. They went to practically every famous attraction in the city, including the museums, the space center, the zoo, and the downtown aquarium. She didn't feel as energetic as she had earlier. But she ignored this. As the evening grew darker, she realized she needed to return to the hotel before it became too late. Both of them were fast to react and arrived near the hotel. In the hotel parking, they saw a light-colored convertible Cadillac.

"Good luck, Fiona. I am going to sit in this convertible Cadillac and relax," Adam said and jumped in the driving seat of the car.

Fiona went upstairs and noticed three people entering the room. She went after them. Fiona realized she was in the right place at the right time as the door banged shut on her face. She stood outside the room for a few seconds before passing through the locked door. When she entered the room, she noticed a stunning white lady passionately kissing a black man. A young black girl sat in the same chair where she had been in the night before. She was terrified of black women. She's heard that some of them use black magic and have the ability to capture spirits.

"Fear of being caught never permitted you to give completely," she remembered the Lord saying. Her heart was encircled by that emotion once more. She was thinking about whether or not to join them when she noticed a magazine on the side table with her picture on the cover. She took it as a lucky omen and decided to try her luck.

The couple was now undressing each other. Fiona took advantage of the fact that the lady was still kissing the man. She merged with the white lady's body. The white lady knelt on the floor, unzipped the black man's pants and took out his penis. She was ecstatic when she saw the size. She popped it into her mouth. The black man yanked her penis out of her mouth and whacked her twice on the cheek. The lady took it in her mouth once more.

Fiona had been feeling nothing until that point. The man flung the lady on the bed and spread her legs after a while. He began licking her vaginal area. Fiona began to feel a delicious sensation, and the white lady began to shout with delight. Fiona gained total control of the white lady's body. She was now free to move her body as she pleased. But she was deeply concerned about the presence of the black girl in the room. She was curious as to what she was doing at the moment. As she lifted her head, she noticed her reading the magazine. But, all of a sudden, something extremely awful occurred. "Paulina, please come and join us, sweetie," the white lady said to the black girl. The black girl rose from her chair and approached them. Fiona was terrified. Paulina's gaze pierced into her soul from the moment she walked into this room. She was terrified that she was aware of her presence in the room.

The white lady undressed Paulina and kissed her on the lips. She then sat next to her and shoved the black man's penis into Paulina's mouth. Fiona avoided eye contact with Paulina by twisting the white lady's body and forcing her to lick the black man's ass.

Paulina lay on her back on the bed when the black man began licking her vagina. The white lady sat on Paulina's face. Paulina began licking the white lady's vagina. Fiona began to experience that lovely pleasure once more. That enormous black penis inside her vagina was now eagerly desired by the white lady. "Come on, you naughty boy. Let's take the party up a notch," the white lady said as she drew the black man over her body. Fiona felt something she had never felt before when the penis penetrated her vagina.

Was it the magic of the black penis? Fiona was so pleased with herself that she forgot about the black girl in the room. She knew she'd have that orgasm right now, and her task was almost complete. But it was again another unlucky day for her. The white lady shifted her position and began anal sex with the black male. Although Fiona had complete control over the white lady's body most of the time, her desire for anal intercourse was so intense that Fiona was unable to prevent her from changing position.

The entire scenario altered when the black penis entered the white lady's ass. Fiona had never done anything like this before. It completely disrupted her mental state. There was no longer any room for orgasm. The white lady, on the other hand, was ecstatic. The black dude was likewise having a great time. Fiona was at a loss for what to do next when she noticed the black girl was fingering her vagina. Suddenly Paulina opened her eyes and made direct eye contact with Fiona.

Fiona was terrified once more. Paulina rose from her seat and approached the couple. She then grabbed the white lady's arm and yanked her away. Fiona had a sneaking suspicion that something horrible was about to happen to her. She flew out of the room like a bullet, leaving the white lady's body behind. She had no idea what transpired inside the room after that. She was so close to having an orgasm, but her luck was not on her side.

Adam jumped out of the car as she approached him.

"Dear, what happened? Can you tell me why your face has turned pale?" He inquired inquisitively. "Is everything all right?"

"Don't know how to explain. However, I'm certain it was an awful day for me."

"I wasn't getting any positive vibes here either. Let's get out of here as soon as possible. I'm curious as to who used to operate this vehicle. I'd just been sitting there for 40 minutes and I was getting this strange feeling that my ass needed a hard pounding."

Day 5

Fiona had trouble sleeping the entire night. When she closed her eyes to try to sleep, she could see Paulina staring at her. Even if she dozed off for a short time, Paulina's face would show up in her nightmares. As soon as her gaze met Paulina's, a shiver ran down her spine. She spent virtually the entire night awake due to her exhausted mind.

She got up with a great deal of uneasiness. She was beginning to believe that completing her task was nearly impossible. Her peace of mind had been severely disrupted by the happenings of the previous four days. The Earth was nothing like she imagined it to be while she was alive. Almost everyone is a cheater at some point in their lives. She glanced down from the branches of the tree. Adam had awoken and was now strolling on the ground. She, too, descended but wasn't in the mood to chat with Adam. Adam wished her good morning and inquired about her health. She informed him about her nightmares and how uncomfortable she was. At the time, Adam didn't take it seriously. He stated that while she was in Room No.107 with Luna and Karl, she didn't sleep. Her sleep was disrupted again the following night by nightmares. With the passage of time, her condition would begin to improve. Fiona believed him.

She then told Adam, with a sad tone in her voice, "I think I won't be able to finish my task because the time I was given is almost up. We must now get ready to return."

Adam chuckled and said, "We didn't have any luggage to pack. So, what kind of preparation is needed? Also, since today is your final day on Earth, I recommend you ignore whether or not you complete your task. Simply enjoy yourself to the fullest on this special day. Nothing will ever change if we try to change things. It doesn't matter what we want."

His words helped Fiona relax a little.

When Fiona's condition deteriorated in the afternoon and she began to falter as she walked, Adam smacked his forehead with his left hand and said, "Jesus, sweet Jesus. Now I understand what's going on with you."

"What is it?" Fiona inquired.

"I thought I told you that when a soul is out of heaven, it is prescribed to spend every night under the stars," Adam continued.

"When did you inform me? I recall you saying something that you forgot to mention."

"Perhaps you are correct. I occasionally forget things. Stars nourish your soul. Music has the same effect. That night while staying in Room 107, you lost contact with the stars. Also, you couldn't sleep last night, as the fear was still haunting you. As a result, your situation is now analogous to a phone whose battery could not be charged for two nights."

"So, what am I supposed to do now?"

"Use your abilities to figure out where music can be found at the moment."

"What kind of ability? I'm completely powerless right now. I'm having trouble seeing things clearly."

"Okay, then, wait. Allow me to do it for you."

For a little while, Adam closed his eyes. Then he said, "I see a place for bikers nearby. There's some lovely music playing there. Let's go check it out and see if it's of any use to you."

In the heart of the city, there was a Native American biker club. The group was known as the Apache Riders. Adam and Fiona arrived at one o'clock in the afternoon. Outside, there were a few motorcycles in the parking lot. Inside, rock music was playing. Adam told Fiona, "Dear, go inside and spend some time. I am confident that your condition will improve over time. This is my tried-and-true solution. I also need your approval to go away for a little while. I'll meet you here in about one hour."

"But," Fiona inquired, "Where do you wish to go?"

"After sitting in that Cadillac last night, I told you that I started having some problems too, a weird desire is gnawing at my mind," Adam remarked nervously. "It is quite tough for me to continue in this situation. I'm looking for a remedy as well."

Fiona managed to hold back her laughter and gave him permission to leave.

Fiona remained surprised as she walked into the club. The club was not unduly busy, but the atmosphere was unlike anything she had ever experienced anyplace else on the planet. However, she had sensed it during her short stay in heaven. The atmosphere on the inside was out of this world. The club was gleaming from top to bottom. It reminded her a lot of heaven. Wonderful Rock music was playing inside. Fiona began to feel more invigorated after hearing the music. There were so many cheerful faces throughout the place. They were ecstatic for no apparent reason.

The bikers in the club were giggling uncontrollably. Fiona had been there for about ten minutes, and her condition had significantly improved. She continued to move around.

She noticed that not everyone there was Native American but a few white Americans were present as well. There was also an elderly native woman sipping beer at the bar. Fiona's gaze met the woman's, who looked at Fiona with surprise. Fiona reasoned that because she was invisible, no one could possibly see her. She's probably staring at someone else. Fiona tried to look away from the woman. But that woman had been staring solely at her since she arrived at that location. A shudder rushed down Fiona's spine when Paulina's eyes met hers the night before. She was concerned that Paulina would see her and harm her. Fiona, on the other hand, was not frightened by the sight of this woman.

The woman set her beer mug on the counter after emptying it. She then beckoned Fiona to come close to her. Fiona took a peek around. There was no other person near her. This indicated that the woman was attempting to contact her. But how was she going to be able to see her?

Fiona's thoughts were interrupted when the woman began heading toward her. Fiona became frantic and planned to leave. She didn't want to get into any trouble on her last day on Earth. Before she could even get close to Fiona, she bolted through the locked back door and began galloping. But just as she turned around to see if the woman was still following her, she collided with a tree, fell down and fainted.

Fiona regained consciousness after around ten minutes. As she opened her eyes, she saw the same woman leaning on her head and looking at her with adoring eyes. "Why did you flee from me, my child?" the woman inquired. "There is no need to be afraid of me."

"How can you see me?" Fiona responded with another question while lying on the ground.

"Leave it. That is an irrelevant question," the woman inquired in a solemn tone. "What is that desire that drew you back to Earth?"

Fiona exhaled deeply and continued, "It's a long story."

"I'm interested in hearing your story," the woman said and then took Fiona's hand in hers and lifted her off the ground. Fiona was surprised by the woman's ability to touch her when she wasn't pressing her fingers together.

"There's a park behind there," the woman added, pointing in one direction. "Let's have a conversation there. Otherwise, people will believe I'm talking to myself."

"Actually, I need to listen to some music. I'm not feeling particularly energized."

"It is not necessary to do so, my child." The woman placed her left hand behind Fiona's head and drew it toward her. A spark surged through Fiona's body as her forehead met Fiona's forehead, and she suddenly felt full of energy.

While sitting on a park bench Fiona asked the lady, "If it's okay with you, could you tell me a little about yourself before you listen to my story? It will help me in overcoming the mixed sentiments of fear and astonishment that are currently occupying my head."

"Sure, why not," the lady said. "My name is Martha Gaylord. I belong to the Cheyenne tribe. I'm 62 years old and a motorcycle enthusiast."

"But I'm curious how is it possible for you to see me? You can also touch me. Are you from another world?"

"I've lived my entire life with a high level of self-discipline. I had attained sainthood in my early years of life. As a result, I have the ability to see and touch souls," Martha said.

Fiona's expression changed when she heard this. "Now I am sure there's no reason to be afraid of you."

Martha tenderly took both of Fiona's hands in hers and asked, "Now tell me which desire has brought you back to Earth."

Fiona began sharing with Martha the entire story after her death. Martha sat with Fiona's hand in hers, listening closely and looking into her eyes as she continued to speak. Her face was riddled with enigmatic expressions.

After Fiona had finished telling her everything that had occurred to her, Martha took a deep breath and said to her, "Very few are given another chance in that world. However, if you've been able to obtain it, there must be a reason behind it. Perhaps death took you instead of someone else."

Hearing those words from her, Fiona should have become very upset, but instead, she sat there appearing entirely calm. She didn't appear to be upset about dying instead of someone else. This was due to two factors. The first was that she discovered multiple facts while roaming this planet as a soul. She was well aware that honesty, loyalty, and truth have no place in this world. She also noticed the deception of those she considered to be her own. The second factor was that after spending some time in Heaven and experiencing the incredible calm there, she had fully lost her attachment to this planet and was eager to return as soon as possible.

Martha broke the silence after a few moments, "So, today is your last day?"

"Yes, and I've given up hope for a good outcome."

"There is still plenty of time. You can achieve success if you take the steps in the right direction."

"Are you implying that I can still find someone who can help me to achieve my goal?"

"I can state unequivocally that your death came too soon. You had a little knowledge of human character in this world. You would not have squandered four days like this otherwise. Why do you believe you require another person to perform this sacred mission? No one is pure in this place. You have the capability within you. You do not need anyone. Whoever led you here has no idea what this is all about."

"But I was told that this was the easiest way."

"Don't be fooled by smooth roads. Only tough roads lead to beautiful destinations. First of all, I believe this concept is ludicrous. You were given five more days by the Lord to accomplish your unfinished work. A person who has reached the point where he will experience full orgasm will have no desire to touch another person's body. He will prefer adventure over sex. Entering someone else's body for sex is pointless."

"So, according to you, there's another way for me to find what I'm looking for?" Fiona got a glimmer of hope.

"The goal is to achieve orgasm. There are a million ways to get there. Sexual intercourse is just a path to reach there. Another path is one of adventure."

"You're speaking as if you've dealt with similar situations before."

"You are not the first person to come here, and you will most likely not be the last. Many souls have arrived here in quest of this thing before you and will continue to do so after you. Here, everything revolves in a circle. You must have noticed that some events in your life are also occurring in the lives of others. Or you're meeting people with the same name again." Martha continued, "People with similar names will enter your life, and their work will be similar as well, leaving you with the same impression."

Fiona remembered Adam, who had taken over as her manager. She would never have taken his services if she had known this earlier. Fiona regretted bringing Adam along. Martha read the thoughts that were forming in her mind. She said, "The soul who has been sent to assist you is not a genius as you were led to believe. Instead, he falls into the category due to whom they had to revise their terms and conditions."

Fiona was shocked. She stated, "But Adam never told me all of this."

"The Board of Directors has no authority to send anyone to Earth as a helper who has gained access to Heaven. Such a mission will be assigned to someone who still has something to accomplish. Adam, like you, is on a mission."

"What's going on is completely beyond my comprehension," Fiona said in confusion.

"You don't have to comprehend anything, my darling. With the limited time you have left, my recommendation is to focus solely on your task. I'll assist you in finishing your incomplete task. Just keep in mind that if your mission is successful, Adam's mission will be considered a success as well. Whether you want to give him credit or not is up to you."

"That so-called genius had already ruined four of my days and was on his way to ruin the fifth. How am I supposed to give him credit?"

"If you don't want him to take the credit, you must leave him behind and travel to heaven on your own."

"But it's nearly impossible for me to return without him."

"You've already done that before. You'll have to focus a little more. I will also assist as much as possible."

"Your words gave me a great deal of courage. Inside, my heart is pleading with me to completely trust your words. Please tell me which method I should use to attain orgasm that isn't the same as Adam's suggestion. And have you ever experienced that kind of orgasm yourself?"

"My child, as I previously stated, I have attained sainthood. A saint experienced orgasms with his every breath. A saint, on the other hand, cannot allow any soul to enter his body. This jeopardizes his chastity. Otherwise, I would have completed your task in a flash while sitting here."

Fiona was surprised by Martha's answer. She'd never read or heard anything like this before. Martha continued, "Now, I'll respond to your first question.

What is another method of obtaining orgasm? You were inside that club not long ago. You must have seen a lot of bikers there. Have you ever met somebody in your whole life who is happier than them?"

"I had noticed it as well. What might it be that makes them so happy?"

"The key to their happiness lies in their way of living. They do not seek wealth, but rather happiness. They believe in equality and justice. Their life revolves solely around adventure. That's why they rode bikes."

"If I understand your point correctly, you probably want to say that I need to ride a motorcycle in order to experience orgasm."

"Yes. You only have a limited amount of time left, so this is the only way to succeed. I won't let you enter into my body, but you are welcome to ride my bike with me."

"Thank you so much." Fiona said, "Will you respond to my question? I've always wondered since I was a kid why some people prefer bikes to cars."

"In a car, you can't feel the wind and the motion at the same time. Your spirit will stay unfulfilled without it. While driving a car, people feel trapped behind metal and glass. However, the situation is not the same in convertible cars. The inclusion of sunroofs in recent car models demonstrates that people miss the wind while driving. By the way, this discussion will never come to an end. We need to get on the mission as soon as possible. My bike is parked in the parking lot. Allow me to take you on the most exciting journey of your life."

Martha took Fiona's hand in hers and led her away. Suddenly Fiona's gaze was drawn to Adam. He was entering the club to look for Fiona. Fiona did not want him to be able to track her down. As a result, she rushed to the parking lot. Martha's opulent motorcycle, 'Indian Chief Dark Horse' was parked there.

Fiona sat in the back seat while Martha mounted her motorcycle. Then another rider asked, "Martha, where are you going at this hour?"

"On a covert mission," Martha smiled and shouted. Then she ignited the motorcycle's engine and said to Fiona, "We say here—Always follow your soul. It knows the way. And look here. A soul is following a body to find its way."

Adam had sensed Fiona's presence outside the club by this time. When he heard the motorcycle engine starting, he ran outside and saw Fiona seated in the back seat of Martha's motorcycle. The motorcycle accelerated out of the gate so quickly that it was out of sight in an instant. He remembered the occasion when Luna was riding on Ricardo's motorcycle and the two of them had left the Wicked Queen Studio while he and Fiona were both rendered helpless.

It had been about half an hour till they had left the club. Fiona sat in the backseat of Martha's bike. The motorcycle appeared to be flying through the air. Fiona gripped Martha tightly. Fiona was so confident in Martha after speaking with her that she didn't waste any time in deciding to leave Adam and follow her.

The road was full of rolling climbs and gentle turns. At one point, Martha came to a halt on the motorcycle and said to Fiona, "My child, listen closely. The route we're on is known as the Good Ol' Texas Loop. The entire route is 150 miles long, which we complete in a single day. Riding a motorcycle down this road is the greatest adventure. We just have a half-day to work with. However, I am confident that that amount of time is plenty for you. I know I shouldn't share any secrets, but you are a very pure soul, so I'm telling you that this way was the only thing that helped some souls who had come here in a similar state before you." Fiona remained silent. She only smiled. The route offered a pleasant ride through oak-covered hills, wildflower beds, limestone cliffs, and numerous crystal-clear streams and lakes.

It was almost impossible to put into words what Fiona had started experiencing after a 45-minute continuous motorcycle ride. That experience can be understood by either a biker or a saint. Martha used to fit into both of these categories. Some of the readers will undoubtedly fit into one of these categories as well. I am trying to put that limitless experience into words for others. When Fiona was sitting in front of the Lord, she felt that her body parts were melting and flowing down her vagina. But as soon as the Lord was gone, she was back to her old self. Similarly, while she was sitting in the back seat of the motorcycle, she felt as if all of her parts were dissolving in the air. Along with the organs, many of her emotions, such as fear, jealousy, worry, and greed, were also fleeing from her. There was no communication between the two during this time. When Martha halted the motorcycle after a two-and-a-half-hour excursion there was nothing like Fiona left in Fiona. She was nothing more than an oval-shaped swarm of light, similar to the Lord's appearance. When Fiona got off her bike and looked inside herself, she was astonished. She could see the entire cosmos within herself.

The only question that remained in her mind was, "How did you find out that I've achieved this state, dear Martha? You came to a complete stop on the bike at the appropriate time."

"You were sitting on my bike, sweet child. I realized the work was over when your weight was merely reduced to 21 grams."

This was not a part of their conversation, but rather an exchange of thoughts between them. Because it was no longer possible to speak to her, Martha communicated with Fiona through her thoughts.

"It's time to say goodbye, my child. As you reach the summit of that modest hill in the west, just remember the Lord. You'll begin your journey to heaven." Martha couldn't keep her tears from streaming down her face.

Fiona likewise bid her goodbyes to Martha and headed down the winding road that led to the western hill. As she looked around, she noticed the wildflowers smiling at her.

She reached the top of the hill after about 20 minutes. She raised her head and remembered the Lord. Some unknown force drew her upward. She was now flying above the earth's surface. She peered down from a great height. Martha was waving at her from the distance.

Book Three
Sailors Without a Compass

After the Christmas holidays of 1996 were over, one morning Paula Sandler was dropping off her five-year-old son Rick at Ralph Straus Elementary School in her old Mazda MX-5 Miata. She was a single mother who worked in a dry-cleaning establishment. Her economic condition was bleak. Her husband died two years ago from an incurable disease. Because of her unwavering love for her kid, she did not even consider being married again. A long with meeting household expenses, the child must receive a good education, so she worked very hard day and night. She had recently given up on living for herself. Her world appears to have begun and ended with her only son. She was well aware that if Rick received a good education, he would undoubtedly progress in his life. And when she would see him growing up, she would be overjoyed.

Paula was driving the car, her mind on the complications of her life, and Rick, sitting in the back seat, was excited to see the snow on the road outside the window. Paula's eyes were clouded with worry, while her son's eyes sparkled with delight. He was returning to school after winter vacation. Reuniting with his classmates was a pleasure. Paula arrived at Rick's school after a 20-minute drive. She pulled into the parking lot, parked her car, and exited. Then she opened the back seat door and Rick quickly jumped out of the car. Paula took his right hand and proceeded toward his classroom. Rick walked in a relaxed and carefree style.

He enjoyed attending the class. Paula escorted him into his classroom. Ms. Laura, Rick's teacher, greeted them and asked Paula to come pick up her son at 3:00 p.m. Paula left after giving her approval with a nod. Rick was directed to sit on a bench by the teacher.

Rick noticed a new kid sitting on the bench. Rick had never seen him before in his class. Rick sat alongside him, and neither of them said anything. The teacher was reading a rhyme 'Down by the Station' from the English book, and they both became preoccupied with listening to the teacher.

During the lunch break, when Rick asked about him, he revealed that his name was Chad.

"I've never seen you here before," Rick asked.

Chad replied that his father had a new job in this area. Last week, they had just arrived in Manhattan. They had previously resided in Fairview. While they were conversing, Chad opened his lunchbox, and Rick noticed a chocolate muffin inside. Rick's lunchbox contained a cheese sandwich. Rick hesitantly asked Chad if he could eat his muffin. Chad said, "If you will give me your sandwich then you can eat my muffin." They both agreed and ate each other's lunch.

The exchange of lunch on the first day of their meeting became the foundation of their friendship. Every day, they sat on the same bench and ate lunch together. Their strong bond was not kept hidden from their class teacher. The other students in the class would frequently observe them both together, either on the playground or in the classroom. If one of them was absent one day, the other would be sad all day.

Eight weeks later, one night at about ten o'clock, Rick was watching Disney's Duck Tales cartoons on TV while Paula was preparing his school bag. Suddenly, Paula's gaze was drawn to a pencil box in Rick's bag. She took out the box from the bag and asked Rick, "Sweetie, where is your new pencil box that I brought you two days ago?" Rick was busy watching television so he most likely did not hear Paula's question.

When Paula asked him again, Rick replied, "Mom, I exchanged that with my friend."

"But why, dear?"

"Chad liked my pencil box, and I liked his."

Paula stated, "I brought the box of your choice. You should've told me you didn't like it at the time of purchase."

Rick remained silent. Paula didn't ask again.

***

A much more interesting incident occurred in the vicinity of Rick's pencil box in a rented apartment on Stone Street, Manhattan's oldest area. Paul Brown and his family were having dinner. It was 9:30 at night. He sat with his wife Sandra, their 11-year-old daughter Suzie, and their five-year-old son Chad. Paul and his wife sat at the table facing each other. Suzie's head was filled with a lot of jumbled thoughts. She was irritated with a classmate boy who had an ugly face and kept pinching Suzie. Suzie was unsure whether she should complain to her teacher or her father. If she complained to the teacher, her friends would begin to tease her by mentioning that boy's name. If she complained to her father, perhaps he would change her school. She didn't want either of these things to happen. Suzie's biggest issue was that she was hesitant to share her feelings with anyone. Sometimes she lacked the courage, and other times, the situation was such that she felt it was best to remain silent.

Sandra spent the entire day alone in the house. A few days were spent setting up household items after moving to the new location. She used to be free in the afternoons and would watch a movie on TV.

She had watched a James Spader movie on TV this afternoon and was infatuated after seeing the erotic scenes in that film. She developed a great craving for sex and waited for her husband until dusk. She was aware that she would only be able to spend time with her husband at night. Sandra was only thinking about sex while eating dinner. Suddenly she felt something on her leg. She noticed that her husband was moving his toe up and down on her leg. Sandra had an odd sensation. She knew that Paul never did such things. He was a solemn man. In many species, the male detected sexual arousal in the female. This hadn't been tested on humans yet. But Paul probably sensed that something dark was messing with Sandra's head. She was in a very naughty mood.

Only Chad was enjoying himself while eating. Upon first glance, one may conclude that he was ignorant on all sides while remaining calm within him.

Paul began to caress his wife Sandra's leg with his foot while sitting at the dining table. Sandra realized he was in the mood for sex as well. She didn't stop him. Paul's foot eventually reached between Sandra's thighs, and Sandra motioned for him to be patient. The kids went to their rooms after dinner. When Sandra was washing the dishes in the kitchen, Paul came and grabbed her from behind. "Let the kids go to bed first," Sandra mumbled in his ear. Paul, though, had no desire to wait. He inserted his tongue into Sandra's ear. He pressed Sandra's left boob with his right hand at the same time. Sandra became excited and asked Paul to go to the bedroom and wait. She would finish her work quickly and come to him soon. Paul walked out of the kitchen. Sandra finished all of the kitchen work in about 15 minutes. She then went to the kids' room.

Chad and Suzie were doing their homework. She instructed Suzie, "Honey, after you two have finished your homework, assist your brother in packing his school bag. And, yes, don't stay up too late." It wasn't the first time Sandra had said this to Suzie. Suzie was given the same instructions almost every night before she went to bed. Suzie nodded and Sandra left their room. She then departed for her room. When she opened the door, she noticed her husband sitting naked on the bed. His penis was totally rigid. Sandra's excitement reached a peak when she saw him like this. She jumped over him and started kissing his lips. She was so excited that she forgot to lock the door from inside.

After a long French kiss, Sandra slipped off her nightgown. The only thing left on his body was her panties. With Paul's help, it too vanished in approximately ten seconds. Sandra climbed onto the bed and grabbed Paul's head from behind, pressing it between her thighs. Sandra's excitement was unusually quick for Paul. He positioned her on the bed, parted her legs, and then began to move his tongue over her genital area. Sandra was pressing Paul's head from behind while clutching her left boob with her left hand. Sandra eventually grabbed Paul's penis and began rubbing it on her vagina. Paul signaled her to stop; Sandra asked the reason.

Paul said that he desires a blowjob from her prior to sex. Sandra, on the other hand, was unable to halt. She requested Paul to have sex first, and she promised to give him a fantastic blowjob later. Paul agreed and put his penis inside Sandra's vagina. Sandra let out a long yawn. She then wrapped her arms around Paul. Tightened her legs around his waist and whispered in his ear, "Fuck me harder, James."

Paul came to a halt and inquired, "Who is this James, dear?"

"Please don't stop," Sandra said, "James Ballard was a character in a film I saw today." Paul grinned and began fucking harder. He was well aware that Sandra enjoyed watching movies and that she occasionally interacted with the characters in those movies. The movie characters have a profound impact on her mind. Nevertheless, he himself had no desire to watch movies. He wasn't even familiar with the actors' names.

Suzie finished her homework in about 20 minutes. After that, she turned toward her younger brother. Chad had completed his homework as well. Suzie began to stuff her notebooks into her bag. Then her gaze was drawn to Chad's pencil box. Her expression was exactly the same as Rick's mother Paula's when she spotted a different box instead of Rick's pencil box at roughly the same moment. Suzie picked up the box and examined it carefully.

"Chad baby, when did you receive this box?" Suzie asked in amazement, "This one is more attractive as compared to the previous."

Chad informs her that he exchanged it with his friend Rick.

Suzie: "That is wrong, dear. You are unaware that this is a bad habit."

Chad didn't even pay attention to her. Suzie said, "Look, dear, the first thing you'll do after you go to school tomorrow morning is get your pencil box back from your friend and return this one to him. Will you do it or not?"

Chad shook his head and said, "I like this box, and I'm going to keep it."

Suzie became enraged and declared, "If you do not listen to me, I will complain to Mom about this action of yours."

Chad repeated, "I'll keep this box. I like it very much."

Suzie slammed the pencil box on the bed angrily, stormed out of the room and raced to her parent's room. When she banged on the door with both hands, it immediately opened, and she was stunned to discover what was within.

Paul was lying naked on the bed in front of her, his penis was in Sandra's mouth and she was sucking it. Spotting Suzie inside the room, Paul hastily covered his naked body with a sheet and Sandra covered her breast with a pillow. Suzie was so thoroughly taken aback by this spectacle that she lost track of her original reason for being there.

"You should be ashamed," she shouted at her mother, "Few years back, you used to yell at me constantly for sucking my thumb, and now look at yourself." Paul and Sandra were stunned and embarrassed, and they lay motionless like statues. Suzie slammed the door shut and dashed toward her room.

Suzie was put in the same situation where she couldn't decide whether to tell her parents about Chad's actions or to tell Chad about her parents' actions. After some consideration, she decided to remain silent once more.

***

The following day, on Sandra's recommendation, Paul made an appointment with a well-known child psychologist. They were given time after three days. Three days later, at the scheduled time, they were both driving to the psychologist's office in Paul's car. They were both so shocked by the incident that night that they were both in a bad mood for two days. The car's cassette player was not working. To pass the time, Paul decided to strike up a conversation with Sandra.

Paul asked Sandra to change her mood, "Darling, this guy, James, you were mentioning that night, is he really so seductive?"

Sandra responded, "Yes, sweetheart. James Spader is both attractive and talented as an actor." The response astounded Paul.

"But that day, you were referring to a different James, not James Spader. Sex was dominating my mind at the time, so I can't recall the name at the moment, but I'm positive you didn't say James Spader."

Sandra: "How is this possible, my love? James Spader was in the movie I saw that afternoon, watching some great erotic scenes of the same, my arousal flared up. That's why we started having sex untimely and as a result, we got so embarrassed in front of our daughter."

Paul remained silent, but his doubts persisted. He kept trying to recall the name his wife whispered that night. His memory, however, did not support him. He was certain the name wasn't James Spader. He began to doubt Sandra in his mind. Perhaps she was seeing someone named James and was cheating on Paul.

But, in order to investigate this matter, first of all, he needed to recall the full name of that James. He was silent for the rest of the journey. About half an hour later, they reached the office of the child psychologist in the Bryant Park area. Five minutes later, they were sitting in front of Dr Maksim Hartshorn, a Russian psychologist who was about 50 years old. Paul attempted to discuss their issue with Dr Maksim, but he felt as if his tongue had become paralyzed. His brow began to perspire and he was unable to talk. He gave his wife a helpless gaze. Sandra realized that she would have to speak up now. In hushed tones, she recounted the events of that night to Maksim. Maksim listened carefully to everything being said.

After she had finished, Sandra said, "Doctor, we are really upset. What impact would the event from that evening have had on my daughter? After that day, I am unable to even look into her eyes."

Doctor Hartshorn exhaled deeply and said, "Look, madam, this is not unusual. Kids in many families often see their parents having sex. On many occasions, parents are not even aware of this." He continued, "And you will be surprised to learn that this has no negative impact on their personalities, but rather has a positive impact."

Sandra responded, "But doctor, my daughter is only 11 years old."

"You shouldn't worry at all, madam," Maksim retorted with a smile. "Everything is understood by 11-year-olds. You must treat her like a pal. Everything will return to normal in a few days, and one more thing, when kids witness their parents cheating on each other, only then there is a negative impact on their personalities."

Paul cocked an eyebrow at Sandra when he heard this. After a ten-minute casual conversation, they both got up and walked out.

Note for the Readers

That afternoon, Sandra was watching a movie named Crash, starring James Spader. The character played by James Spader in that movie was named James Ballard, and Sandra whispered the name of James Ballard that night, which she later forgot. But this had raised doubts in her husband's mind that his wife was cheating on him.

***

The following evening, Paul was once more seated in front of Dr Hartshorn. He made an attempt to introduce himself, but the doctor claimed to have already known him. Paul added, "Doctor, we came to talk to you about a situation yesterday. And your response left us both feeling largely satisfied."

The doctor inquired, "So, what brings you back today?"

Paul: "You had mentioned that kid's personalities are negatively impacted if they witness one of their parents cheating with the other."

The doctor answered with a nod, "That is correct. You carry on speaking."

Paul mustered the courage to say, "Doctor, I am aware that this is not your specialty. I've come to you with hope because I am new to this area and I don't even know many people." Paul's dried throat made it difficult for him to speak. "I have a feeling that my wife is cheating on me."

Doctor: "Sir, I can't help you on this. You should hire a good detective who will keep an eye on your wife's movements and bring you the truth."

Paul responded hesitantly, "But, Doctor, I only have doubt. I came to you because you are a psychologist. Could you kindly provide me with a method to eliminate my uncertainty over my wife's loyalty?"

The doctor exhaled deeply and said, "Mr. Brown, we live in a very immoral world where many people do not even understand the value of loyalty. Our environment is extremely unethical. Many people think it's normal to cheat on their partners. But they are unaware that by doing so, they will never be able to reach the depths of love. They are also unable to experience the peak of an orgasm. These types of people can never live a complete life, no matter how wealthy they are."

Paul was completely absorbed and paid close attention to the doctor. Even his conscience recognized that the doctor was correct. He stated, "How can this message reach all of the people who are doing a lot wrong by cheating on their partners?"

The doctor said, "As people's education levels rise, they become arrogant rather than humble. They do not easily listen to anyone. Only the Lord can now explain such profound things to the people."

"You are right, Doctor," Paul said, "People will only listen to the Lord, and won't pay attention to anyone else."

"Let them handle it themselves." The doctor continued, "Mr. Brown, now to your problem. There are numerous such things from which we can ascertain the truth. Are you aware that the non-living things around us reveal a great deal? Unfortunately, we lack the ability to hear them." In awe, Paul continued to listen to the doctor.

"Now, please respond to my question, Mr. Brown. Are you wearing torn socks right now?" This question perplexed Paul.

He responded, "No, doctor. They are completely new."

"Is your underwear or vest ripped?" The doctor inquired further.

Paul stated, "I didn't pay attention. The vest is quite old, and it may have been worn out and torn somewhere."

"Had it ever happened that your shirt got worn out but you didn't notice?"

"No doctor, this never happened."

"You don't notice the undergarments because they aren't visible to those outside. Mr. Brown, am I correct?"

"You are absolutely correct, Doctor."

"However, you pay close attention to the rest of your clothes that are visible to the public. Your wife is the only one who has access to your undergarments. Only your wife is aware if you are donning a torn vest, no one else is. You also don't give a damn about your wife. You always treat her casually."

Paul: "You are absolutely right."

Doctor: "Now listen carefully. If you had a girlfriend, would you still be unconcerned about your vest?"

Paul: "Never doctor, how could someone expose a torn vest to their girlfriend?"

"That's exactly my point, Mr. Brown," the doctor said. "Before you succumb to any other delusion, go check your wife's undergarments. They will tell you whether or not she is cheating on you. If she consistently wears fresh undergarments, then clearly someone else has access to them in addition to you. Furthermore, you should have known whether she trims or shaves her pubic hair on a regular basis."

Dr Hartshorn's every word helped to eliminate Paul's mental confusion. He shared a lot of wonderful stuff with Paul. In fact, non-living things could reveal so many secrets, if we have the ability to listen to them.

After their discussion ended, Paul left for home.

His heart was profoundly affected by the doctor's words. He was committed to finding the truth. But how could he examine his wife's underwear covertly? He went to work every day, but Sandra stayed at home. There was no such occasion when he was at home, but Sandra had gone out.

Every night when she was in the bedroom with him, he was unable to see her undergarments well due to the dim light. But he knew very well that Sandra shaved her pubic hair regularly. He thought that he could have a chance at night when Sandra was cooking dinner in the kitchen. So, that evening while Sandra was in the kitchen, he went to the bedroom and shut the door from inside. Then he slowly opened the wardrobe where Sandra kept her undergarments. He thoroughly examined every pair. Each one appeared to be brand-new. Doubt grew in his mind. He needed to find out who was sleeping with his wife as soon as possible. But first, he had to remember that bastard's full name.

As Dr Hartshorn suggested, first check yourself, if the suspicion was confirmed, it was best to hire a private detective. Private detectives charged a hefty fee. Paul decided to wait a few weeks before taking a step in this direction.

He was deeply immersed in these ideas when Sandra's voice announced that dinner was ready. He finally joined his family at the dining table after approximately ten minutes. While eating, Suzie told her mother, "Mom, from tomorrow onwards, I'll be arriving from school an hour late."

Mom inquired, "Why?"

Suzie stated, "James, our basketball coach, has announced a one-hour after-school practice session for the next two weeks. As the game period is only half an hour long, there is not enough time for practice."

Paul was startled and asked, "What's the name of the coach you just told?"

"James," said Suzie.

"No, what is his full name?"

"James Baxtor."

"Ohhh," Paul exhaled coldly.

"Papa, what happened?" Suzie inquired.

"Nothing, baby. I'm looking for another James. He's also an excellent player."

***

There was a coworker named Shobha in the dry-cleaning shop where Paula worked. She was an Indian and was a single mother like Paula. She married an American but divorced after four years. Shobha's son was of the same age as Rick. Despite the fact that Shobha was gorgeous, she had gained a lot of weight since getting married. Her obesity became a hindrance in her way of getting married again.

Shobha and Paula had a great deal of respect for one another. Paula would frequently ask Shobha to lend her money, and Shobha would never refuse. Paula used to return her money as soon as she received her pay check. Even today, Paula had to borrow money to pay her electricity bill. She asked Shobha for money without hesitation, and Shobha smiled and gave it to her.

Paula thanked Shobha and said that her expenses were increasing day by day. She was not sure how she was going to run the house on one salary. Shobha suggested cutting back on expenses. Paula said that she wanted her son to have a bright future, so she sent him to an expensive school. Shobha claimed that many affordable schools also offered high-quality education. It was not necessary for only those children who attended expensive schools to succeed in the future. Her son attended St. Aiden School and was making excellent progress. Also, that school charged half the fees as Ralph Straus. She ought to consider this as well.

After listening to her, Paula nodded, but she didn't truly agree with her.

***

Ms. Laura, Rick and Chad's instructor was examining the student's assignments. Ms. Sonia, the math instructor was seated nearby. Laura held the notebook belonging to Chad. Chad's lewd handwriting had caught her eye several times. She decided to speak with Chad today.

She had taken English period before the break and gathered the kid's notebooks. She had another period in 30 minutes. When it was time for her period, she went to the class, and said to Chad, "Chad Brown, you must improve your handwriting a little. Your handwriting is extremely difficult to read."

Ms. Laura noticed that Chad wasn't even glancing in her direction. She repeated her point, but Chad kept his head bowed and his eyes glued to a book. Ms. Laura approached him, "I'm talking to you, Chad," Ms. Laura shouted as she shook him while holding him tight.

As he raised his head Ms. Laura saw that it was Rick. Then Chad's voice came into his ear, saying, "Miss, I'm here." Ms. Laura noticed Chad sitting next to Rick on the chair. She was perplexed as to how she had made this mistake. Then she realized that Rick was wearing the same blue and white striped T-shirt which Chad was wearing when the teacher took his English period earlier in the day. Later in the lunch break, both of them had exchanged their clothes with one another. This was the reason why the teacher had a misunderstanding. She inquired as to why they had switched your clothes. Both continued to lower their heads, but neither responded to the teacher's question.

Chad removed Rick's shirt when he got home in the evening and hid it in a cupboard because he knew his sister would be furious. Suzie did not come to know about his actions that day. However, Rick's mother caught him wearing a different T-shirt that didn't belong to him. When she asked his son, Rick told him the whole truth that this T-shirt belonged to Chad. He liked it so Chad exchanged that T-shirt with his shirt. Paula informed Rick that this was not a good habit at all. She instructed him to remove his shirt right away, adding, "I'll put it in your school bag. Return it to your pal early morning tomorrow." Rick removed his T-shirt, as directed by his mother. Paula, as soon as began putting the T-shirt in his school bag, realized that even the school bag was not Rick's.

Paula was so upset about his son's behavior that she decided to meet with Chad's parents and discuss it with them. In order to meet them in person and discuss this issue with them, she called the class teacher and requested Chad's address. The next Sunday, Paula arrived at Chad's home on Stone Street. She made an introduction and revealed that her kid and Chad were close friends. She then informed them about their children's practice of exchanging items. They were unaware of their son's peculiar habit.

When Paula Sandler informed them about their kid's terrible habit, Sandra took it seriously, but Paul was unconcerned. The reason for this was that he was preoccupied with something far more serious. And that was his wife betraying him. In comparison to that problem, he thought this one was minor.

Sandra assured Paula that she would speak with her son tonight and try to sort this out. Paula asked about their house's landline number. Sandra quickly jotted down the address and phone number along with Paul's office and handed it to Paula. Paula then left from there.

Sandra spoke to Chad that night, but nothing changed. Within a week, every book, notebook, and even water bottle had been replaced with Rick's.

One afternoon, Rick's class teacher called Paula to let her know that the school would be holding a parent-teacher meeting this coming weekend. Paula contacted Paul Brown at his office as soon as she got the phone call and informed him about the parent-teacher meeting. A few minutes prior, Paul had also received the same call. He typically didn't attend meetings of this nature, and her wife Sandra attended these meetings. But because Paul had misgivings about his wife, he preferred to go out and let Sandra remain in the house. He consequently agreed that he would accompany Paula to their class teacher and inform her about their kid's habits. Perhaps she could provide a solution. At the appointed hour, Paul arrived at the school. They discussed it in depth with the teacher, but she expressed her helplessness in this matter. She suggested they should consult with a child psychologist. Again Dr Hartshorn's name came into Paul's mind. He suggested to Rick's mother that they should meet with this child psychologist. Paula stated that she was a single mother who could not afford to pay the psychologist's fee. Paul said that she must accompany him and that he would pay the fees himself. Paula agreed, and a few days later, Paul scheduled an appointment with Dr Hartshorn.

Paul Brown, Sandra, and Paula Sandler were seated in front of Dr Hartshorn one evening. Paul requested Paula to tell Dr Hartshorn about their kid's peculiar habits. Dr Hartshorn was astonished after hearing what she had to say. He claimed to never have witnessed such a thing in his entire career. Nothing could be done about this because they were just five years old. As they grew older, they would realize that it was a bad habit and would stop doing it. Paul agreed, but Paula Sandler was concerned. She asserted that he must offer a remedy as she disliked his son's habit very much. The doctor expressed regret for being unable to offer a remedy to this issue. All he could suggest was that they should change their schools so that they did not meet each other. According to Dr Hartshorn's advice, if either of the two children's schools were changed and they were separated from each other, this strange habit would vanish automatically. Both liked it, but Paul stated that he had only been here a few weeks. He was unable to change his son's school so soon. He needed to do some research to determine which school was best for his child.

The doctor gave Paula a glance. Paula gave off an air of hesitancy. She was worried by Rick's peculiar tendency. Her friend Shobha's words were echoing in her ears at the same time, "Quality education is also available in many economic schools. It is not necessary that only those children who attend expensive schools succeed in the future."

She began to consider that enrolling Rick in another school would also enable her to save some money. This one action would resolve her two issues. She said that she was ready to switch her son's school.

***

After two weeks, Paula Sandler transferred her son Rick from Ralph Straus to St. Aiden Elementary School. Rick was devastated. He didn't eat properly for several days. He didn't even want to study. He was frequently silent. Nobody ever saw him laughing at school. On seeing this, Paula realized she had made a huge mistake by taking her son away from his friend. But afterward, he reasoned that everything would eventually work out on its own. She began to spend more time with her son.

After a while, Shobha's son Shiva became friends with Rick at school. Rick's old smile returned after about eight to ten weeks. Perhaps he had forgotten about his friend Chad. Then he became interested in studies as well. Paula was happy to see the changes. On the other hand, because of the low cost of her education, she was now able to save some money.

Paul Brown hired a detective named Philip Walker to monitor his wife Sandra. The detective tracked Sandra for four weeks. But he didn't notice anything out of the ordinary. Sandra didn't frequently leave the house. Her friendship was limited to a selected group of women in the neighborhood. After a month, the detective gave his report to Paul Brown, in which he stated that Sandra had not even spoken to a man at that time.

Paul took Philip's report and kept it in his drawer. Then he took out his checkbook from the same drawer and filled in the amount owed to Philip as a fee. Then he addressed Philip, saying, "Sir, could you please give me your full name so that I could write it on this check? Is that the same Philip Walker?"

Philip: "Sir, please make the check payable to Philip J. Walker, my full name."

Paul's brow furrowed, and a strange doubt crept into his mind.

"Mr. Philip, is this 'J' from James?" he inquired.

Philip: "No, sir 'J' is for Jonathan. My full name is Philip Jonathan Walker."

Paul heaved a sigh of relief, wrote his full name on the check and handed it to him.

***

Winter had arrived in New York in the year 2015. The nights were no longer as scorching as they had been. Rick Sandler, then 24, was locked up at a police station that evening. Late yesterday night, during a brawl in a nightclub, he smashed a liquor bottle on the skull of another boy, severely injuring him. The root of the argument was the boy's inappropriate behavior with his girlfriend. Rick was picked up from his house by the cops this morning. He spent the entire day in the police station reflecting on the good and bad times in his life.

Rick worked as a client service associate at the London Stock Exchange Group (LSEG). He used to invest his own money in the stock market as well. He no longer lived with his mother. After working for two years, Rick purchased a house in Carnegie Hills. His girlfriend's name was Fiona Rios. They had been dating since their senior year of high school. Nearly five years had passed since he graduated from high school. Despite being in a relationship for such a long time, they did not live together. There was a rationale for this. They were both aware of how living together caused relationships to end quickly. People frequently didn't take each other's habits lightly. People who lived under the same roof grew tired of one another. It was vital to keep some distance between them so that their attraction to each other did not fade. Fiona promptly joined a modelling agency after high school because of her stunning appearance. She rose to the ranks of supermodel in less than two years. During her five-year career, she had amassed considerable wealth.

She had a highly compassionate personality and was passionate about donations. Fiona, who was of Spanish descent, was Rick's first romantic partner.

As dusk loomed, a middle-aged man entered the police station. He approached Rick and informed him that his girlfriend had hired him as his attorney. Then he explained to him that he was delayed in coming here since he had been working all day to settle with the other side. He continued by saying that he had arranged his station house bail so Rick could get out of there.

The attorney then handed over certain papers to the officer in charge of the police station, who examined them carefully before releasing Rick from custody. The attorney assured Rick that he would notify Fiona as soon as he knew the date of the hearing of this case in court and that in the interim, he would work to resolve the issue with the other side. Rick had nothing to be concerned about in this situation.

When the attorney emerged from the police station with Rick, he noticed Fiona's Lexus RX parked outside. He had intended to drop Rick off at his place, but when he saw Fiona's car, he realized she had come to pick him up. He bid Rick farewell and walked toward his car. Rick was pulled like a magnet to Fiona's car and sat in it. When he saw his lover in the driver's seat, he forgot about his problems and felt at ease.

Fiona was dressed in a black top and jeans. Her cheeks were flushed with rage. Rick saw her angry expression and remembered how she kept stopping him from fighting, but he didn't listen since he was inebriated. Rick clasped her hand in her and apologized. Immediately, the fury on her face vanished, and love began to flow from his eyes. She smiled, hugged Rick, and asked in his ear, "Your place or mine?"

"Now it's up to you to choose whether you want to make love on the terrace or in the garden," Rick chuckled in response. Fiona's face flushed bright red once more.

She smacked Rick on the shoulder and yelled angrily, "Why can't you get this disgusting thought of outdoor sex out of your head? I'm not at all comfortable in it."

Rick laughed and replied, "I know, darling. But I'm quite tense today. Please help me to feel normal again."

Fiona smiled and drove the car in the direction of her residence. Her house was spacious and had a garden. Rick's house in Carnegie Hills was substantially smaller than Fiona's. He liked to have sex on the terrace while he was at his house with Fiona. When they both were in Fiona's house, he chose the garden. Fiona found it all quite bizarre, but Rick thoroughly enjoyed it.

Fiona was quite unhappy about last night's incident, and now she had to make love to Rick in the open. After having red wine with dinner, she had become a little relaxed, but she was still irritated at Rick. Due to these circumstances, the sex between them was going to be a mixture of love and quarrel. It was about to be midnight. Both were in the garden located in Fiona's house. The clothes had vanished from their bodies. Fiona was on her knees on the floor sucking Rick's penis. Rick suddenly asked her, "What did you see in that rascal Jimmy Seymour that made you accept his invitation to dance with him? You should be aware that he is a disgusting person."

Fiona yanked his penis from her mouth and said, "Now don't start all that again. How am I supposed to know what kind of man he is? I have never met him before." Saying this, she put back Rick's penis into her mouth.

Rick added, "But you should have understood when he was touching you here and there while dancing with you."

Fiona yanked his penis from her mouth once more and muttered, somewhat angrily, "Sometimes all this happens under the influence of alcohol. This shouldn't be taken too seriously."

As she was about to put Rick's penis in her mouth once more, Rick grasped her hand and pulled her upward. She got to her feet and stood. Rick gestured to her that he wanted to have doggy-style sex with her. She quickly adopted the posture Rick had requested by bending her knees and supporting herself with her elbows.

Rick knelt down behind her and gently pushed his penis into her vagina. Then he began softly sliding it in and out. He went on, "And this is what I'm trying to make you understand, fights happen under the influence of alcohol as well."

"But you knocked the booze bottle on his head," Fiona remarked. "That was excessive. Did you know how many stitches he got?"

"So you care more about that jerk than me? What does he possess that I do not? Yes, he has far more money than I do." Rick accelerated the action of thrusting his penis in and out while saying this. His thighs began to collide with Fiona's thighs.

Fiona's cheeks became red with rage. "If you had said these words two minutes earlier, I would have severed your penis with my teeth," she added. "You're aware of my rage, perhaps that's why you didn't put your penis in my mouth again. Rick, you're such a jerk. I arranged for your bail, and you're blaming me in this manner." Fiona began thrusting her buttocks backward and striking Rick's thighs as though she intended to injure him.

Rick accelerated his movements and stated, "Fiona, my blood was boiling when you were dancing with him. My heart desired to murder both of you. But then I decided I should first teach that jerk a lesson. I would talk to you later." Saying this, Rick smacked hard on her bum. Fiona grew enraged and seized Rick's balls, pressing them firmly. Rick screamed and yanked his penis from Fiona's vagina. Then he yelled, holding his balls in his hands, "What have you done?"

Fiona said, "Do you think you'll slap my ass and get away with it?"

"Darling, there was a mosquito sitting on your bum," Rick whispered helplessly. "I killed it before he could bite you." Fiona remained silent for a moment and then burst out laughing.

She apologized, saying, "I am sorry." Then she embraced Rick, and their naked bodies entwined on the grass until their lust was quenched.

Both of them went into a deep slumber on the grass owing to exhaustion from the day and the intoxication of alcohol. When Fiona awoke at about 7:00 a.m., she felt a burning feeling beneath her left breast. She sat up and noticed that a mosquito had bitten her there, leaving a large red welt. She began to caress that spot with her finger. Rick awoke and sat up at the same moment. As soon as his gaze rested on Fiona's face, he started laughing. When Fiona questioned him about it, he said it was because her nose had also become red from a mosquito bite. As soon as Fiona touched her nose with her finger, she experienced a scorching sensation there as well. She looked at Rick with a furious look on her face and stated, "This only happens to me because of your perverted demands."

Rick told her, "Seeing you like this, you remind me of that red-nosed writer friend of yours."

"You must accompany me to the launch event of her new book this weekend," Fiona said to him. "She wants me to launch her latest book, which features a love triangle with a dark ending." Then, in a frightened tone, she questioned, "Will my nose return to normal by then?"

"If it doesn't return to normal, people will then believe you two to be biological sisters," said Rick.

***

Three days later, on Saturday evening, Fiona and Rick showed up for her friend Amelia Martinez's book launch party at a Loft Gallery in the Lower Manhattan area. Amelia, who was of Fiona's age, had Rosacea, and the red patch on her nose was highly obvious owing to her pale complexion. However, because it was her evening, she attempted to conceal the red area with thick makeup, and she was successful in doing that. On the other hand, the red mosquito bite welt on Fiona's nose had also disappeared.

Amelia's third book was being launched today, and her model friend Fiona Rios was there to launch it. There were around 50 people in the hall. As they both moved slowly and reached inside, Rick's eyes caught sight of a young man wearing a black linen shirt sitting on a chair holding a drink. It sparked a very odd desire in Rick. They both walked by him and sat down in their chairs.

A tiny stage was set up in front of which Amelia stood to deliver her speech. She waved at Fiona as soon as she spotted her, and Fiona waved back. Then Amelia began to address the guests, but Rick's gaze was fixed on the young man in the black shirt. He didn't stop staring at him. That young man was immersed in his phone while drinking. He appeared to be uninterested in the event, just like Rick.

After approximately ten minutes had elapsed, the young man with the black shirt got up from his seat and headed toward the toilet. No one knew what occurred to Rick, but he swiftly rose from his seat, whispered in Fiona's ear, "I will be back soon," and followed the young man to the toilet.

Rick entered the toilet and noticed that there were only two of them inside. As soon as their eyes connected Rick questioned him without waiting even a second, "Excuse me, brother, can you tell me where you got this shirt, it looks quite appealing to me." The young man continued to stare at Rick's face without responding. Rick asked the same question again but he continued to stare at him, puzzled, without responding as though attempting to identify him. Then, it appeared as though an old recollection had flashed into his consciousness.

He pointed his finger toward Rick's chest and asked him, "Are you Rick, who used to study at Ralph Straus in childhood?"

Rick was astounded that the young man recognized his name and school. He said, "Bro, have we met before?"

The young man inquired, "First, let me know if I identified you correctly. Is your name Rick?"

Rick informed him that his assumption was accurate. The young man's face lit up with delight. He asked, "Don't you remember your childhood friend?"

Rick had been staring at his black shirt up until now. He attentively examined the young man's face after listening to him. Suddenly childhood memories were refreshed in his mind. It was undoubtedly his pal Chad, without whom he could not have spent a single day of his childhood. Today, after so many years, they had reconnected. Rick took a step forward and hugged Chad. His eyes welled up with tears. He said, "We have met again today after so many years solely because of your shirt."

Chad said, "When we were kids, we were both drawn to each other's things. I'm not sure what type of connection we had."

Rick remarked with a dejected tone, "You know, my friend, because of this habit of ours, we both had to part."

Chad put his hand on Rick's shoulder and murmured, "Now we're both adults. So no one can force their will on us anymore, bro. We may now be friends again, just like we were in childhood. We can reestablish our friendship. Today is a really memorable day since it reunited us. You loved my shirt, didn't you? You are free to keep it, my buddy. From today onwards, it is yours." Saying this, Chad began unbuttoning his shirt. Rick also took off his beige-colored shirt and both of them handed their shirts to each other. After that, they opened the toilet door and stepped outside while wearing each other's shirts.

Chad questioned Rick, "Who did you come here with, bro?"

Rick indicated where Fiona was standing on the stage, carrying her friend's book in her hands. He informed Chad, "That girl launching the book is my girlfriend. I came here with her."

"If I'm not wrong, this girl is a model," Chad added. "I've seen her images in several magazines." Then he stroked Rick with his elbow and said, " You proved to be an experienced player. I can't believe what I'm seeing. Only a lucky person can have such a lovely girlfriend."

Rick grinned and asked Chad, "Did you too come here with your girlfriend?"

Chad pointed to a photographer taking pictures of the individuals on stage and added, "That's my friend Andrew. He is the one who dragged me here. However, I have no interest in such events."

The event was now moving toward its conclusion. They parted ways by exchanging cell phone numbers and agreeing to meet again soon. Then they returned to their respective seats. Fiona's steps abruptly came to a halt as she approached her seat from the stage. With an odd smile on her face, she cautiously came closer to Rick and murmured, "So, it is you. I had the impression that someone else had taken your seat. Rick, how did you get your shirt changed? You were wearing another shirt."

Rick opened his mouth to answer her question, but then kept mute, fearing that if he told her about his childhood habit, she would think him insane. Then he just said, "It's a long story, Fiona. I'll explain later."

On the other hand, because men are careless, Andrew didn't even realize that his friend who came with him was now wearing a shirt of a different color.

***

Fiona spent the next two weeks following that event reading Amelia's book. Although she was not fond of reading, every now and then she would pick up a book. Amelia's novel had a love triangle in which an American girl and an African girl both fell in love with the same man. That man was likewise African, and he was more attracted toward the American girl. When the African girl learned of this, she used witchcraft to control the guy and caused immense suffering to her rival American girl, both physically and emotionally. Amelia had emphasized in her book the fact that certain African girls were specialists in witchcraft who had the power to hurt their opponents even when they were not in their direct line of sight.

Fiona's thoughts became extremely troubled after reading this book. This was not without cause. She was an extremely sensitive young lady. She became upset by books or movies that did not have a happy ending. Her thoughts began to draw parallels between the story's events and those in her own life. This time, too, her mind formed links between two events from her past life and those described in the book.

In her third year of high school, she had a weird incident for which she was unable to comprehend the cause at the time. However, after reading this book, she began to realize the true cause of such situations. The third year's events began to play back in her head like a reel.

In the last week of June, the Miss High School America Pageant was scheduled to be held. The winning girl would receive over $75,000 in scholarships, excursions, outfits, travel, services, and other awards. Girls were crazy about this contest. The name of the strongest contestant was Grace. Everyone was sure that the same girl would be the winner of this contest. The second chance was Fiona's. Apart from these two, there was a third strong contestant named Zuri who was African. All three of them labored day and night practicing as the competition date drew near.

Then, though, something odd and unexpected occurred. Grace unexpectedly became ill two days before the competition and had to be admitted to the hospital. She was disqualified from the competition, and the third contestant Zuri was declared the winner. Fiona stood second.

After reading the book, she began to suspect that the cause of the occurrence a few years ago was likewise witchcraft. Zuri must have done something to make Grace sick, causing her to lose the title. Fiona, on the other hand, was unconcerned. She had previously been in the second position and had remained there. But she felt awful for Grace.

A significant modelling project had mysteriously slipped out of her grasp a year ago. The agency signed a black model and erased her name without even providing a justification. Despite the fact that she had a lot of other work and that his manager Adam was busy all day due to work, being removed from a project was not going to make a difference to her, so she found it quite weird that she was abruptly replaced. People frequently used the term 'Black Girl's Magic,' she began to think that what had transpired in her life was not any black girl's magic but simply black magic.

Fiona's mind was extremely fragile and sensitive, and anything might swiftly have an impact on it. She had moments when she thought she was going to die. When she went to see a psychiatrist, he examined her and told her she had nothing to be concerned about. She was simply very sensitive, and with some group treatment, she would be fine. Fiona then included yoga into her daily routine and began attending group psychotherapy sessions twice a month.

Fiona was depressed after completing Amelia's book, and on the other side, Chad Brown was also depressed for a different reason.

Chad experienced some internal shifts after meeting Rick. Particularly, his sexual life had lost some of its heat. He continued to schedule frequent dates with his girlfriend but his interest in her had waned significantly. His girlfriend had also realized this but she did not talk to Chad about it. She suspected Chad might have some problem, as his conduct had altered and he was no longer as amorous and passionate as before. She didn't feel the need to inquire since she believed that if Chad intended to tell her something, he would have done so without her asking. She believed that when some time had passed, he would return to being the same.

Chad, on the other hand, took many days to figure out his problem. He eventually discovered what had caused him to lose interest in his partner. And then, one night, while having sex with her, he made a bizarre decision in his head. He stopped his girlfriend from putting her clothes on after sex and then shot some naked images of her on his phone with her permission. That girl didn't object to this in the least. She adored Chad with all her heart and saw no reason to reject his demand. She assumed he did this to recall the wonderful times he had with her while he was not with her.

***

The following day, after Chad got home from work, he contacted Rick and requested a time to meet. Rick informed him that owing to his tight schedule, he would be unable to meet with him before Friday. They both met together on Friday night at the designated time and location. When Rick was about to order beers Chad stopped him and said, "Wait a moment, bro. I want to discuss something really important with you."

Rick stared at him, surprised, and requested the waiter to return later. When the waiter went away, Rick turned to Chad and said, "Tell me, bro, what you want to discuss?"

Chad retrieved his phone from his pocket, unlocked it, and placed it on the table in front of Rick. Rick saw the picture of a fair-skinned female completely nude on the phone's screen. That girl was seated on the bed, cross-legged. Rick started feeling uneasy.

Why is his friend showing him this image? In a perplexed tone, he asked, "Whose picture is this, bro? And why are you showing it to me?"

"I'll tell you everything right now," Chad said. "Do you mind telling me whether or not you felt something within after seeing this picture?"

Rick was even more surprised. He took the smartphone off the table and examined the snapshot carefully. The girl was really stunning and there was no denying the girl's beauty. He said, "This girl is attractive, but so are many others. I didn't find anything noteworthy about it." Rick put the phone back on the table after saying this.

After a little pause, Chad added, "Bro, this girl's name is Liza Petrov, she is Russian and she is my girlfriend."

Rick smiled and replied, "That's great dear. You are quite fortunate. However, no matter how close someone is to you, you should never share a photo of your girlfriend with them." Rick finished his words with a trembling voice. Chad sat calmly, observing his expressions. Rick's expression began to shift quickly.

He once more picked up the phone that was on the table. The display was still active. Lust began to appear in his eyes after viewing Liza's picture. He swiped his finger across each of the succeeding images to examine them all as well. No one knows which evil spirit had whispered in his ear that there would be more comparable photographs following this one. Chad had never revealed this to him, though. He continued attentively examining each image one at a time, and Chad kept seeing how his facial expressions were altering.

After a while, he passed the phone to Chad and said, hesitantly, "Man, she's really hot. I hadn't realized it before."

Chad stared him in the eyes and inquired, "Are you desperate to get her?"

Rick responded, "Certainly, my friend. I'll do anything to get her."

Chad's face lit up with a smile. He took Rick's hand in his and said, "You know, buddy, you got interested in this girl when I told you she's my girlfriend. We both are well aware of this instinct of each other. I'm not sure which power has imprisoned both of us in this bizarre circumstance. But it is certain that this scenario affects both of us. And I have no idea how or when it will all end. But for the time being, however, I currently feel like a puppet being controlled by an unknown force."

Rick paid close attention to him. Chad said, "That evening when we met and you pointed to Fiona and said she was your girlfriend, believe me, I haven't been able to sleep properly since then. Her face keeps flashing before my eyes all the time. I completely lost interest in Liza. That evening was not the first time I had ever seen your girlfriend, in any way. I've previously told you that I've seen her images on several magazine covers and centerfolds. But I never had such thoughts about her after viewing her photos. I grew concerned about what was going on with me. Then I realized that the reason for this desire was because she was your girlfriend. My heart yearns to own all that is yours. And the same thing occurs to you."

Rick nodded yes while remaining silent. Chad further said, "If I had gotten right to the point after meeting you, you might have thought wrong about me. That's why I had to deliver such a lousy presentation so you could comprehend my situation."

Rick burst out laughing. He asked Chad, "Now tell me what do you intend to do next?"

Chad took a big breath and stated, "As we have done in the past, we both have to swap girlfriends."

Rick said, "This is not possible, brother. The girls are not non-living items that we can just trade with one another."

"I know this won't be easy," Chad replied as he held his hand. "But we'll try our best. We will create a sound plan in order to make this job viable. If not, we shall have to live a restless life."

Following that, they ordered drinks, had dinner, and then said their goodbyes and parted ways.

They both met again after two weeks of this meeting. This time, instead of going to a public spot, they went to Rick's residence. They sat for hours discussing the secrets of their love lives and telling each other about their girlfriends' strengths and shortcomings. After three hours of diligent labor, they both came up with a workable strategy.

***

Let's go back in time when Chad and Liza first met. It had been roughly two years. Chad Brown was employed at North East Community Bank. The colleagues at his office were all men. There was no female coworker. He was 22 years old. He'd had three or four casual affairs until now, but no such female had entered his life who he felt he needed. He also didn't have a very active social life. He only had two high school buddies with whom he kept in touch. One was a cop, while the other was a photographer.

On weekends, Chad would see his photographer friend Andrew, who had his own studio. Andrew was usually involved in some sort of photo session due to his extensive workload. Chad took pleasure in seeing his studio work. Andrew's new assistant was a young Russian girl, Liza Petrov. She stood 5 feet 7 inches tall and had a curvy body type. The haircut was a high bob cut, and the facial shape was round. Chad was drawn to Liza the moment he saw her. But he'd kept his emotions to himself.

When he visited Andrew's studio one Saturday afternoon, he noticed that some furniture was being fixed in Andrew's office. As he approached, Andrew urged him to have a seat in another room where he would be doing a photo shoot. As soon as Chad entered another room, he noticed Liza mounting the camera on the tripod. When Chad said hello, she smiled and said hello back. Chad sat quietly in the corner on a stool. At the same moment, a model emerged from the makeup area, shrouded in a white sheet. For a brief second, her eyes met Chad's, yet there was no unusual expression on her face that should have arisen when she saw a stranger there. Andrew took his position behind the camera at about the same time, and Liza stood a bit further away from him.

Chad realized that a nude photo shoot was about to take place here. He thought he had no business being here. However, there was nowhere to sit because repairs were being made in the office outside. He then reasoned that Andrew himself had permitted him to sit here. He should remain seated here if those folks have no objections to his presence.

After a short interval, Liza approached the model and took the white sheet off of her shoulders. Chad was stunned when he saw the model's bare physique. His mouth watered after spotting the model's bell-shaped boobs. He continued to sit silently at his spot while attempting to suppress his feelings. Andrew began taking pictures of the model. She continued following Andrew's instructions, while Andrew kept photographing her from every angle to capture her beauty. Chad continued to savor the sight of her physique as he also began to get a tingle between his legs. He had a hard erection that was obvious through his jeans. Before he could do anything about it, he heard the sound of a really pleasant chuckle. He observed Liza was laughing while examining his pants. He became embarrassed and placed both hands on his pants. Both Andrew and his model paid no attention to him because they were both focused on the photo shoot. Liza became aware of the thing right away because she was standing in a fully unfettered stance. She continued to smile mischievously at Chad even after this. Her smile told Chad that she liked him.

Andrew finished the photo shoot in twenty minutes, and after the model departed, the three of them stayed in the studio and continued chatting. When Andrew went to the restroom after a while, Chad immediately asked Liza for her phone number. Liza gave her phone number without hesitation. Chad's assessment of her was spot on since she liked him as well. The next evening, they both had a lengthy phone conversation that started happening practically every day. They both started meeting on weekends. Chad and Andrew met less frequently, as was to be anticipated, but their friendship persisted. Chad was now spending all of his free time with Liza. Liza was a kind and open-minded young lady. She was three years younger than Chad. She, like other Russian females, enjoyed Vodka. Golubtsy and Schi were her favorite dishes. Chad once asked her at lunch, "You're so attractive, why you don't try modelling? Or are you content with your current job?"

"It has always been my dream to become a model," she replied with a smile. "However, I haven't had a chance yet. I had applied to several agencies even before working with Andrew, but nothing worked out."

"But Liza, working with Andrew can also be advantageous to you," Chad remarked. "He keeps doing photo shoots of so many models. He is well-known in the fashion industry. He has a lot of model friends. You ought to get in touch with them."

Liza had a sad expression on her face. "Chad," she said. "I tried several times. Many models have also suggested that I should consider modelling. However, no one steps forward to provide assistance. Perhaps they fear that if I venture into modelling and become successful, I may become a threat to their career."

Chad remained silent after listening to her. They had intended to spend the entire day together. They strolled around the lake's shore till late at night. Today was almost two months since they had become friends. Chad noticed that Liza was constantly holding Chad's hand all the time today. Chad gently pulled his hand away from hers while walking, placed his arm over her shoulder and whispered in her ear, "Liza, if you don't mind, stay at my house tonight."

Liza's eyes twinkled with mischief, and she punched Chad lightly in the stomach, saying, "Okay, but you won't keep me awake for long, right? I'm an early riser."

Chad chuckled and promised, "I won't keep you awake for long."

That night was one of the best nights of Chad's life. They both continued to drink till ten o'clock while dancing in one other's arms to slow romantic music. After some time, Chad placed the order for dinner from his phone. Once dinner was finished, they both entered the bedroom. They were going to make love today for the first time in their two months old friendship.

While they were kissing each other's lips, their hands began to move over different parts of each other's bodies. Within a few seconds, none of them had any clothes on. They were entirely engrossed in each other as soon as they took off their clothes. It was an incredible experience for both of them. Liza had an extremely flexible body. She provided Chad with such a pleasant sexual encounter that he developed an obsession with her. After approximately 40 minutes of jumping in the bed, they both became tired and fell asleep.

It was 5:30 in the morning. Chad was dozing off soundly. His mind suddenly experienced a very powerful and joyful sensation. It was so powerful that it jolted him awake. As soon as he opened his eyes, he noticed Liza sucking his penis. For the first time, he went through anything so amazing. The experience of having sex at night seemed little in comparison to this one. This fantastic technique for awakening someone from a deep slumber must have been discovered by some great individual. He glanced at her with amazement and Liza smiled. Chad embraced her and began kissing her lips. He was starting to think that he would be in a long-term relationship with Liza.

They both began having sex at regular intervals after that day. Liza would sleep with him two or three times a week. And every time she awoke early in the morning and used the same technique to rouse Chad from his sleep. Chad appreciated her style so much that he preferred Liza's distinctive method of waking him up in the morning over sex in the night. Their love became stronger over time. Their intense love lasted almost two years and then one day Chad met his childhood buddy Rick Sandler.

***

In those days, the Denim-Fashion Frontier Exhibition was going on in a fashion museum located on 27th Street in Manhattan, which explored the diverse history of denim and its relationship with high fashion from the nineteenth century to the present. Liza had come to see that exhibition. The reason behind this was her immense love for denim being a Russian. She came here by herself today; her boyfriend Chad did not accompany her. When she requested Chad to go with her, he made a strange excuse. It wasn't like she'd told Chad about her plans today. She told her four days ago that she needed to visit this exhibition. He may have made some sort of arrangement to accompany her if he wanted. Liza, on the other hand, did not push him to join her. For some time, Liza had noticed certain changes in Chad's conduct. She began to suspect that Chad was growing tired of her.

She moved slowly and came to a gradual halt in front of a mannequin dressed in Gianfranco Ferré's blue denim jacket. She really loved that jacket. She continued to look spellbound at the garment for two minutes. Then she heard someone say, "This jacket will look great on you."

She glanced in the direction of the voice, startled. A charming young man was smiling at her. He repeated it again, "You should buy this jacket. You'll feel even better wearing this than you do when walking down the ramp."

Liza stared at him, surprised, and replied, "I've never walked on the ramp before."

He said, "Is that true? Aren't you a fashion model?"

"No." Liza said, "I am a photographer."

"So, no one has ever told you that you can become a successful model?"

Liza exhaled deeply and said, "Many people have told me. But, thus far, fortune has not been on my side."

The young man approached her and said, "There is nothing like luck, and so on. You just need one opportunity. You will never look back after that."

Liza's face began to show signs of disappointment. She said, "Opportunity also comes with fortune."

"No. You should be aware that good networking is necessary to seize opportunities. Do you know anyone who works in the fashion industry?"

"No."

"However, I have a large network of contacts. Many people in my social circle work in the industry. We can try if you wish."

Liza smiled for the first time. She began to believe that other female models had complemented her features but all of them were unwilling to help her. This is the first time a man has said something like this to her. Men are not as envious as women. Perhaps this guy truly wants to help her. She smiled and said, "If this is possible, I will be really thankful."

"Give me your phone number," he said. "I'll contact you in a few days."

Liza gave him her phone number, which he saved on his phone.

"Your good name?" he inquired.

"Liza Petrov."

"Nice to meet you, Liza," the young man remarked as he shook Liza's hand. "My name is Rick Sandler."

***

Late-night phone conversation between Chad and Rick:

Chad: "Bro, did everything go as planned?"

Rick: "Yes, of course. I think I've done a very good job of impressing her. And she gave me her phone number."

Chad: "She instantly gave her phone number to anyone who asked for it. There is nothing to be happy about. What are your plans for your next meeting?"

Rick: "We'll need to put in a bit more effort before our next meeting. I bragged to her about the several fashion industry contacts I had who might help her. But this is not true. We now need to identify a person who can assist us with this task. We can't take any kind of help from Fiona. I'd like to keep her fully out of this situation."

Chad: "No way, don't involve her in all this. Otherwise, things will get extremely messy. I'll check with Andrew."

Rick: "Who is he?"

Chad: "The same guy with whom Liza works. You've seen him before. He was present at that book launch ceremony with me. He has a lot of connections. However, even while speaking with him, we must use extreme caution. We can't even tell him everything, since Liza could find out."

Rick: "Try approaching him in your own manner. If he can acquire an appointment from someone, this task will be made easy. That appointment will serve as the foundation for my second meeting with Liza."

Chad: "However, Liza's odds of receiving a chance following her meeting with someone from the industry are extremely slim…"

Rick: "Bro, all we have to do is pretend to help her. My main goal is to impress her, not to make her career. It is not on our agenda whether she finds a job in the industry or not."

Chad laughs. "You're a big bastard, man. Now I must hang up."

Rick: "Is she going to be with you tonight?"

Chad: "No, I called her, but she refused. Don't worry; I'll speak with Andrew tomorrow. I also need to create a reason to end my relationship with Liza. Good night."

Rick: "Good night, bro."

***

Rick and Fiona went on a long drive in Rick's car on a Sunday afternoon. While returning, they were still 20 miles from New York City when night struck. Rick turned on the car's headlights and changed the song playing on the stereo. The song 'Fire Meets Gasoline' by Sia began to play on the player. Rick's face revealed a diabolical grin. He didn't say anything and continued driving quietly. After a few seconds, he heard Fiona's voice, which he had been anticipating.

"Do you remember Rick, the last time we passed by this location, the same song was playing?"

Rick responded, "I don't remember clearly, dear," without glancing at Fiona. "Perhaps this is what took place."

"Although you might not recall the song, you will remember its effects for sure." Fiona said, "Our lives were only barely saved that day."

Rick claimed to recall and said, "Yes, I remember. But we had also made a fantastic memory."

"However, if any of us had been shot, we, too, could have become a memory."

"That was not the case, Fiona. He merely wanted to frighten us, and he succeeded."

Fiona became silent and got immersed in the recollection of that three-month-old incident. They were both traveling via this location that day around midday. Sia's song 'Fire meets Gasoline' was quite popular at that time. Fiona recalled that song's sizzling music video while she was listening to it. In the video, the girl walks into a field with her partner, where they both lie down on the ground and make love. Fiona became thrilled after hearing the music and placed her hand on Rick's thigh. Rick immediately acknowledged her invitation and stopped the car on the roadside. Then they both emerged from the car and entered the neighboring field holding each other's hands. There was no one nearby. They both got in the middle of the field and started making love there, just like in the music video. They were both passionately kissing each other, completely ignorant of their surroundings. The clothes on both of their bodies gradually began to disappear. But before any of them could strip nude, the sound of gunfire echoed in their ears.

Both of them became terrified and turned to gaze toward the direction of the sound when they saw an elderly, overweight bald man approaching them with a gun in his hand. At the same time, he was abusing and yelling at both of them, saying, "Get off my property right now or I'll shoot you."

They both became quite terrified and fled toward their car at a great pace. Some of their clothes were left behind in this haste. They heard the sound of gunfire once again as they fled. Like the first time, aerial shooting was done this time. Despite stumbling and rushing, they both managed to get in the car and then drove away from there.

That was the first time Fiona agreed to have sex outside. Otherwise, she would constantly object to this act. Perhaps it was the song's effect. Rick had played the same song again today.

Then, no one knew what came to his mind. Suddenly he parked his car on the side of the road and turned off the engine. Fiona stared at him, surprised, and inquired, "What happened, Rick? Aren't you eager to get home? We're already running late."

"Fiona, I want to finish the work that was left unfinished at this place that day," Rick remarked with a smile while looking at her.

Fiona's face became enraged. "No way. I'm never going to step into that field again."

"It was high noon. It was a horrible idea, I admit. But no one will notice us at this moment."

Rick flung out of the car. Fiona also emerged, shouting with rage, and stepped in front of Rick.

"Look, Rick," she said, "get back in the car right now and leave from here. I never want to step into that scumbag's property again."

Rick did not appear to listen to her and instead embraced her. Before she could say anything Rick planted his lips on her lips. Fiona's rage seemed to subside abruptly. Even now, that song had an effect on her.

Rick whispered in her ear, "Darling, screw that old man, let's make love here."

"It's hazardous here, Rick," Fiona warned. "The road is open to anyone."

Rick said, "Fiona, I don't think there's anyone around here. The night has also arrived. We will leave immediately if we notice any headlights."

Following that, Fiona kept quiet. Neither concurred nor disagreed. Rick pushed her right boob while inserting his hand into her top. She became horny.

She sat down and unzipped Rick's pants, revealing his penis. Then she began wiggling her tongue on its tip. She took the penis in her mouth when it became absolutely rigid. Rick closed his eyes in contentment. After a while of ecstasy, he took Fiona's hand in his and laid her on the bonnet of the car. Then he removed her jeans, followed by her panties. He then slid his head between her thighs while her legs were stretched apart. He continued to lick her moist vagina. He recognized after a while from Fiona's look that she was now eager to feel his penis inside her. He rose up straight and dragged Fiona, who was resting on the bonnet, closer to him, stroking his penis on her vagina. He was ready to slide his penis inside Fiona when a dreadful issue arose. They heard the sound of a siren and noticed a police vehicle approaching them quickly. They both became quite frightened and hurriedly grabbed up their clothes and jumped into the car. Rick started the car right away and drove away. The closer the police car got to them while they were having sex, there was absolutely no chance that their activity would have gone unnoticed by the cops. Just before the cops could exit the vehicle and arrest both of them, they hurriedly left the place.

Fiona was short of breath as a result of her anxiety. She began babbling rubbish to Rick and started blaming him, "We're going to be in a lot of trouble because of your actions." Rick sat quietly listening. He didn't say anything. The police car was still following them. Rick pressed the accelerator harder, increasing the space between both vehicles. The police vehicle was left far behind as they entered the city. The threat was almost over.

Rick stopped his car in front of Fiona's house. It was nine o'clock at night. Fiona jumped out of the car and stormed into her house, roaring. He didn't see the point in inviting Rick inside. If Rick didn't want to escalate the fight, he might have left quietly. But something different was going through his head today. Perhaps, how awful things had gotten, he didn't want to reconcile with Fiona. He also followed Fiona into her house.

Fiona gave him a startled glance before turning her head away. She turned on her laptop to avoid Rick. It was evident that her mental condition was rather unstable at the moment. When a woman's body is filled with a tremendous desire for sex and she is forced to flee at that same time, her mental condition frequently develops like this.

Rick had a thorough understanding of everything going on. "It is simple to place the entire blame on me, Fiona," he remarked to her. "You are equally responsible."

Fiona was irate as she said, "How am I responsible? Did I ask you to stop there? I'd been rejecting since the beginning."

Rick said fiercely, "But nothing will ever get better if you vent all of your rage on me. I did not rape you. You too had a say in what transpired."

Fiona yelled, "You didn't rape, but you know very well that when you get close to me, I can't stop myself. You ought to have avoided approaching me. This situation would not have happened if you had even the slightest sense. I'm not sure what you get from doing all this in the open."

"However, I am the one who got you out of that mess," Rick remarked. "You can at least say 'thank you'."

Fiona pointed toward her laptop screen and said, "Look at this. I've just received an email from the attorney. He has claimed that an out-of-court settlement had been reached with Jimmy Seymour. You are no longer required to attend the hearing. I got your bail and resolved your case, but I didn't expect to hear a 'thank you' from you."

Rick remained silent.

Fiona continued, "And if we were caught by the cops today, we'd be in far more trouble. We may have received a hefty fine. There would have been widespread mockery if this had been reported in the press. Let me tell you the truth, I'm sick of you, Rick. I'm sick and tired of your foolish acts. I'm not sure when you'll reach adulthood. When are you going to act like normal people?"

Rick made his final move after listening to her. "You vented your heart's rage on me, Fiona. But I never did anything like this to you. I adored you. I never made a complaint to you…"

Rick had hardly finished his remark when Fiona lifted her right hand and stated, "This is my only request to you, Rick, please do not try to contact me for a few weeks. Until I get over this shock. Lest I decide to leave you."

These final words she spoke melted like honey in Rick's ears. This was exactly what he wanted to hear from her at this moment. He swiftly turned and went out of Fiona's house.

She would show up to say goodbye to Rick at the door every time he left Fiona's home. However, she didn't get up and go to the door today; instead, she continued to stay in front of her laptop. Rick stormed out of her house, seeming to be enraged. As soon as he stepped outside, his facial expression transformed and a smile spread across his face.

***

Late-night phone conversation between Chad and Rick:

Chad: "Bro, did everything go as planned?"

Rick: "Yes dear, it was great. She was terrified to death by you folks."

Chad: "Do you think she will soon break up with you?"

Rick (laughing): "I did my best. She's not going to see my face after today. Please tell me how much you paid to the cop. We will split the cost 50-50."

Chad: "Hey, never bring up money in friendship."

Rick: "But, bro, we each have our own interests in this task."

Chad: "I wanted to mention that I had a close friendship with that cop. He has voluntarily helped us. For this service, he made no demands for payment. Tell me whether our timing was impeccable. We followed your car for a long time with the headlights turned off. When you stopped the car, we did the same. Then we spent some time watching your roadside romance. We entered the situation when I believed it had gone too far. We weren't late at all, were we? Did you succeed in fucking her?"

Rick burst up laughing. "You arrived at the right time, friend. If you were even a little late, I would have succeeded. Even I was infuriated to see your timely entry. Whatever occurred, it was to our advantage. Sometimes it's necessary to make minor sacrifices for a bigger goal. I got into a heated argument with Fiona following that event. She has asked me to stay away from him for a few days. I'm sending you an SMS right now with her two-week schedule. Only two weeks remain for you to make arrangements. After that, I won't be able to learn about her schedule. Do you get what I'm saying?"

Chad: "Yes, I do."

Rick: "How far has our other strategy progressed?"

Chad: "It has, indeed. I'm just sending you a phone number and an address. Talk to him and arrange Liza's meeting with him. They are on the lookout for a new model."

Rick: "Many thanks, dude. Good night."

Chad: "Good night."

***

The next day, Rick took a day off from work and drove Liza to the address Chad had provided. It wasn't a well-known modelling agency. They had a meeting with the talent manager. Liza had brought some of her photos with her. The manager was somewhat impressed by Liza as well. He assured them that he would definitely promote Liza. He kept Liza's phone number and photographs, and they both left from there.

After a while, they were both sitting in a coffee shop. Liza was flipping through the pages of a fashion magazine. She appeared to be in a good mood.

She thanked Rick for his efforts and remarked that only a true friend could be so helpful.

"If you've considered me a good friend, can I ask you a personal question now?"

"You can, indeed."

"Do you have a boyfriend or are you single?"

"Definitely, I have a boyfriend. But what are your intentions?"

Rick simply smiled at her without saying anything.

"Answer my question with complete honesty," Liza commanded, "as I might expect from a true friend."

"I think you're incredibly gorgeous. I fell in love with you the moment we met. I wish you had met me earlier."

She sat silently for a while, thinking about something. She then revealed, "I've been having an affair with that boy for two years. Everything was going well until recently when I began to notice that the passion in our relationship had faded."

"Do you intend to break up with him now?"

"No, I won't make a decision that quickly. I definitely need some time to consider it. But I can hang around with you for a while. Nowadays, cheating is considered as normal. However, you may be aware that girls prefer boys who say romantic things. Say anything that will make my heart melt."

Rick saw this as his opportunity to woo this girl and win her heart. He used his hazardous mind and said to Liza, "It is said that a person looks very beautiful when he is in deep sleep. You are so gorgeous while you are awake. I really want to know how gorgeous you appear while sleeping. Because there is no other way to know this, I just want to be in the same bed with you to witness it."

Liza burst out laughing after hearing him. Rick grew tense and asked Liza, "Did I pass or fail?"

Liza gently smacked the fashion magazine over his head and said, "Pass."

***

They had a great time at Liza's house that night. Liza's living room was the starting point for the sex game. After a lengthy foreplay on the couch, Liza grabbed Rick's penis and started climbing the stairs. Rick quietly followed him. He assumed Liza's bedroom was on the first floor. However, after mounting the steps, they both arrived at the terrace. Rick's enthusiasm doubled as soon as he stepped outside. He learned that Liza had no issues engaging in outdoor sex. As they reached the terrace, Liza drew him to her by putting her hands on his ears and started kissing Rick's lips. She then sat down and enjoyed sucking Rick's penis. Liza elevated Rick's pleasure by utilizing her supple body in various settings. While engaged in the sexual activity on the terrace, Liza appeared careless as if she didn't mind if anybody from the neighborhood would see her. Rick was simply carefree. No one knew here who he was. Anyhow, after their first night together, Rick had come to the conclusion that Liza was the ideal girl for him.

Both of them were resting on the terrace gazing at the stars after having an amazing sex session. It was 10:30 at night. Liza's eyes were filled with sleep. Perhaps she had a tendency to go to bed early. Rick took Liza's hand in his and asked, "How much time do you need to make your decision?"

"Not sure. No doubt I had a great time with you. But I'm unable to tell him the truth. There must be a justification."

"If you want to come with me, you can call him and right now and explain everything. Just a little courage is needed."

"He'll feel terrible." Liza's words made it clear to Rick that she was really worried about Chad.

He put her hand on his heart and added, "God is the one who looks after us all. Soon he'll find another girl and forget about you. I can't share you with him in this manner."

Liza's eyes were welling up with tears. "I understand," she said. "I'll try to speak with him about it tomorrow."

***

Chad calls Rick the next afternoon to inform him that Liza has broken up with him. Half of their plan had worked.

Chad carefully examined Fiona's schedule, which Rick had texted to him. An event piqued his interest, and he began creating plans in his head. Exactly ten days later, there was an open session on mental health awareness where Fiona was supposed to participate. Rick had informed him that Fiona was very sensitive and that she was frequently gripped by an unexplained fear. She was concerned about her illness and had attended numerous such seminars. Many people who had gotten rid of their mental disorders also used to attend such seminars, and they came just to help others.

The session was scheduled for 4:30 p.m. that day. It was a form of group conversation in which ten people who had never met before talked about their issues. The seminar's organizer was also sitting among them. All of them sat in a circle with their chairs facing each other. When one of the participants described his issue, the other participants would recount their own experiences one by one in an attempt to solve his problem. Fiona had been sitting quietly till now.

After some time, a 30-year-old woman began to tell that she frequently experienced nightmares. She could never sleep soundly as a result of it. She finished speaking and then turned to gaze at other people's faces. Perhaps she thought someone would step up and assist her in solving this issue. There was nearly two minutes of silence.

Then someone said, "Ma'am, it is not true that you experience nightmares and are unable to sleep properly as a result. The issue is with your sleeping. You experience nightmares because you can't sleep well."

Fiona looked toward the direction of the voice and noticed a young man wearing jeans and T-shirt with light blue and white stripes. The young man continued, "My girlfriend also experienced this issue, but she's now been cured of this illness. Sound sleep is the only method to put an end to nightmares. It is the answer to many of our mental health issues. And nice and healthy sex leads to sound sleep. As a result, I can confidently predict that there will be a problem in your sex life. When a person has sex half-heartedly or is terrified of being caught while having sex, that sex ruins his mental serenity. Make sure you enjoy sex wholeheartedly."

Fiona believed the young man had spoken something more profound than his age. This could not have been based on his personal experience. He must have read about it somewhere. But none of that mattered. What was important was that the young man had provided a solution to Fiona's problem. Today was a particularly fortunate day for her. She received the remedy without disclosing her issue. This was exactly what was happening to her. While having sex, she constantly worried that someone would see her. Her lover, on the other hand, was not ready to accept. So she kept getting these nagging feelings that she was going to die, and the consequence of this was that she was unable to enjoy sex and was also unable to sleep deeply. Fiona examined the guy closely for the second time. He was also extremely appealing to look at. Fiona decided that she would see him in person after this session was over.

After the session was over, all of the participants were provided with hot coffee. Fiona took the cup and walked around the corner to where the young man was standing alone, sipping coffee. Fiona approached him and said, "Hello, my name is Fiona."

The boy smiled slightly before saying, "My name is Chad Brown. Have we met before?"

"No," Fiona responded, "we have never met."

"So why does your face seem so familiar to me?"

"I'm a fashion model, Mr. Brown," Fiona replied as she took a sip of her coffee. "You may have seen my face on a magazine cover or a billboard."

Chad placed his left palm on his head and, as if recalling something, replied, "Oh yes. I have seen a large billboard with your picture near my house. I consider myself really fortunate to be speaking to a celebrity today."

Fiona smiled. Despite his best efforts, Chad's happiness was not being masked. Fiona went on to say, "Actually, I wanted to talk to you about something very important. What you just said to that woman piqued my interest. I'm also dealing with a similar issue."

"So why didn't you bring your situation to the attention of everyone? As far as I recall, you were always listening to people. I didn't hear about your difficulty. You didn't mention your problem."

"I arrived here for that reason. However, while I listened to you, I had the impression that you had provided the answer to my query. Therefore, speaking was not required. But the reason I'm speaking to you is because I was impressed by you. I want to learn a little bit more about this from you."

"Please tell me what you want to know."

"I don't experience nightmares, yet I am constantly terrified. It's the fear of dying. My departure from this world seems imminent. Perhaps this is due to my hypersensitivity."

Chad was quiet for a few moments. Then he told Fiona, "Look, oversensitivity isn't a problem, it's your strength. It simply indicates you are more human than others. You should be proud of yourself. And while you sleep soundly, whatever fear that is plaguing you will dissipate. Is your sex life normal?"

Fiona was a little hesitant to speak about it herself. So when Chad asked her about her sex life, she breathed a sigh of relief. She informed Chad about her boyfriend's peculiar tendencies. Chad, acting a little worried, said to her, "Madam, you should talk to him about this as soon as possible. This tendency of your boyfriend is disturbing your mental calm. This could have serious ramifications in the future."

Fiona informed him that her partner had lately committed a grave mistake, for which she was furious and refused to see him for a few weeks.

Chad listened to her with amazement, like he was unaware of what she was saying. Then he uttered the words, "Look, Madam, just give him one more chance and see. However, if he continues to engage in such behavior, it is best for you to avoid him. Sex should only be performed in a private setting because it is such a delicate matter. Lighting should also be avoided if possible."

Fiona listened intently as he spoke. Every word Chad spoke appeared to be finding a place in her heart. And this is just what ought to have occurred. Chad had put in a lot of effort to prepare for this meeting.

Fiona then questioned him, "Has your girlfriend completely recovered? Have both of your love life returned to normal?"

Chad smiled and continued, "Madam, the first thing she did when she recovered was break up with me."

Fiona was surprised and asked, "But why?"

Chad said, "It is difficult to understand girls these days. Now that I'm single, I'm looking for someone who thinks exactly like me."

Fiona averted her gaze shyly. Chad did not squander the opportunity and said to her, "If your boyfriend is unwilling to change his habits, and you decide to break up with him, please notify me. You know what I mean, don't you?"

Fiona looked up and inquired, "Mr. Brown, don't you think that went too fast?"

"It doesn't matter if you're fast or slow, ma'am. What counts is whether you are heading in the right direction or wrong. If you are confident that you are on the right track, then moving fast is always the better option."

Fiona's cheeks flushed with shyness. Chad realized that his efforts were bearing fruit. He quickly invited Fiona out to dinner. Fiona agreed but also put a condition that he would not make any additional demands.

***

Chad Brown visited a local park an hour after this meeting. A 30-year-old lady who had discussed her problem in the session that Chad had responded to was seated there on a bench. Chad sat alongside her on the bench and handed her an envelope. Opening the packet, the woman took the money out and began counting. She counted every dollar and had a surprised expression on her face. "This sum exceeds the amount that was requested," he told Chad. Chad agreed with a smile.

"Are you so pleased with my performance?" She questioned Chad.

"I am quite pleased with the outcome," Chad retorted.

***

Chad and Fiona met again for dinner that evening. They talked about a lot of stuff. No one could tell by looking at them that they had only met today. Their facial gestures gave the impression that they were longtime friends. Fiona found Chad Brown to be quite alluring. The only purpose of the condition she had set was to determine whether Chad is truly as gentlemanly as he appears to be.

Chad was able to infer the truth that Fiona was going to put him to the test. He spoke carefully while eating dinner. He didn't demand anything to which Fiona may object. They did, after all, share mobile phone numbers. After bidding their goodnights to one another after dinner, they parted ways. On his first day, Chad made more progress than he could have imagined.

The first 'good morning' text on Chad's phone the following morning came from Fiona. Chad also responded although he made no mention of wanting to meet Fiona. He really did not want Fiona to suspect that everything was happening according to a carefully thought-out plan. Although he was desperate to meet her and spend time with her, he wanted Fiona to show her interest in doing so. Three days later, his wish came true. When Fiona contacted him, she requested a meeting. Chad concurred. They shared another meal after which he brought Fiona to his house with her consent.

They both spent the night together. Fiona had expected to have carefree sex for the first time in her life today, followed by a good night's sleep. But, while having sex with Chad, she was worried about what her boyfriend Rick would think if he found out she had cheated on him. She wasn't sure if she should continue her affair with Rick or end it. She expected to make a decision after giving it some thought.

It was more enjoyable to have sex with Chad than with Rick. She also made an effort to love Chad as best she could. They both dozed off after midnight. She made love to Chad once again after waking up in the morning. Since it was the weekend, they both remained at his house till the afternoon. They also took a shower together. The string of meetings between them thereafter continued. In the meantime, Chad kept updating his friend Rick through phone calls about the situation.

Fiona and Rick neither broke up nor saw each other again for a long time. Fiona had been so impressed with Chad Brown's personality that she had totally forgotten about Rick. She appeared to have forgotten that she also had another innocent lover with whom she had an argument and had refused to meet for a few weeks.

Rick, on the other hand, got busy with Liza. Liza began to receive some minor contracts in the industry as a result of his efforts. She was grateful to Rick for this and did her best to keep him happy. Rick would occasionally remember Fiona and pray that she would never remember him. He was ecstatic about Liza. This joy was greatly influenced by the fact that Liza had once been Chad's girlfriend. Time flew by. Both of them were content in their relationships. They always discussed their experiences with one another whenever they met. Their entire plan was successful. Both of them engaged in such a risky activity due to a childhood habit. They both began to feel as though they had arrived at their destination. However, they were unaware of their true destination and what game would take place next.

***

One evening, on her way home from a photo session, Fiona made a surprise visit to Chad by stopping in front of his house and ringing the doorbell. After a little delay, the door opened, revealing an unidentified young lady standing in front of Fiona. "Is Chad Brown at home?" Fiona asked her.

The lady replied, "No, he is not at home. He has gone out."

Fiona experienced an odd sensation. He continued by asking the lady, "Who are you? I haven't seen you here before. As far as I know, Chad lives alone in this house."

"My name is Suzie," the lady said with a smile. "Chad is my younger brother. I've come to meet with him today. Please tell me about yourself. Who are you?"

Fiona told her, "I'm Chad's girlfriend."

"I can't believe this," Suzie muttered with a little surprise. "I've already met that girl. She is a photographer."

Fiona informed her, "I only met Chad a few weeks ago. He told me that his girlfriend had dumped him."

Suzie's face dropped. "What? He didn't inform me of this? Please come inside."

Fiona entered the house. Suzie made her a drink. They both then sat down on the couch and began conversing. Suzie claimed, "I'd only ever met Chad's ex-girlfriend once, and it was at the same house. She was a very intriguing young lady. I had a great time chatting with her. I'm shocked to know that she left such a nice boy."

"Even Chad was surprised why she left him," Fiona added. "This type of thing happens all the time nowadays. So, please tell me a little about yourself."

Suzie informed Fiona that she taught psychology. And she resided in Cove Haven, Green Pond, about an hour from New York. She remained busy in her research. She had never married or had an affair.

Fiona tried to hide her curiosity after learning about Suzie, but then she questioned, "Your brother works in finance, and you teach psychology. This is the first time I've noticed such a distinction between brothers and sisters."

Suzie laughed when she heard this. She told Fiona, "I experienced a tumultuous, perplexed childhood. My thoughts were jumbled. Also, I was hesitant to share my feelings with anyone. I never even mentioned it to anyone. When I grew up I began investigating my own mental issues, and I developed my interest in psychology. I received my master's degree in this field without any difficulty."

Fiona was surprised that Suzie had not said the exact words she expected from every stranger: "I've seen you somewhere before." And then she would proudly tell them that it was because she was a fashion model. Knowing Suzie, Fiona reasoned that she was probably too engrossed with her work and studies to notice what was going on in the outer world.

When Suzie asked about her profession Fiona said that she is a fashion model. Suzie smiled and remarked, "My brother has really good fortune."

Fiona talked to Chad Brown's sister Suzie for roughly 40 minutes at his house. Both were profoundly inspired by the other. Fiona then left from there. When Chad returned home late that evening, Suzie informed him that his new girlfriend had arrived to meet him. She didn't, however, ask about the break-up that she had learned from Fiona.

***

Likewise, three more months went by. The lives of the two friends appeared to be entirely normal from the outside. However, something was going on deep inside that would have a significant impact on their lives in the future. In the middle of 2016, a lot of people lost money in the stock market due to the recession induced by the sharp drop in oil prices and the inadequate handling of currency. Rick had also made significant financial investments. He had also endured a great deal of loss. His financial situation had deteriorated. His salary was reduced, making it difficult for him to pay the EMI on his house and car. Despite numerous efforts, no funds were forthcoming. His challenges were becoming more severe by the day. Then one day he felt obligated to seek help from his wealthy ex-girlfriend.

On the other hand, Chad Brown was happy with Fiona but missed the experience Liza gave him early in the morning. Fiona woke up late in the morning and Chad woke up earlier than her. There was almost no chance that Fiona would wake up Chad the same way Liza did. That was the one pleasant recollection Chad had of the lovely times he had with Liza. He loved that early morning sensation , which he could no longer get. The lack of that sensational experience made his sexual life with Fiona less exciting. On the other hand, he couldn't abandon Fiona and return to Liza. Liza was a kind and caring girlfriend. He felt in his heart that if he expressed his desire to meet Liza, she would not turn him down. And if he asked her for a favor at the moment of meeting her, such as spending the night with her, it was unknown if she would comply or not, but she would not be furious.

One Saturday afternoon, Fiona and her boyfriend Chad Brown were eating lunch at Fiona's favorite restaurant. After having lunch, Chad expressed his desire to have coffee and Fiona also agreed. They were both making plans for the evening while eating. After watching the nighttime show of a movie, both of them intended to spend the night at Fiona's place. While Chad was placing the coffee order with the waiter, Fiona's phone rang in her handbag. She was shocked to see the screen as she took out her phone. Rick, her ex-boyfriend, was calling her. She started to wonder why Rick was calling her after such a long time. Fiona did not disconnect his call. She slid her phone back into her handbag and rose from her chair.

She informed Chad that she needed to use the restroom for five minutes. Chad was talking to the waiter at the moment and was unaware of the phone call. Fiona hastily retrieved her handbag and headed to the restroom. The phone started ringing again as soon as he got inside. She hurriedly received the call, held the phone to her ear with her heart pounding, and whispered, "Hello."

"Hello, Fiona," Rick said from the other side. "How are you doing?"

"I'm fine, Rick," Fiona said. "How about you? How come you remembered me after all these months?" Her heart appeared to be pounding with excitement.

Rick's voice said, "Fiona, I'm in trouble. And I need your help. Not everything can be discussed over the phone. Could we meet up?"

"When do you want to meet, Rick?" Fiona asked as she placed her hand over her pounding heart.

The voice from the other side said, "As soon as possible. It would be amazing if we could meet tonight."

After giving it some thought, Fiona said, "I'll try. Where would you like to meet?"

"Groove Nightclub," said Rick. "10:00 p.m. sharp."

After hanging up the phone, Fiona sat on the toilet seat, with her palm on her rapidly racing heart, waiting for her excitement to fade. She didn't want her boyfriend Chad to notice anything unusual about her by looking at her face.

Chad Brown while sitting at the restaurant table was waiting for coffee and his girlfriend. There was a delay in the arrival of both. He was restlessly scanning the area. The restaurant's walls were covered with photos of numerous foods. One ad featured a girl munching on a banana. When Chad saw the poster, his thoughts began to spiral out of control. His heart got even more restless than before. He'd really lost control of himself. He hurriedly took his phone from his pocket and dialed Liza's number. The voice from the other side caused Chad's throat to get dry. He wiped the sweat from his brow and said, "Hello, Liza. Do you remember me?"

Chad heard the sound of laughter from the other side. He asked once more, "Liza, did you recognize who is speaking?"

Liza said, "I haven't yet become so renowned that I'd forget about my old buddies. Please tell me why you called."

"Liza, I don't think I can talk much longer here," Chad said after taking a deep breath. "I'd like to meet you once. Can you give me some time next week?"

Liza responded, "I'm afraid I can't confirm anything about next week, Chad. But I have the entire evening free today. Please let me know if you wish to meet."

Chad began to consider how to cancel tonight's movie plan. It was also critical to meet Liza. Who knew if she would make time to meet after today? "Okay, Liza," he said. "Let's meet for dinner tonight. I'll text you the location's name."

Liza: "All right, Chad."

As soon as Chad disconnected the phone and put it in his pocket, he spotted Fiona leaving the restroom and coming toward him. She approached and took the seat in front of him. The waiter delivered coffee after two minutes. Chad took a sip of coffee from the mug. He was unaware of Fiona's expression of intense perplexity. Engrossed in himself, he said to her, "Darling, I was thinking of cancelling tonight's movie plan. I don't feel well. I desire to go home and get some sleep. In order to prevent any interruptions, I will also turn off my phone. Let's get together again tomorrow evening. What do you think?"

As soon as Fiona heard him, the perplexity on her face vanished. She was considering what reason she might come up with to cancel tonight's program. Chad made her job easier.

"As you like, dear," she said with a smile. "You sleep without any worries today. Nobody will disturb you."

Around nine o'clock that same evening, Chad Brown and Liza Petrov met again on the rooftop of a continental restaurant. Liza had arrived wearing an extremely seductive outfit, and Chad's heartbeats were racing out of control. Liza asked Chad while they were eating, "Tell me, Chad, what important thing you wanted to talk to me about?"

Without establishing eye contact with her, Chad began, "Liza, there is no doubt that we both had a wonderful time together. You still have my undying love. I didn't object when you broke up with me because of how much I loved you. But as soon as you left, my life lost all of its joy."

Liza started to feel a little emotional. "What are you saying, Chad? Don't you have any girl in your life right now?" she asked, taking hold of his hand.

"It's not like that," Chad said. "Although I have a girlfriend, I really miss you."

Tears welled up in Liza's eyes. "I also didn't want to leave you, Chad," she said. "However, I came across someone who was giving me a lot of support as I made my way into the fashion industry. It is because of that guy that I have a couple of projects today. Chad, I was under his influence. I couldn't say no when he demanded my love. Please forgive me. I hurt you."

"Whatever happened is no one's fault, Liza." Chad asked, "Tell me, do you live with that boy?"

"No, Chad. He resides in Carnegie Hills. He sometimes visits me, and sometimes I visit him. We don't see each other all that much these days since he's a little worried about something."

"Would you mind if I make a request, Liza?"

"I won't mind, Chad. You are free to speak anything that comes to your mind."

"Liza, I'd like to spend more time with you. After meeting you, my mind has become completely fresh. Can you come to my house tonight if you don't mind?"

Liza sat still for a time. Then she murmured quietly, "Okay, Chad. But make sure that no one should know about it. And please don't make it a routine after today. Okay?"

Chad's face lit up with a smile. He said, "No one will know about it, Liza. You can switch off your mobile." Then he asked, "Liza, do you still get up early in the morning?"

Liza replied, "Yes, I always get up early."

Chad asked, "And do you still wake up your partner in the same manner?"

Liza remained silent. She shrugged her shoulders and smiled.

***

After this encounter, two more ex-lovers met in Groove nightclub. Fiona was dressed in a rust-colored sleeveless shift dress, which was popular in the 1960s, with her hair left untied. She appeared to be extremely content but Rick's face was very sad. He had a mug of beer in front of him. Fiona was also sipping Nebbiolo wine. She noticed Rick's condition and worried. "What's the problem, Rick?" She asked, "You didn't contact me for so long? Did you find what I said to be so offensive? Or perhaps you fell in love with someone else and forgot about me?"

Fiona's final question was exactly about what had actually occurred. But Rick lied to her because he desperately needed Fiona's help. He said, "Until now, no other girl has entered my life except you, Fiona. My love is solely for you."

Fiona then asked, "But it appears that the smile has faded from your face. What type of mess have you gotten yourself into?"

The club was playing really loud music. Rick brought his lips close to Fiona's ear and softly informed her of his financial situation. Then he explained that he had called her to meet so that she might help him.

Fiona asked him to be calm and continued, "Rick, tell me whatever amount you want. I'll transfer the amount into your account tomorrow morning. You may return it whenever your condition improves. It doesn't matter if even you couldn't return it. You have nothing to be concerned about. It's our duty to help each other in the times of need."

Rick's mood improved significantly after speaking with her and watching Fiona's reaction. He was no longer concerned about anything. Fiona had previously helped him financially, but Rick had returned her money after two months. He wasn't sure how long he'd be able to return her money this time.

Fiona and Rick talked for quite a long time. He then conveyed his desire to dance with Fiona, and she promptly said yes. They both began dancing on the floor. Fiona had a lot of alcohol, and her steps were shaky. Her hands began to crawl over Rick's body. She had possibly grown a little excited as a result of wine's effect. Then something happened that fueled the fire. The DJ began playing the same song sung by Sia, 'Fire Meets Gasoline' that Rick had purposefully played in his car.

But today, it wasn't Rick who was responsible for playing that song, but some unknown entity who wanted to see this meeting end on a high note. As soon as the song began to play, Fiona grabbed Rick in her arms and sobbed, "Oh Rick, this song drives me crazy. I can't stop myself when you're around me. I'm losing control of myself. Rick, please tell them to stop otherwise I don't know what I will do." Saying this, Fiona placed her lips on Rick's lips.

Now Rick was no longer in a position to speak so that he could ask the DJ to change the song. He only needed to signal the DJ to do that. But after tasting the moisture on Fiona's lips, which was like dewdrops on rose petals he realized that this endeavor would have required a lot of courage, which he most certainly lacked at the time. Fiona passionately hugged him after the long French kiss. Rick was feeling her hot breath on his neck. She found it difficult to wait much longer at this point. "Please don't start here," Rick mumbled in her ear. "It's not the right place, let's go somewhere else."

Fiona grabbed his hand and rushed toward the toilets. They were both aware that the only safe location to have sex in such places was in the toilets. They both went through all of the toilet doors. They were all occupied. Fiona's respiration became more rapid. She exited the club with Rick. Her car was parked on the opposite side of the street. She got into her car with Rick and began kissing him profusely.

Rick removed her dress. Fiona was only wearing panties underneath her outfit. Then she swiftly removed Rick's clothes. Then, for some unknown reason, she turned on the car's ignition. Rick looked at her with surprise. Fiona pressed a button, which opened the car's sunroof. Then she said to Rick, "You must be missing outdoor sex with me. I can't help you any further today. This is all I can do for you right now."

Rick's eyes welled up with tears. He wrapped his arms around Fiona's naked body and the two of them had fantastic sex in the car.

That night was bizarre. All of the former lovers had been reunited. The amusing thing was that everyone had turned off their mobile phones so that their new lover could not contact them, the same new lover who was occupied with his old lover somewhere else.

Everything returned to normal the next morning. On Sunday evening, Chad and Fiona watched a movie and spent the night together. Rick's anxiety was significantly reduced when he received the desired amount of money in his account from her ex, and he called Liza and extended an invitation to visit his house.

Liza had said good morning to her ex-lover in her own unique style this morning. Chad felt really content after spending the night with her. He had persuaded Liza to meet with him at least once a month, if not more frequently. Rick, on the other hand, knew after meeting Fiona that Fiona had not yet been able to remove him from her heart. She still harbored the same feelings for him. They made a pact that night to meet again as soon they got a chance.

More time elapsed. The four of them continued playing this nefarious game in this manner. The fact that the two friends were still in contact with their ex-girlfriends was a secret they both kept from one another. But there are those people who cannot be kept in the dark. Suzie, Chad's older sister was one of them.

***

One night Chad and his ex-girlfriend Liza spent time together at Chad's house while cheating on their lovers, Liza habitually took Chad's penis in her mouth as soon as she woke up in the morning. Chad awoke and began running his fingers in Liza's hair. His phone rang at that very moment, so he scooped it up off the edge of the bed with half-open eyes and answered the call. It was a video call from his sister Suzie. Chad suddenly realized that he had made a mistake by accepting the video call because both of them were in a compromising position. He attempted to press the call-disconnect button, but unfortunately, the camera switch button was accidentally pressed, turning on the phone's back camera. Suzie caught a glimpse of Liza's face as she sucked on her brother's penis.

She screamed. "Oh God, Why do I have to see this scene in my family?" She then hastily disconnected the phone call. As soon as she regained her composure, she realized that Liza had broken up with her brother. She texted her brother. 'As soon as you're done, call me right away. I have an urgent need to speak with you.'

Liza left to take a shower after a while, and Chad called back his sister.

Suzie asked, "What is this girl doing with you now, Chad? I learned she had broken up with you."

Chad wiped the sweat from his brow and whispered softly, "Suzie, that was correct. She left me a while back."

Suzie asked, "If she had left you, has she come to apologize to you now? And I thought her manner of apologizing was odd, Chad?"

"Suzie, let it go. It is quite complicated." Chad tried to dodge the subject, but Suzie insisted on knowing the truth. "You've been telling me everything since childhood," she said, "Chad, I am not only your sister but also your friend. Please tell me if you are cheating on these two girls. If this is true, Chad, you are doing something terribly wrong. The results can be disastrous."

Chad had to give in to her obstinacy. "Do you remember my boyhood friend Rick, Suzie?" He questioned.

After a ten-second pause, Suzie remarked, "Is this the same Rick whose stuff was often found in your bag and yours in his bag?"

"Exactly Suzie, he's in touch with me again. And we'd both swapped our girlfriends. Fiona was Rick's prior girlfriend. And Liza abandoned me for Rick. My affair is solely with Fiona. Liza occasionally pays a visit."

Suzie smacked her forehead and replied, "I've studied psychology, Chad, and I also teach the same topic. But after learning about your situation, I'm also perplexed. This is shocking to know that this world is filled with weird people. I cannot fathom what is happening to you people. My suggestion to you, Chad, as your older sister, is to halt everything as soon as you can. Select one girl, and stick with her solely. You can end up in trouble if you carry on in this manner."

Chad remained silent. He didn't want to make any false promises to his sister. His silence gave Suzie the impression that nothing would change. She quietly hung up the phone.

***

Liza Petrov began to participate in modest fashion events. Since Fiona was a supermodel, she used to take part in a lot of fashion shows. Rick frequently accompanied Liza in these fashion events. But anytime he found out through Chad that Fiona had to attend the same occasion, he would fabricate an excuse for Liza and refuse to accompany her. Chad Brown did the same thing. Liza was supposed to participate in a similar fashion week in Houston in the spring of 2017 but Fiona was not coming.

Rick also applied for leave from his work and traveled to Houston with Liza for six days. They had a great time the entire week. It was Saturday, and it was the final day of fashion week. The next day, Sunday, both of them had a ticket back to New York. Liza had to perform in a 45-minute show that evening. They were both free throughout the day. They woke up late, dressed, skipped breakfast and boarded a taxi.

They were almost starving in the afternoon. Rick requested the taxi driver to drop them at a reputable restaurant. The taxi driver stopped the car at one point and asked them to move in a particular direction. He informed them that the Lake Club restaurant is only a two-minute walk away. It was a nice place to eat. Both of them could go there. They stepped out of the taxi and began strolling in that direction. Soon they saw the restaurant.

Liza's phone rang at that precise moment. She immediately began to cross the street while talking on the phone. A pink Cadillac then unexpectedly and quickly passed extremely close to her. Rick seized her by the arm and immediately hauled her away from the road. If Rick had been even one second late, Liza would have been run over by that speeding car. In a fit of rage, Liza spat insults at the black girl driving the Cadillac.

Rick attempted to soothe Liza. They were both still out of breath. Liza was going to need some time to recover from the shock. They stood still on the roadside for a few moments before proceeding to the restaurant. As soon as they stepped inside, they noticed that the entire hall was occupied. They were both shocked, wondering why the driver had sent them to such a packed location. Then a waiter approached them and said, "You will have to wait for some time, sir. After a while, some tables will become unoccupied." Despite the fact that they were both starving, Rick agreed and told the waiter that they would wait. This was because they were both unfamiliar with the area and didn't know if there was another restaurant nearby where they could eat.

The waiter left, and Rick and Liza stood there looking around the hall. His gaze was drawn to a man sitting in a corner, dressed in a blue shirt and glasses, who was presumably staring at him intently. His expression had a peculiar familiarity to it. It seemed as though an artist was looking at his creation. A stunning woman wearing a yellow corset dress sat in front of him. They were both eating.

Rick tried to remember if he had ever met that man before. But he was certain he had never seen him before. Then what could be the reason for that man to look at him? It may be possible that Rick's face resembles someone he knows. Rick, confused, shifted his gaze away from the man and started looking in another direction. Both of them stood there for about five minutes. Then Liza shook Rick's hand and gestured to one side, where there was a table recently vacated. They both went and sat at the table right away.

Rick looked at the man in the blue shirt again as soon as he sat down, but this time he was engaged in conversation with his friend while eating.

After a while, a waiter brought the menu card to their table. They both decided on what to eat and ordered lunch and wine. The food was served after 15 minutes. They both sat quietly and began eating. Liza's face revealed that she had not yet recovered from the shock of what had occurred on the road some time ago. Rick was considering what topic he should bring up to make Liza feel more normal. However, he was unaware of the impending catastrophe that would befall him.

Rick's phone, which was placed on the table, began to ring while he held a glass of Pinot Blanc in his right hand. Liza also looked at his phone. The message on the phone's display read, 'Bestie calling…'

Rick held the glass of wine in his left hand, picked up the phone in his right, and answered the phone. On the other side was Chad. Rick had purposefully not saved his phone number in his name so that if he was with Liza and got a call from Chad, their secret would not be disclosed. Chad's frightened voice sounded from there as soon as Rick said hello. He asked, "Where are you, Rick? There's some bad news."

"I am in Houston." Rick became nervous as well and stated, "What happened, bro?"

When Rick heard what Chad had said on the other end, his wine glass slipped from his grasp.

Chad said, "Bro, Fiona just died on the set in an accident."

"W…W…What exactly are you saying, bro? Why are you uttering such nonsense? Are you conscious? This is not possible." Rick's voice appeared to be trapped in his throat. His entire body was saturated with perspiration.

Liza assumed that something really horrible had happened when she saw Rick's condition. She inquired about what had occurred, but Rick motioned with his hand and told her to wait. The sound of glass breaking also grabbed the attention of the individuals seated at the neighboring tables, and they all began to turn their heads in their direction. Just then, a waiter appeared with a tray, picking up the fragments of glass that were shattered on the ground and placing them on the tray. Then he questioned Rick, "Are you all right, sir?" Rick indicated that he was all right. Chad, on the other hand, described Rick the entire scenario in detail, stating that Fiona was shooting on a set when a giant light from the ceiling crashed on her, killing her instantly.

Rick was still in disbelief. He continued asking Chad over the phone if he was kidding with him over and over again. Chad struggled mightily to persuade him that what he was saying was absolutely true. Following that, Chad questioned Rick about their return date. Rick informed him that they would arrive in New York the next day, on Sunday afternoon.

As Chad hung up the phone, Rick covered his face in his hands. His heart wanted to cry loudly, but he couldn't because he was sitting in a public place. Liza grabbed his shoulders and asked, "Whose phone was it, Rick? Tell me what happened that has disturbed you so much."

"Liza, I've suffered a great loss," Rick said after a few moments of silence. "I had made a large investment in a stock, and its value had abruptly dropped. A significant amount of money is lost."

Liza trusted him. "Rick, profits and losses keep on going," she consoled him. "Don't be concerned. The money you have lost will come back to you some day."

Rick was unable to swallow the morsel after this. He left the food behind. Liza completed her meal and paid the bill. Then they got up, came out, sat in the taxi, and proceeded to their hotel room.

The news of Fiona's death circulated quickly. All TV channels were broadcasting the same news. Everyone who knew her or loved her was heartbroken.

Rick declined to accompany Liza to the event that evening. Since Liza was aware of Rick's distress, she agreed to leave him in the hotel and attend the event by herself. Everyone was talking about the unexpected death of a supermodel even throughout that event.

Rick sat alone and depressed in his hotel room. Tears continued to pour from his eyes. Today had to be the worst day of his life. What was the awful circumstance that attempted to snatch both of his girlfriends? He was able to save Liza because he was with her. He pulled Liza from the road in time otherwise the black girl was about to hit her with her car. Fiona, on the other hand, was far away from him and was now in the grip of death. Both of these incidents occurred at the same time and caused a storm in Rick's life.

Note for the Readers

The thoughts racing through Rick's mind at that time had nothing to do with reality. What transpired was as follows: That day was Liza's last day on earth. But there was some mysterious force present at the moment that intended to influence the events of that day so that the story could take a different turn. Rick was not fast enough on his own to rescue Liza's life. Liza's life had been saved by the same mysterious force. When Liza was dragged out safely from that moment, the awful Death suddenly turned toward Fiona and seized her. This was due to two factors. The first was that both girls (Liza and Fiona) were having sexual intercourse with Rick at the same time. The second reason was that Fiona's heart and intellect were filled with fear of death, which drew that evil toward her.

***

Rick flew back to New York with Liza the next day, his heart aching. Liza was overjoyed about the event, but Rick's grief dampened her spirits. Neither of them spoke much during the journey. After dropping Liza at her residence, he went to his house. He went to see Chad late at night. He sobbed as he hugged Chad. Chad's tears were similarly not stopping. Both of them were missing that stunningly attractive girl named Fiona terribly. Perhaps no one could fill the vacuum created by Fiona's departure.

Fiona Rios' funeral was held at St. John's Cemetery on Monday late morning. Along with individuals from the fashion industry, some Hollywood stars also came there to pay their tribute. Fiona's parents looked very sad. Apart from them, the two other people who were very sad were Rick and Chad. They were both madly in love with Fiona. Chad couldn't stop crying. Rick comforted his friend by giving him another embrace and rubbing his back. Chad wiped his eyes with a handkerchief he pulled out of his pocket. When he opened his eyes again, suddenly he received an abrupt and powerful shock. He noticed Fiona perched on a tree branch from a distance. She wore nothing on her body. She appeared for a split second before disappearing. Chad trembled all over. "What happened, brother?" Rick asked. "Why are you shaking so badly?"

"Dude, I just saw Fiona on that tree branch over there," Chad said, pointing his finger in that way. "She was completely naked while she sat there."

Rick hugged him once more and murmured, "She's gone, my friend. She won't be coming back at this time. You had immense love for her, that is why your mind keeps bringing up images of her. You close your eyes for a few moments. This will make you feel more normal."

Chad saw some truth in what he had said. Suzie, his sister, had told him that when a person is in a state of shock, he often experiences hallucinations.

Both of them went back to their homes after the funeral was over.

Rick invited his girlfriend Liza to his place on Monday night. Liza also brought dinner when she arrived. Rick was unable to conceal his melancholy from Liza. They talked together till late at night. Liza was also made aware of the unfortunate death of Fiona Rios, a Spanish model, through the news, but she did not bring it up in her conversation with Rick. Despite having sleep in her eyes and a habit of going to bed early, she chose to stay up with Rick a bit longer. She was thinking that Rick had suffered a significant financial loss. But the truth was that he was no longer in financial trouble. Rick was no longer required to repay the large sum of money he had borrowed from Fiona. But Rick's anguish over her departure was so intense that he was unable to restrain himself. Rick couldn't have proper sex with Liza that night because he was depressed. Liza, too, made no demands of him and went to sleep.

Liza woke Rick up around 7:00 a.m. and told him, "Rick, I should leave now."

Rick took her hand in his and murmured, "Stay with me for a little longer, darling." However, Liza turned down his plea and apologized profusely. "Rick, this is a very hectic day for me. I have a lot of people to meet. I am pursuing a career in the industry as a result of your efforts." She kissed Rick's lips and murmured, "You look after yourself, Rick. I'll see you again in a couple of days."

Rick got out of bed and walked with her to the front entrance of the house. When Liza emerged, she immediately gave Rick another embrace and whispered in his ear, "I love you, baby. Please take care of yourself."

Rick kissed her lips while he was still in her hug. After a few moments, he opened his eyes and saw something really weird. At a short distance from his house, a girl who looked like Fiona and was completely naked appeared for a short moment and then quickly slipped behind a tree. Rick drew Liza away from him and began to rub his eyes with his hands. Then he peered in the same direction again, but there was no one there. He remembered that Chad had previously told him that he had seen Fiona sitting naked on a tree branch, which Rick interpreted as a hallucination. Was he also experiencing hallucinations, or was Fiona's soul wandering? After saying goodbye to Liza, he entered his house entangled in this mess.

That same evening at 7:30 p.m., Chad received a call from Liza, who asked, "How are you, honey? Are you free tonight? Can I have dinner with you at your place?" Chad, like Rick, was saddened by Fiona's passing. He did, however, accept Liza's offer and invited her to his home. Chad was the one who always called Liza after they broke up. But today it was Liza who was thrilled to meet Chad after spending the night with Rick and not having any sexual satisfaction.

Chad's doorbell rang one hour after receiving Liza's call. Liza was standing in front of the door when he opened it. Chad ordered dinner after receiving Liza's call, and it arrived shortly before Liza arrived. While they were eating, Liza told Chad that she needed to have her car checked by a mechanic.

Chad asked, "What's the problem with the car?"

Liza explained, "The car has not been running smoothly since this morning. Throughout the day, I've seen decreased handling and performance, with stopping, starting, and turning all negatively impacted. I was the only one in the car, yet it felt like other people were also sitting in it."

Chad said, "A good mechanic is just a short distance away from here. I'll text you his phone number and address. Get the car checked by him while leaving in the morning."

At night, Liza experienced another disappointment. Even the sexual encounters she had with Chad Brown fell short of her expectations. She was baffled as to why this was happening. She was aware of Rick's distress and his inability to love her properly, but Chad had not experienced any negative events.

Chad had no desire to have intercourse with her either. Chad had already informed Liza that he had found a new girlfriend after she had left him. But he missed Liza terribly. Liza had agreed to meet him again just because of this reason. But it appeared that he had lost interest in Liza and was now entirely focused on his new girlfriend. If such was the case, why did he allow her to visit his home? He could have turned her down over the phone. Liza fell asleep naked, embracing Chad, thinking about all of this. And the next morning, she showed no interest in even greeting Chad a good morning in her unique style.

After this episode, Liza bounced between her two partners like a tennis ball for the next two months, but she was unable to find happiness. Now neither of them called her on the phone. She called them herself whenever she wanted. Both her lovers had failed in bed. She never went out with Chad because their relationship was strictly limited to the bedroom. Meeting in the open carried a great deal of risk. Their secret might have been discovered. But Rick used to act completely normal whenever he was out somewhere with her. He was never frugal when it came to spending money and never demonstrated any financial restraint. If he was in serious financial trouble, as he claimed to Liza, he would have changed his way of living. This situation was beyond her comprehension. However, Liza's boyfriend's spending habits were not her concern. She only desired physical fulfilment, which she could not find from any of them. If one of them had lost interest in her, she would have completely embraced the other, but this was an unusual situation. She eventually stopped calling both of them out of frustration and started dating a Chinese man.

***

Suzie, Chad's sister, learned about Fiona's untimely death after watching the news, and she called Chad and spent a considerable amount of time comforting him. After two months, he called his brother again and inquired about his well-being. She noticed a change in Chad's behavior after speaking with him. She inquired as to whether Chad was still seeing his former girlfriend after Fiona's departure. Chad admitted to her that he was seeing Liza, but that he was no longer interested in her. Furthermore, he had no desire to love any girl. Suzie was alarmed when she heard what her brother had said. She recognized his problem. Suzie continued by probing Chad with further queries, such as whether he still saw his childhood friend Rick. Chad stated that he frequently spoke with Rick over the phone and that he, too, was going through a similar mental crisis.

Suzie was silent for a while after hearing his remarks before she resumed thinking. Then she said to Chad, "Listen, brother, I believe both of you friends have succumbed to depression. Depression can have an impact on all aspects of your life, including your sexual life. Low self-esteem, hopelessness, and physical exhaustion can all reduce libido. Anorgasmia can also be caused by depression. Furthermore, prompt treatment is crucial. Do you agree with me?"

Chad agreed and inquired as to how it might be treated.

Suzie informed him, "I'm leaving for Japan this weekend for two weeks. At that time, you and your friend are welcome to stay at my lake house. Staying away from the hustle and bustle of the city and close to nature will help both of you regain your mental stability. Can you both do this?"

Suzie has made a good point, but Chad wasn't sure whether Rick would agree to go. He promised to tell Suzie tomorrow after speaking to his friend about it.

Suzie went on to say, "If both of you come to stay at my house, keep a few things in mind. You must spend the most of your time fishing and swimming. You must maintain a worry-free state at all times. Additionally, always keep in mind that you both prepare your own meals. This is my tried-and-true way of bringing anyone's mental stability back to normal. All of these actions help a person recover from depression. Playfulness can aid in the treatment of depression."

Chad assured Suzie that if they planned to visit her, they would take care of these details. Chad then disconnected the phone. At night, he discussed it with Rick. Rick was initially hesitant, but when Chad persisted, he agreed. The next day, both of them applied for leave in their respective offices. Later that evening, Chad called Suzie to confirm that both of them would be staying at her house.

On Saturday, both of them packed their belongings and drove to Green Pond in Chad's car. They arrived at their destination in under an hour. The residences in that neighborhood were all 40–50 meters apart from one another. In the center, there were dense bushes. It was 10:30 in the morning at the time. Suzie was waiting for them at her opulent lakefront house. Suzie's house was pretty spacious.

In the backyard of the house, there was also a basketball court. Suzie had loved basketball since she was a child. Her flight to Japan was scheduled for 2:00 p.m. Rick and Suzie had just met for the first time. Suzie informed them that the groceries in the kitchen were sufficient for two weeks. Other than fresh milk and fruits, they don't need to buy anything.

Suzie was about to leave for the airport around noon. As she was departing, she added some more instructions to both of them. She said, "Both of you keep your phones turned off throughout the day. Simply switch them on for an hour at night. Forget about anything throughout the day and simply live without stress. No interaction with the outside world is permitted. Your playfulness is your therapy."

She then got into a cab and left for the airport.

On Saturday, they both stayed inside the house the entire day and only went for a walk in the evening. They continued to listen to music throughout the day, and they both cooked their own lunch and dinner. The following week, they spent as it was instructed to them. They'd both lie out in the sun on the wooden dock in front of the house. They went fishing and swimming while leaving their phones at home for the entire day.

They turned on their mobile phones an hour before preparing dinner in the evening and read and responded to urgent texts and emails. Once or twice, they both attempted to play basketball, but they soon recognized that this sport was not for them. In this way, a whole week went by. The following Saturday night, they were both watching a movie on TV. As soon as a romantic scene appeared in that movie, Rick grabbed the remote and switched the channel. Chad did not object to his action either. Both of them were obviously uncomfortable with the situation. They had entirely altered their lifestyle and had been removed from the outer world for a week, yet they were still not showing any signs of recovery. The ice that was causing both of their brains to become frozen was not dissolving. It was a pitch-black night with no chance in hell of the sun of hope rising. Both of them went to bed dejectedly at midnight as usual.

On Sunday noon, they were both relaxing on wooden sun loungers on the dock near the lake while sipping canned fruit juice. They had only swimming trunks on their bodies. Even though the sun was almost directly overhead, it wasn't that hot yet. Despite the fact that excessive heat had begun throughout most of America, the region's profusion of trees kept the weather comfortable. Chad was holding a men's magazine and had goggles covering his eyes. They were conversing with one another.

Rick asked, "Do you feel like going back?"

"I'm not sure. Neither that world nor this world contains anything valuable." Chad responded with disappointment. Rick rose from his sun lounger and walked to the lake's edge. He shifted his gaze here and there. There was silence far and wide. The sound of a pelican was heard from somewhere in the distance. Suddenly, Rick said to Chad, "There is no other house nearby. What if I swim in the lake entirely naked, with no one around to see? I believe I require a skinny dip."

"Do whatever comes to your mind, bro," Chad murmured as he set the open magazine down on his chest and turned to face him. "Suzie has given us similar instructions."

Rick removed his swim trunks and plunged into the water, leaning forward.

Chad's mind flashed with lightning as soon as he saw his friend's nude bum. He stood up swiftly and started glancing at him speechless. It appeared as though a tiny fragment of the block of ice, which had been frozen in his mind for months, shattered and dropped, chilling his heart. He set the magazine down and began watching Rick swim. Rick returned to his seat after 15 minutes. He wrapped a towel around his lower half. Then he opened the nearby juice can and began to sip. Chad had a gentle smile on his face. Rick asked, "What happened, bro? You appear to be quite cheerful. Tell me the secret of your happiness."

Chad remarked, "You know, it's pointless to explain when I have to prove something. A demonstration is the best course of action."

Rick said, "I don't understand anything. What do you want to say?"

Chad got up from his place and said to Rick, "I'm going to do the same thing you just did. You just have to focus."

Rick gave her a perplexed expression. Chad reached the lake's edge and turned his back to Rick and removed his shorts. He then leaned forward and leapt into the water in the same manner. Rick's mouth opened wide. His mind started longing for something. With startled eyes, he watched Chad dive into the lake.

Chad didn't swim for 15 minutes as Rick did. He emerged from the lake within five minutes and came to sit next to Rick. He placed the magazine he had been reading some time ago on his thighs. His priority at the time was not swimming because he had just solved a deep mystery, and he was anxious to talk to his friend about it.

He reached for his juice can and opened it. He then asked Rick, "Rick, what did you feel when you saw me jump into the water?" while smiling at him.

With some hesitation, Rick said, "I felt like a sailor who had been stranded in uncharted waters for quite a long time and then all of a sudden discovered his lost compass. My mind is right now filled with immense happiness, but I'm also extremely uncertain of my chances of getting it."

Chad exclaimed, "You idiot," while laughing aloud. "There was no point in showing it to you if I had to refuse to give it to you. But what I want to hear from you right now, my friend, is whether or not you felt relaxed when you saw the item you were keen to have. Did you, like me, have a brief feeling that your despair had lifted?"

Rick nodded confidently and said, "I felt it exactly. My mind suddenly became as fresh as it had been a few months before. In addition, I experienced an erection. If you don't believe me, you can examine by lifting up my towel."

Chad responded, "No need for that, friend. I have complete faith in you. The same thing happened to me today. So, should I accept that our friendship has reached a new dimension?"

Rick grasped his left hand and gently pressed it. Then he gazed tenderly into his eyes and said, "Now we are not only friends but lovers. We'll be living together after today. We don't require anyone else."

Chad extended his right hand and ran his fingers over Rick's hair, saying, "I am surprised to realize, dear, that until now I have been delighted by having so many things of yours, but the true gem was kept hidden by you until now. I would not have realized my true goal if the concept of skinny dip hadn't crossed your mind."

Rick said, "Now that nature has made us realize our real destination after so much time, I am sure all the bad instincts within us will vanish. And now that we've become so close, I feel compelled to confess something to you."

Chad asked, "What do you want to confess, Rick? You can tell me without any hesitation."

"Even after I started dating Liza," Rick said, "I kept seeing Fiona. All of our previous actions kept going uninterrupted. I apologize for it."

Chad received a mild shock. Then, after giving it some thought, he uttered, "If you forgive me, then I will also forgive you, Rick."

Rick gave him a tender shoulder bump and asked, "So, have you been fucking Liza as well? This is exactly what I expected from you."

Both burst out laughing. Rick added, "If I look at the lives of both of us, I find that whatever has been happening to us up to this point, we had no intention in it. We continued to dance as nature had been forcing us to do up until this point. But today I think the wandering is finally over. The days ahead will be peaceful. I'm going to ask you again, Chad, do you feel like going back?"

Chad said, "No, bro. Now I want to settle down here. There is nothing worth living for in that place."

"But staying here would also not be appropriate," remarked Rick. "There is still one week until Suzie comes back. And when she returns, she will instantly realize that we have overcome our depression. Then she'll expect some girls to enter our lives, which is not feasible. We can't trick her in this place. We'll have to return to New York for that. We can have all the fun we want in the one week we have left."

"Rick, you're correct," Chad admitted. "The sun has grown hotter. Let's go inside the house."

They stood up, gathered their possessions and began to make their way toward the house while still being completely naked. "We boys have a lot of sex with girls, but they require a lot of training," Rick said as he walked with Chad. "They frequently treat the penis roughly. It's a highly delicate thing, and only a man would know how to handle it better."

Hearing his words, a thought arose in Chad's mind. He told Rick, "I want to tell you why I kept seeing Liza even after we broke up. She used to wake me up in her own unique way in the morning, and I really missed that experience when I was with Fiona. That's why I used to call Liza over sometimes."

Following that, Chad described Liza's 'unique style' to Rick, who was already familiar with it. Then he questioned Rick, looking at him with interest, "Can I expect the same experience from you, Rick?"

"Chad, I'll do my best to make you happy at all times," Rick added with a smile.

It appeared as though Chad's mind was free of yet another weight. Then he began to giggle and said to Rick, "But in return for this demand of mine, you should not begin demanding outdoor sex from me. I can tell you right now that it is not my cup of tea."

They both chuckled and entered the house holding each other's hands.

***

Book Four
The Ballad of Lily

The year was 1981. One afternoon in the month of February, in an undisclosed location in the San Fernando Valley, Dakota Fawkes, a gorgeous 29-year-old woman with shoulder-cut coiled hair was lying completely naked on the bed. The bed was lavished with rose petals. Dakota rested her hands on her torso, one leg straight and the other folded at the knee. A black bandage was wrapped across her eyes. Her figure was really alluring. That figure is named as hourglass. It is believed to be a very unique and appealing figure in a woman. Her skin tone was fair, her eyes were brown, and her hair was black. The room was dark, but the bed was illuminated. Her body appeared to be the source of the dim light that extended over the room. Dakota was slowly moving her left hand from her torso to her chest. She eventually straightened her other leg also, and she began to rub her feet together. She continued to squeeze her lower lip in between her teeth.

After some time, a six-foot-tall and muscular man entered the room. He had wavy hair, thin eyes, and a moustache. He was also completely naked. He moved slowly toward Dakota's head. Then he touched Dakota's lips with his right hand's finger. Dakota's face lit up with a lovely smile as she recognized that touch. She seemed to be waiting for him. He moved his finger from her chin to her neck. As soon as his fingers reached down from her neck to her breasts, Dakota grabbed his hand with both hands. She slowly got up and sat down. The man got down on his knees and kissed Dakota on the lips. Dakota put her right hand behind his head and began sucking on his lips. The man, too, had closed his eyes. Their kiss lasted two to three minutes. He then repositioned Dakota on her back and spread her legs. Between her thighs, there was a clump of dark hair over her vagina. He put his face between her thighs. He started moving his tongue over Dakota's vagina. Dakota moaned with delight. She began running her fingers through the curly hair of the man. This game lasted nearly five minutes. The man then pulled his head out from between her thighs, grabbed Dakota's right hand, and lifted her off the bed. She was now sitting on the edge of the bed, with the man standing alongside. Dakota grabbed his penis with her right hand, which was completely stiff. She grasped the penis, drew it toward herself, and then popped it into her mouth. For five minutes, she continued fervently sucking it while occasionally running her tongue around the penis. He kept stroking her hair with his fingertips. That man's mouth kept erupting in gratifying moans. The penis sighed in relief when Dakota removed it from her mouth. The man slowly removed Dakota's blindfold by placing both of his hands behind her head.

As soon as their eyes met, Dakota's eyes lit up with a sly glint, and she yanked his penis back into her mouth. The poor penis's brain was on the edge of exploding from the overdose of satisfaction from the magnificent blowjob it had just received. Going through the same process again was quite challenging for it. It managed to survive somehow. Dakota had already provided a blowjob, so why did she feel the need to repeat it? She was the only one who could respond to this. We can only speculate that she may have done it to appease her own eyes. Or perhaps she just needed a little more stimulation on her dripping tongue.

After a short while, Dakota removed the penis from her mouth. They both started sucking each other's lips. The environment in the room had started to get really exciting. Maybe Dakota's vagina was starting to feel the desire for firm penetration now. While sucking the man's lips, she pushed him from the right side, causing him to tumble into the bed. Then she spread her legs and sat on his stomach. She then began clawing her chest with her nails. The man grabbed his dick and stroked Dakota's hips twice. Dakota quickly pressed her knees on the bed and elevated her hips above the man's abdomen. Then she slid her right hand between her thighs, grasped his penis, and inserted it into her vagina diligently.

Once the entire penis had entered her vagina, she slowly began spinning her hips counterclockwise. The man was grunting in delight. Dakota's groaning began to reverberate in the space along with his voice. Dakota gradually accelerated the pace. She rotated her hips for a moment and moved up and down the next. Both of them felt the urge to shift positions after a while, but the penis probably didn't want to come out of her vagina. It sent a signal to its owner. The owner responded to its signal by dropping Dakota to the side and climbing on top of her without pulling it out. Dakota was groaning as the invasion into the vagina persisted. She had both hands on the man's back at times, and behind his head at others. With each thrust, she also elevated her hips.

After a while, the posture changed again, and they had sex in the doggy style for the next few minutes. The sheet on the bed had multiple wrinkles at this moment. And the rose petals were severely crushed. The man then extracted his penis from Dakota's vagina, after which Dakota made him lie down on his back and rode him in reverse cowgirl style. She took the penis in her hand once more and inserted it into her vagina. Then she began caressing his balls. She now started to move back and forth. This went on for around two minutes. Then all of a sudden, the man abruptly touched her back with his finger. She immediately detected his signal and yanked the penis out of her vagina and began vigorously shaking it. The man ejaculated immediately after that. Her thick pubic hair was splashed with hot sperm. Dakota let go of the penis and ran two of her right-hand fingers through her pubic hair. When those fingers were completely covered in white sperm, she brought her hand to her face and protruded her tongue out of her mouth. Instead of licking both fingers, she turned her palm toward the front, made a victory sign, and winked her left eye.

Then someone shouted, "Cut," and there was a sound of applause. In addition, the room was filled with light. There were five other people present in the room. "Well done, Dakota," exclaimed a man in a polo cap sitting in the director's chair. "You've brought this scene to life. There is no one else in the entire industry with your level of skill."

Dakota replied, "Thank you, dear," and she arose from the man's abdomen. "My compatibility with Danny is excellent. The public has loved a lot all of the scenes that we have performed together."

"Yes, you're absolutely right," Danny answered as he jumped from the bed. "You can't feel normal with everyone."

Dakota picked up a hand towel and rubbed it firmly between her thighs. She then used the same towel to clean her hands. "Now both of you sit in the adjacent room and enjoy coffee while we get this room cleaned," the director remarked. "I'll join you in a moment."

Danny put on his briefs, while Dakota stepped out of the room naked and entered another room. On a table, there were two coffee mugs. She sat in one chair, while Danny sat in the chair opposite from her. They both began sipping coffee.

"Hasn't it been a really wonderful day? It's sunny too," Danny sought to start the conversation.

"Yes. The day is wonderful and very special," Dakota agreed.

"What makes today so special?" Danny asked.

"I've been working in this industry for ten years now. I shot my first scene on this day in 1971," Dakota replied.

"Wow, that's great. Congratulations, Dakota."

"Thank you, Danny."

Danny placed the coffee mug down on the table. Then he brought his right hand closer to his mouth and made a pose as if he was holding a microphone in his hand. Then he asked, "Will you tell our audience about your experience in this industry?"

Dakota burst out laughing. She eventually regained herself and replied, "I would say it was pretty good. I got everything from the industry. Moreover, the industry introduced me to a lot of wonderful people. I can say with assurance that the quantity of imaginative and creative people I have met in this industry will not be found anywhere else."

"Tell us about your early days. How did you get into this profession? And who did you film your first scene with?"

"I formerly worked at a gas station. I was 19 years old at the time. Toby Ziehm, a filmmaker, stopped by to fill up his car. He was 45 years old at the time. He introduced himself and told me that he had shot some documentaries as well as some adult films. He said that he found my figure really appealing and that he wanted me to work in his film. I felt bad for what he said. He realized it by the look on my face. Then he said solemnly, 'Look, if you don't like what I said, forget it here. However, if you wish to do this, please keep my card and contact me anytime. I firmly believe that you have a talent that will propel you to fame's pinnacles.' He hurriedly handed me the card and drove away. Perhaps he assumed I would become enraged."

Danny continued to listen to her, surprised. He then set the invisible microphone on the table and picked up the coffee mug. He took a sip of coffee and said, "This was a very good start. What happened after that?"

Dakota continued, "My financial situation was not very good. I've been here for two years. I worked really hard but did not make much money. I thought for three days before making a decision. I contacted Toby one evening and told him I was ready to work on his film. He was delighted. He gave me his studio address and urged me to visit the next day. I arrived on time. He was thrilled to see me. He revealed that he had been seeking a model for his new film and that his search was now over. He started shooting the next week. He also played the lead role in that film. My first sex scene was with him, and that film was very successful. I became famous overnight."

"He was an extremely brilliant personality. He is no longer with us, yet he is an inspiration to many young directors," Danny's voice reflected his grief.

"Of course," Dakota replied. "He was aware of his illness but didn't tell anyone until the very last moment. He was like a father to me. Nobody ever helps their own child as much as he did for me." Tears welled up in her eyes.

"Miss, I also want to make an open confession here." Danny raised his right hand and said after feeling her grief.

Dakota gestured with her hand, "What?"

Danny replied, "I was lured to join this industry because of your debut movie. That movie inspired me to choose this profession."

Dakota inquired, surprised, "Really?"

"Yes, it's true. I was in high school when I saw that movie of yours," he said. "I was blown away by your beauty and amazing figure. I made up my mind to work in the industry as well. After finishing high school in two years, I started trying my luck. I was given a chance after three years of hard work. I've been in the industry for five years. From the beginning, I was excited to shoot with you. But I didn't get the opportunity for three years. I had to shoot scenes with a lot of different models. Following that, God answered my prayers, and I was given the opportunity to sign a contract for a film in which you were in the lead role. I was walking on air that day. I was overjoyed. And then the scene featuring both of us became so popular that the filmmakers began to sign both of us together."

When the conversation started, Danny's tone was as if he was taking Dakota's interview. However now he resumed speaking in his natural style. Dakota said, "We've shot about 30 scenes together so far. Is that correct, Danny?"

"Dakota, you are absolutely right. Today's scene was the thirty-first. And I wonder how many other young men would be there dreaming of you and yearning to do scenes with you, and that's why they would have joined the adult industry?"

"What else can I say, Danny?" Dakota remarked, "I pray to God that all of their wishes get fulfilled soon."

They both burst out laughing. Danny's focus then shifted to Dakota's shoulder. A stink bug was sitting there. These bugs were found in large numbers in this area. He asked Dakota if he might touch her shoulder and then shook the bug away with his hand. The same person who had just fucked this woman in another room felt it was inappropriate to even touch her without her permission as soon as the camera had been taken away.

They chatted in that way for fifteen minutes. Danny inquired, "When is the next shoot?" She explained, "My periods will shortly begin, so no shooting for the next few days. After that, I have to shoot a gangbang scene for Tim's upcoming movie. That scene is one I'm extremely excited to do. Then I'll take a two-week vacation in Miami."

"Where are you going to stay in Miami? I own a house there. Please let me know if you need anything. I'd be glad to help you."

"I'll spend much of my time on South Beach. I've reserved a nearby hotel."

Just then, an assistant entered the room carrying Dakota's dress. Dakota got up from her chair and put on her dress. Before leaving, she bowed down and touched Danny's cheek with hers, saying goodbye to him. Someone beckoned her from behind as she walked toward her car. When she looked around, she noticed the director approaching her. She stopped. The director approached her and handed her the pay check. She thanked him, got in her car, and drove away.

***

Dakota spent the next five days at her residence on Alm Eve Street in Burbank City. She was excused from the shooting since her periods had started. The house was once owned by director Toby Ziehm. And shortly before his death, he transferred it to Dakota's name. Dakota lived all alone. She had neither a lover nor was she married. Never in her life had she felt a need for a man.

Most of the shooting took place exclusively in the San Fernando Valley those days. She could drive to the shooting location in less than 30 minutes. Her neighbors were quite pleasant and cordial. But no one in the area knew what she did for a living. She would tell everybody who inquired that she worked as a salesgirl. A church was within walking distance from her house. She occasionally attended church on Sundays. She liked hearing Father Davis's sermon. She had video cassettes of all the movies she had worked in, which she watched in the afternoon and at night. She, like other ladies, did not enjoy watching porn. But she used to watch all of her own movies over and over again and tried to figure out the flaws in her work. Every time, she made an effort to improve her performance. It was difficult to find someone who was more committed to her work than she was. However, she used to avoid watching porn during her period.

She was sitting idle that afternoon when the doorbell rang. When she got up and opened the door, she saw her next-door neighbor Mrs. Molly standing outside. Molly was around ten years older than Dakota. She lived with her husband and 17-year-old son Jacob. Molly was a housewife who spent most of her afternoons alone. Dakota greeted her and escorted her inside. They both sat on the couch in the living room.

"Tell me, dear, what's going on. I came to meet you when I saw your car parked outside. I haven't seen you in quite some time. Did you not go to work today?" She continued to speak without pausing.

"No. I don't feel well. I'm going to spend the next few days at home."

"Dear, what happened? Should I call the doctor if you want?"

"No, that isn't necessary. I'm just exhausted from too much work. I'll be fine after a few days of rest."

"Certainly, too much work makes you exhausted. I don't even have a job, but even doing household work exhausts me. Can I give you some advice, if you don't mind?" Molly asked, her gaze fixed on Dakota's face.

"Yes please."

"You're gorgeous. Your figure is also fantastic. Why don't you try modelling? There are so many lovely women in commercials. They make a lot of money as well. You will almost certainly get a chance if you try. You won't have to work as hard as you do today."

Dakota was getting bored of her. She tried to get rid of her by saying, "You are right. I'll try."

"When I was your age, people used to say the same thing to me," Molly added. "But I didn't take their advice seriously. And now I'm regretting it. I spend the entire day doing household work. My husband has gone to Utah to visit his sister. He'll be back in ten days. Until then, I must manage all his work also."

Dakota remained silent. Molly turned to look around the living room and noticed a 19-inch color TV with a VCR on top. In one corner, there was also an upright vacuum cleaner.

"By the way," she went on to say, "if the company is giving such a good salary then there is nothing wrong in this job too."

"Can I get you something to drink?" Dakota inquired.

"No. I don't need anything." She got to her feet. "I should go now. I'll see you later."

Dakota sighed with relief.

The next evening, when Dakota came out of the store after buying groceries she noticed Father Davis arriving from the front. Father Davis was in his fifties. He had a very peaceful demeanor and was constantly seen smiling. The face was quite radiant. He was always willing to help others. He earned a lot of respect in this town.

When she said 'good evening' to him, the Father's face cracked a smile. He asked, "I learned that you are not well. How do you feel right now?"

Dakota was surprised by how quickly news circulated in this town. She smiled and said, "Now I feel better than before."

Father asked, "Do you attend my sermon on Sunday?"

Dakota said, "I don't visit church every Sunday, but when I am free, I definitely attend."

"We shouldn't ever turn away from God," Father said. "He is the only one who can set us free."

"Yes, you are absolutely right, Father," Dakota said goodbye to him and continued on her way.

Dakota had a terrible dream that night. She was strolling naked down a secluded trail in the dark. Nobody could be seen nearby. Only a few trees were visible. On the side of the road, thick grass had also sprouted. She was walking barefoot. The path around her suddenly got covered with Napier grass. She moved a little further and noticed that the ends of the long grass were attached to human penises that were touching her shoulders. She walked forward in an effort to get away from them, but after a while, all of the penises, numbering in the hundreds, became aggressive. They started slamming into her shoulders, thighs, and face. Dakota ran more quickly. A penis then attempted to enter between her legs. She became terrified and ran even faster. She found herself surrounded from all sides by these penises. She covered her vagina with both hands, but as she did, the penis began to strike her hands forcefully. It wanted to enter there at any cost. Dakota got quite upset. A little penis jumped and tried to get inside Dakota's mouth, but Dakota prevented it. She struggled against them valiantly. During the struggle, her body began to sweat and her breathing grew hard. She then abruptly wakes up. She rose and sat down. It was 2:30 in the morning. She'd had similar dreams two or three times previously, but today's was particularly terrifying. Her eyes were utterly sleepless, and she spent the rest of the night tossing and turning.

***

Tim was a veteran filmmaker who never gave the models commands while shooting his scenes. He was always recognized for trying new things. He used to offer his models free hands and ask them to bring the most intensity to the action. Models adored him as well. By nature, he was a philosophical type. He was five years younger than Dakota. The final scene of his film, a poolside gangbang, was scheduled to be filmed today.

The shooting was to be held at a villa. Four muscular men were going to have wild sex with starlet Dakota Fawkes at the open pool. Dakota, like all other directors, was Tim's favorite model. She used to shoot with great ease and was never irritated. Nobody had ever heard a complaint from her. There was still half an hour till the shooting began, but Dakota's car arrived ahead of schedule. Tim rushed toward her as soon as she stepped out of the car.

"Hello, Miss Fawkes. You look ravishing today," Tim said.

Dakota embraced him in her arms. "How are you, Tim? What special are you planning to do today?" She inquired.

"Who am I to do anything, Miss Fawkes?" Tim laughed. "Whatever occurs, occurs on its own. I just don't place any obstacles in the way."

"I have never understood why you are so hesitant in taking credit for something?"

Without responding to her question Tim said, "Your screen partners will be arriving soon. By then, you should wait in the makeup room."

Dakota's elegant skin didn't require any makeup. Also as she had to enter the water during the action, therefore no makeup was applied. Only the underarms were shaved and pubic hair was clipped. A quick haircut was also performed. Then she was made to wear red two-piece lingerie. When Dakota came out after a while, she noticed that her co-stars had already arrived.

She came over and shook hands with all of them. She was familiar with three of the men, but it was her first encounter with the fourth. The fourth man was about his age. He had an attractive personality. His physique was well-shaped. His face was heart-shaped, with a broader forehead and a V-shaped chin. He also had a scar over his left eye on his forehead.

When it was time to start shooting, the director instructed the cameraman to set up the camera. Dakota went to the toilet room, squatted on the floor and inserted the vaginal contraceptive pill inside her. When she stepped out, the camera was already set. All four males were completely naked and had entered the pool by that time. Dakota started walking slowly toward the pool. The cameraman was following her and taking shots of her rear.

Dakota started to walk along the pool's edge. All the four men turned to face her.

"Good morning, miss," one of them said. "Would you like to swim with us?"

"I'm sorry," Dakota said, "but I do not know how to swim. Do you have anything I can grab so I won't drown?"

"Yes, we all have something like that," the other person answered. "We won't let you drown if you enter the water."

Dakota took off her halter bra slowly. She then removed her thong and stepped into the water, to set the pool on fire. The four men stood apart from one another. The pool's water level was up to their shoulders. As soon as Dakota emerged into the pool, she noticed that Tim had installed an underwater camera in the pool. A smile appeared on her face. She was even more amazed at Tim's creativity. That man left no stone unturned in his pursuit of perfection.

She was shocked when her gaze was drawn to the surface of the water. She noticed sperm floating on the surface. She wondered which among the four of them had ejaculated after having one glimpse of her naked body. She had already worked with three models and knew she couldn't expect anything like this from them. It had to be the fourth person who couldn't stand her heat. She began to wonder if he would remain just a silent spectator during this entire scene. Dakota felt a twinge of sadness. She had a strong desire to have sex with him from the moment she saw him. His personality has a distinct appeal to it. She then tried to concentrate on her task while fortifying his mind and purging it of silly ideas. She slowly approached all of them, pulling one of them closer to her by grabbing his erect penis. As he drew nearer to her, Dakota kissed his lips. The other man rubbed his hand down Dakota's back and up to her hips and ended up grasping her right bum in his hand. Dakota moved away from the first man, turned her face to the second, and began kissing him. After a little while, she knelt down, plunged her head under water and began sliding her tongue on his balls. Then she took his penis in her hand, put it in her mouth, and sucked it for as long as she could hold her breath.

She then got to her feet and emerged her head from the water. She stepped away from that man and approached the other two, one of whom was a newcomer. She cradled both of their heads to her breasts. They both began sucking her nipples. The third man put his right middle finger into Dakota's vagina and began fluttering it in and out. Additionally, he began to wiggle his thumb in her pubic hair. Dakota became aroused and began sucking the man's lips. That man also began to move both of his hands on Dakota's hips. Then he lifted Dakota up and made her sit on the poolside. He spread her legs apart with both of his hands and began to move his tongue across her vagina. Dakota began moaning with delight. The first man lifted her right foot from the water and began licking her fingers. The second man grabbed the third man's arm, turned him to the side, and started licking Dakota's vagina. After that, all of them sat on the poolside, and Dakota entered the water. Then she sucked each of their penises one by one. She found no slackness in the newcomer's penis. If that sperm floating on the surface of the water was actually his, then his masculinity was truly incredible. She was lost in this thought when she noticed the first man extend out his hand to her.

While she held his hand, he pulled Dakota out of the pool. Then he grabbed her up, slung her over his shoulder, and began walking toward the bedroom with her. He was followed by the other three. He carefully lifted Dakota off his shoulders as he reached the bedroom door. The first part of the scene was complete. It was now time for some bedroom sex. Dakota was advised to go to the makeup room once more, which she did. Her body was toweled down, and her hair was dried with a dryer. She began to think that the newcomer had done very little activity in the first scene. There could have been a lot of reasons for this. The first reason could be that he had ejaculated before the action began, which lowered his interest. Aside from that, he was probably a little shy considering it was his first time. Tim, the director, did not provide his models any screenplay. Everything happened according to the models' wishes. It was quite possible that the first three didn't give the fourth one much chance. She tried shaking his head to get rid of the thoughts. When it was time for the next shot, she emerged from the makeup room completely naked and made her way toward the bedroom. Her co-stars were all standing naked outside the bedroom door. When Dakota arrived, the first one lifted her up and put her back on his shoulder exactly the same way while carrying her here from the pool. After that, he entered the bedroom. He was followed by the other three. Tim was sitting on a chair on one side while the cameraman sat alongside with his camera ready. The first man flung Dakota's body on the bed and immediately parted her legs and began licking her vagina.

The other three also climbed to the top of the bed. Two of them approached her head and sat on their knees, while the fourth began stroking her boobs. Dakota noticed that the fourth started doing something on his own for the first time. She took both of the other two's penises in her hands, raised her head, and began sucking them one by one. The first man moved to the side after licking Dakota's vagina for a while, and the fourth rapidly positioned his body between Dakota's legs. Dakota missed the act because her entire attention was focused on the blowjob at the time. The fourth man rubbed his right thumb up and down her vagina before inserting his penis into her. Dakota's attention was diverted as the penis entered her vagina, and she pulled the penis out of her mouth and glanced at the fourth man. Then she realized that the man between her legs had been replaced. He felt a little better knowing that this newcomer had also shown some courage. When the two men sitting near Dakota's head saw the first one was free, one of them moved to the side, and the first one took his spot near Dakota's head.

Dakota now held the first man's penis in her hands. She took it into her mouth without even a second's delay. That newcomer's body was quite shapely, and his penis was also larger than the other three. For the first five minutes, he moved the penis in and out of the vagina slowly. His movement thereafter gradually increased. Dakota's body also appeared to start to tingle with energy. She was in a terrific mood. Despite her shaking head, she kept sucking and didn't pull the first penis out of her mouth. There was a specific cause behind this. She knew from her previous experience that while doing such gangbang scenes when one model stops the action, the others follow him and stop their actions as well and then everyone swaps their positions. Dakota realized that if she removed the first man's penis from her mouth, the fourth man might take out his penis from her vagina, and all four of them would switch positions. She thought the penis ought not to protrude from her vagina. She had never felt such a wonderful sensation before.

After fucking her for quite a long time in a missionary position, the fourth man lay down on his side and made Dakota sit on him in such a way that his penis did not come out of Dakota's vagina. Now it was Dakota's turn to move up and down. She began her contribution to the project with zeal. When the first man brought his penis closer to Dakota's mouth, she accepted it with an open heart and mouth. The other two stood motionless, waiting to take the place of the fourth. They had no idea, however, that their wait would last forever. The fourth man's penis was penetrating Dakota's vagina with gusto, and Dakota's screams echoed throughout the room. The director had a contented look on his face, as though he was satisfied with this scene entirely.

Dakota had positioned both of her hands on the chest of the fourth man. After some time, she lifted them from there and spread both of her hips with her hands. One of the two males standing motionless noticed this and got an idea. He sat down behind Dakota and attempted to slide his penis into her asshole. He was successful after several attempts. This doubled the impact of the impulses that were developing inside Dakota's body. She had reached the peak of her ecstasy. Two massive penises were causing mayhem in each of her holes. She took the first man's penis out of her mouth and began shaking it back and forth while gripping it in both hands at the height of her pleasure. After about a minute, a torrent of white liquid fell over her face. She started shaking the penis more vigorously. The same thing happened twice before the penis finally gave up and bowed in front of her. The man moved a few steps back; the other idle male's penis entered Dakota's mouth knowing it would suffer the same fate as his predecessor.

Dakota defused it in around three minutes. Dakota's face was fully encrusted with sperm. The makeup artist did not see the need for a facial on that face, but those two dicks had done that job wonderfully. Now was the time for the third penis, which had been inserted into her asshole, to come out and puke. Its sperm spilled on Dakota's back. However, the penis that was inside her vagina was not growing tired. Just like the other three, his time arrived after five minutes. Instead of pulling his penis out, the fourth threw the sperm into her vagina. Dakota, too, had experienced orgasm by that time. Her moans had also faded. Dakota leaned forward with her face coated in mingled sperm and kissed the lips of the fourth man. In that kiss, there was an unspoken 'thank you.'

Dakota had noticed that the fourth man wasn't doing much activity throughout the first part of the scene. Her illusion about him had entirely dissipated by the time the second section of the scene was shot. Apart from himself, he did not give anyone else a chance to fuck her pussy.

Dakota rose from the bed and stood up, but her head was spinning. Then darkness enveloped her eyes, and she collapsed. The director's voice reached her ears just before she fell—"Cut".

Dakota regained consciousness after around thirty minutes. She was lying on the same bed. Although she had nothing on, her naked body was covered with a sheet. Her face and the rest of her body were cleansed of the sperm. Tim sat close to her head and rested his right hand on Dakota's forehead. When he saw Dakota regaining consciousness, he exhaled a sigh of relief and inquired, "How are you feeling now?"

Dakota uttered a 'hmmm' sound and gazed around the room while lying down. Her three co-stars were standing in a corner. However, the person her eyes were searching for was not present. "What happened to me?" Her mouth made a shaky sound.

Tim stated, "You became dizzy and fell unconscious."

At that very moment, the cameraman brought a glass of water in the tray. Tim supported Dakota's back and made her sit. Dakota took the glass of water and drank it. Then she hung her legs down from the bed and asked the cameraman, "Please bring me my clothes."

"Dakota, I think you should rest a little longer," Tim remarked.

Dakota replied, "No, Tim. There is no need. I'm feeling better now."

She rose from the bed. The cameraman brought her dress. She dressed up and asked, "Tim, who was that newcomer?"

Tim said, "I'm not familiar with him either. I contacted 'All Men Agency' and requested them to send a model. He left without telling anyone after the shooting was over. He didn't even collect his pay check. I'm going to call the agency right now and enquire about it." Tim headed toward the phone in the corner of the room after saying this.

Dakota looked at the other three models and asked, "Don't any of you know anything about him?"

"Not at all, ma'am. We have no information about him. I tried to do an introduction, but he didn't tell us anything about himself," one remarked. "Then you emerged from the makeup room, and we started talking to you."

Tim placed the receiver to his ear after dialing the agency's number. "Hello, I'm Tim," he said as soon as the voice on the other side emerged. "The model you provided for my shooting has already left without collecting his pay check.

I don't even know what his name is. If you provide me his name, I'll send the pay check to your agency."

After hearing what was said on the other end, the receiver slipped from his hands. His hands began to tremble, and his entire body became saturated with sweat. Tim wiped the sweat from his brow and tried to appear normal.

"What's the matter, Tim?" He heard Dakota's voice. "What did the agency people tell about him?"

"Nothing. The receptionist told me that he was a new model and even though she didn't know his name, they'll shortly give me the specifics."

"All right, Tim. As soon as you know about it, please let me know. I must now leave," Dakota said as she fetched the car keys from the table.

"Are you in the condition to drive, Dakota?" Tim asked anxiously.

"Don't worry about me. I can drive, Tim," Dakota replied.

"I was just suggesting that you should take a rest for some more time. You can leave after noon. All of us are staying here for some more time."

"Tim, it's not possible. The day after tomorrow, I had to leave for Miami. And a lot of packing has to be done today. Please let me go."

She then reached over to the same table, picked up the pay check that was issued in her name, and said to Tim, "Thank you for this." She then walked out, sat in her car, and headed back toward Burbank.

On the way, the newcomer's face kept flashing across her mind. She also recalled Danny's words. "How many other men would be there who would be dreaming of you and would be desperate to do scenes with you and that is why they would have joined the adult industry."

Dakota was certain that the newcomer had joined the industry solely because of her. The way he had fucked her, it was apparent that the urge to get Dakota had been present in him for a quite long time. She smiled mischievously and mumbled on her lips, "One day I'll find you, mystery man."

***

Dakota was in Miami for the last five days. She had a great time during these days. She also did not leave any stone unturned when it came to shopping. She discovered that Miami was significantly more expensive than her hometown. She noticed people having fun and being carefree. She was strolling along the sandy shore on South Beach that evening. The waves would come in and strike her feet, getting them wet. While playing, some tiny children were making a lot of noise.

She realized that someone had called her name in the midst of the din. She turned around and noticed a tiny man in a cap staring at her. He waved his hand and said, "Hello, Miss Fawkes!" Dakota approached him. He was smiling. Dakota found her face familiar, but even after racking her brains, she couldn't recall where she had met him before. Her confused expression let the man, who was around 45 believe that she had failed to recognize him.

"Hello, Miss Fawks," he said. "Keong here. Keong Woo. Most likely, you didn't recognize me."

Dakota said. "I'm really sorry. I'm trying to recall."

"I was Sir Toby Ziehm's assistant when he cast you in his film."

As soon as he revealed his identity, Dakota recognized him right away. He was a Korean man. He was the director Toby's assistant at that time. He was ten years younger than him. Toby Zeihm was the one who taught him how to direct movies. But he eventually left him.

Dakota said," I apologize for not recognizing you at first glimpse."

He smiled and said, "However, I recognized you. You look just like you did ten years ago."

Dakota smiled. Then she asked Woo, "Are you here for work or on vacation?"

"Here, I'm shooting a reality show for television. Have you come here to shoot some content?"

"No. No. I am on vacation."

"Oh, okay. Is there anyone else with you here?"

"No, I've come by myself."

She started walking, and Woo joined her. Then he added, "I've got a lot to learn from Toby Sir. I wouldn't be who I am today without him."

Dakota smiled. She thought in her mind that whatever she was today was also due to Toby Sir. Then she turned her face toward Woo and asked, "Then why did you leave him?"

"Look, Miss Fawkes, I learned a lot from him. I learned a lot of new things while filming his documentaries. But later his focus shifted to pornographic productions. I assumed that after making a few adult films, he would return to his original work, but that never happened."

"I'm not sure why he suddenly became so interested in porn. As much as I know him, I can't claim he changed his line of work to make more money. He already had a lot of money. I assisted him for a short period in the beginning. I used to direct sequences when he was performing himself. I was seated in the director's chair when your first scene with him was shot."

Dakota giggled and said, "I remember it vividly."

"However, I envisioned my future in documentaries or television series and never in the adult industry. I wanted to create stuff that, if someone copied it in the future, viewers would instantly notice. That is why I had to leave him. I knew he was upset when I left, but I had my own reason."

"On the other hand, it's me, who sees no future outside the adult industry."

"Your situation is distinct. Anyone who has watched your movies can affirm that you were created exclusively for porn. For the past decade, you have been the face of the adult industry. You are an inspiration to others."

Dakota's lips curled into a smile. She was reminded of what Danny had said.

They had walked a long distance. Dakota said, "I believe we should now return."

Woo said, "If you don't mind, you can join me for dinner tonight." Dakota accepted his proposal.

Woo invited Dakota to dinner at El Exquisito, which was close to his hotel. Dakota boarded a taxi and arrived around 9:30 p.m. Woo was waiting for her. They ordered dinner and began conversing. Dakota inquired about his family, and he revealed that his wife was a fashion designer, and he had a 15-year-old daughter. He now resided in New York with his family. However, he frequently had to travel to different locations for shooting. Dakota then told him that she was still single and intended to stay that way.

Dinner was served after a while. They maintained their casual discussion. Dakota then told Woo, "You had mentioned earlier in the evening that you don't know how Toby Sir became so interested in making porn that he ditched his original profession. Let me elaborate. He used to share with me everything that was in his mind."

Woo stared at him, shocked, and said, "Tell me, please. I really need to know."

"He used to claim that the only thing that is completely honest today is porn. It is even more sincere than religion. He also used to warn that in the kind of circumstances he sees approaching in the near future, the human race will find it difficult to keep its sanity. People's proclivity for drugs will increase much more at that time. What we are creating today will aid in the mental wellness of people. Even if society does not embrace us now, we will be remembered as heroes in the future."

Her words struck a chord in Woo. "I have also spent a lot of time with Toby Sir," he added. "But he never revealed that to me. How much truth do you find in his words? I didn't interact with him after I left because I thought his new work was not eternal. In the coming years, none of this will be created anymore."

"Why did you think that it is not eternal?"

"How many times can you replace the sets and models to present the same thing to the audience? And eventually, the audience will grow tired of seeing the same thing over and over. Then why would anyone want to create all of this if there will be no response from the audience?"

"But why are you forgetting that there will be a new audience in every era? They will watch porn created in their times. Those individuals will not consider performers from the past who would have grown old or dead by that time. Those people will like their contemporary models, and this will go on forever."

Woo was at a loss for words. Dakota went on to ask, "According to you, what will be the age of the porn industry?"

"This, too, will be over by the end of the century, in my opinion. Yes, new experiments in this industry will be required if it is to be maintained alive."

"And what type of new experiments are they going to do? After all, sex is sex."

"Only the filmmakers of that time will be able to tell about this." Woo was quiet for a few moments. "Look, according to me, all the experiments have already been done," he added. "More and more films have been produced in recent years. Some films are even discussed on mainstream television shows. This is known as the 'golden age' of the adult industry. People who grew up in this period and have seen contemporary porn movies will never like porn from another era. Even 50 years from now, they will watch video cassettes from the same era."

"You are right, Woo. But that time hasn't come yet, so why worry about it now?" Dakota said. "Tell me how are things doing in Miami?

"Excellent, Miss Fawkes, this is an incredible place. The people here are also wonderful. Living here is a joy in itself. But I have to return in a few days. I'm thinking about migrating here with my family. However, all of my and my wife's jobs are in New York. I can only consider shifting to this place after the retirement."

Dakota smiled. Dinner was over. After saying Woo goodbye, Dakota stepped out of the restaurant and hailed a taxi to her hotel.

That night, Dakota had a similar nightmare she had a few days before. She was running naked down the same desolate trail when she was attacked by erect penises nearby. They attempted to get in through her thighs. Her hands were not free to defend herself this time, since she was holding something wrapped in a cloth in her hands. She was cautiously carrying that thing when she gets attacked by those bastard penises. She couldn't decide whether to protect herself or that precious thing. She ran around in great confusion and finally woke up. She sat up and wondered why she kept experiencing this dream over and over. And what did she have this time that was more valuable to her than herself? She continued to think about all of this while lying in bed, and after a few moments, she fell asleep again. She was surprised when she awoke in the morning. She had never been able to sleep again after going through a nightmare before. She suspected that this occurred because she was in another city. But she didn't realize the significance of all that happened in her dream.

Dakota went shopping the next day in the afternoon at a branded garment store. A 20- to 22-year-old couple was also in the store. As soon as the boy's gaze rested on Dakota's face, his eyes widened in surprise. He hurriedly murmured something in the ear of his girlfriend. When the girl saw Dakota, she yelled with delight. She dashed over to Dakota and exclaimed, "Hello, ma'am, are you Dakota Fawkes, the famous adult star?" Dakota was hesitant since she didn't want anyone to know anything about her. He looked around the store. Despite the fact that there were few people in the shop, she became worried. The girl did not wait for an answer to her query. Perhaps she was confirmed.

She took both of her hands in hers and said, "You have no idea how much I admire you. I aspire to be like you. My boyfriend and I both enjoy your movies."

Dakota made no attempt to free her hands. The girl said in one breath, "You are as beautiful in real life as you appear on the screen. Your body shape is incredible. All the scenes between you and Danny Sir are my favorite. Will you please give me your autograph?"

The girl took out a little diary and pen from her handbag and handed it over to Dakota. Dakota signed her autograph without even a second's hesitation. The boy then asked, "Would you like to join us for coffee?"

Dakota claimed she was about to leave, and she was already running behind schedule. When the girl persisted, Dakota thought that it would be safe to depart because her true identity might be revealed here just because of these two. Therefore she accepted their offer.

They both were quite delighted and walked to a coffee shop with her a little distance away. Dakota's mood had been much brightened by the hospitality she had received from strangers in an unknown city. She stayed awake till late at night thinking about that incident. At the same time, it occurred to her that if people in her hometown discovered her profession, would she receive a similar adoration? She was unaware when she fell asleep while contemplating.

***

Dakota returned to Burbank after a two-week vacation on Saturday night. Her aircraft arrived at 8:00 p.m., and she arrived at her house around 9:30 p.m. She got out of the taxi, unlocked the main door, and went straight to the living room, where she sat on the couch. After some time, she had a craving for coffee. She got up and walked to the kitchen, opened the packet of cappuccino, and then realized there was no milk in the house. At that time, the market was also closed. She stood there contemplating for two minutes and then decided to pay a visit to the neighborhood and ask Mrs. Molly for some milk. She picked up a cup and walked out of the house. Then she rang Molly's doorbell, and her husband Henry opened the door. Dakota wished good evening to him and he also smiled and said good evening back. Then he stepped aside and Dakota entered the house.

Molly's entire family was having dinner. She, her husband, and her son were seated at the dining table. A 14–15 year old youngster was also sitting with Molly's family whom Dakota had never seen before. Molly felt glad to see her and inquired, "Dakota, how was your trip?"

Dakota replied, "That was fantastic, Mrs. Molly, Actually I needed some milk."

Molly stood up and handed Dakota some milk from the refrigerator. Then she pointed to the youngster and said, "This is Charlie. He is Henry's sister's son. Henry has recently returned from Layton. Charlie accompanied him."

Dakota smiled and cast a glance toward Charlie. She noticed Charlie giving her face a very close look. She ignored it and said to Molly, "Thank you for the milk. The market is now closed and I have recently returned back from Miami. That is why I need to come to your house at this time."

"Consider it your own home, Dakota," said Molly. "You are free to request whatever you wish."

Dakota said, "Thank you very much, Mrs. Molly."

When she turned to go back, she noticed Charlie was still staring at her. She rushed out of their house.

Molly's family finished the dinner at ten o'clock. Her husband retired to the bedroom and got busy reading a book, while Molly started cleaning dishes in the kitchen. Jacob, her son, sat in the living room with his cousin Charlie and turned on the television. Then he connected his 'Atari 7800' gaming console to the television and both kids sat on the ground next to it. Jacob launched the 'Street Racer' game and both of them got busy playing it. Jacob had kept the TV's volume quite low. After 20 minutes, Molly emerged from the kitchen and said, "Jacob, Charlie, son, don't stay up too late," staring at both of them. "Get to bed on time. Even if it's Sunday tomorrow, that doesn't mean you should stay up all night playing video games. Okay?"

Jacob said, "Okay, Mom. We won't play for long."

Molly walked into the bedroom and locked the door from inside.

Charlie continued to peer at the space between Molly's bedroom door and the ground from the corner of his eye. After a while when the light in their bedroom turned off, he stood up and increased the volume of the TV.

"What are you doing, Charlie?" Jacob asked nervously. "Their sleep will be disturbed by loud noises."

Charlie said, "Brother, I turned up the volume so that neither of our voices could be heard by them. I'm going to share some crucial information with you."

Jacob asked, "What are you going to say, Charlie?"

"Bro, have you ever watched an adult movie?" Charlie asked.

"What are you talking about, Charlie?" Jacob said, surprised. "Children should not view adult films. I have one more month till I turn 18. Charlie, you're even three years younger than me. You should not even talk about it."

"And what if I tell you that I have seen many?" Charlie boasted.

"Have you gone insane, Charlie?" Jacob asks, shocked. "Who will provide you with the video cassette of an adult movie?"

"There is a video parlor close to our house in Layton," Charlie replied quietly. "One of my classmates is the owner's son. He secretly retrieves video tapes from his father's store and brings them to me when my parents have gone out and I am alone at home. Then both of us watch it on our VCR."

"Charlie, you are such a devil," remarked Jacob. "Have you ever considered the consequences of being caught?"

"Leave it, Jacob. When we get caught, we'll think about it. Listen carefully to what I have to say next."

"Tell me, Charlie," Jacob murmured softly as he drew nearer to him. "What do you have to say?"

Charlie asked, "Who was the woman who came over to ask for milk while we were having dinner a while back?"

" She is Ms. Dakota. She resides in our neighborhood." Jacob told him.

"What type of job does she do, Jacob?"

Jacob thought for a while and then replied," Probably a salesgirl in some company."

"My dear, Jacob," Charlie said, "she works in adult movies."

Jacob endured a terrible shock. "Oh my God, Charlie, are you telling the truth? You're sure there's no misunderstanding?"

Charlie said, "I'm certain, bro. I've watched a lot of her movies. You'll be astounded when you see her naked body. She performs her role so well that the TV screen catches fire. I had an intense urge to meet her. I had never imagined she would appear in front of me like this. I had an erection when I unexpectedly saw her today. One by one, all her scenes began to appear before my eyes."

Suddenly the bedroom door opened, and Molly stormed out yelling furiously. She shouted, "Why is the TV volume so loud? You are neither sleeping nor letting us sleep. Stop doing everything right now and go to your bedroom. There should be no more sounds. You got it?"

Jacob quickly turned off the TV and rushed to his room. Charlie tagged along with him. They both lay down after turning off the lights. Both of their eyes showed no signs of sleep.

Charlie requested, "Jacob, could you please introduce me to her?"

"Mom has already introduced you to her," said Jacob. "Did you want her autograph now?"

Charlie said, "She believes no one here is aware of her secret. We can ask for any favor in exchange for keeping her secret confidential."

Jacob said, "You're going to get me killed along with you."

Charlie requested, "Just take me to her house once. I'll speak with her myself. You simply sit still."

Jacob said, "All right. Let's see if tomorrow provides an opportunity."

***

Dakota awoke at about 1:00 p.m. on Sunday. She was exhausted from the flight and didn't have any job to do during the day, so she didn't think it was necessary to get up early. She was going to attend a party in Calabasas hosted by a prominent production company that evening. Many well-known industry figures were expected to attend the party. She used to avoid parties, but at Danny's prodding over the phone late yesterday night, she agreed. He got out of bed and made butter toast and coffee for breakfast. Around 2:00 pm, she finished her breakfast and stepped into the shower. She wrapped a towel around her body after taking a shower and then exited the washroom. Her doorbell rang at that very moment.

As she peeked out the window, she noticed two neighborhood boys standing outside. She experienced an odd sensation because no one had ever come from that house before except Molly. She had no idea why the boys felt the need to visit her house. She smiled as she opened the door and saw both of them. As soon as her eyes met Charlie's, a shiver ran through Dakota's body. There was a devilish glow on his face. "Miss, can we come in for two minutes?" Jacob asked. When Dakota stepped away from the door, they both came inside and sat on the couch. Dakota retreated to her bedroom, leaving both of them sitting there. She quickly threw away her towel and slipped into a gown. Then she came out and sat with them on the couch.

"What happened, Jacob?" Dakota asked as she took a seat.

"Ma'am, Charlie would like to speak to you for a moment," Jacob's throat felt dry, and he had trouble getting any words out.

Dakota shifted her gaze to Charlie. Charlie's eyes glowed with lust.

"Tell me, Charlie, what do you want to talk about?" She asked.

Charlie began speaking without hesitation, "Ma'am, I know everything about you. I am aware of the kind of work you do. I have watched your movies. You have lied about yourself and hidden the truth from the people here."

Dakota's throat dried and she remained mute, staring at that kid's face. She now realized why he had been staring at her last night.

Charlie went on, "I need a favor from you. If you do not comply, I will tell everyone about what you do."

Dakota became enraged, "Who will you tell?"

Charlie said, "I'll tell everyone."

Dakota asked, "And why should I fear you? Am I a criminal?"

Jacob started feeling uneasy seeing Dakota so angry. When he stood up, Charlie forced him to sit back while grabbing his hand.

Charlie said, "I don't want any big favor from you. All you have to do is give me and my brother a blowjob."

Dakota's rage had reached a boiling point. She jumped to her feet and yelled at them, "Get out of my house in a minute or I'll call the cops right now!"

Jacob rose to his feet swiftly, while Charlie remained seated. "Think about it, ma'am," he said. "Otherwise, you'll subsequently have a lot to regret."

Dakota overlooked his words and dashed for the telephone set on the far side of the living room. Meanwhile, Charlie stood up and he and Jacob hurried out of her house fast.

This incident occurred around 2:30 p.m. But Dakota's mind remained in turmoil until 6:00 p.m. Even after all this time, she was unable to overcome the shock that two next-door kids had inflicted on her. She lay on her bed, staring at the ceiling. She hadn't eaten lunch and had forgotten she had to go to an evening party. Danny phoned at 6:15 p.m. He inquired if she was ready for the party. Then she remembered that she had an invitation this evening. She once again claimed that she was not in a good mood and that she did not want to attend the party. But Danny insisted that she must go. According to him, going to the party will do wonders for the mood. Danny's words appealed to her. Maybe while attending the party, she might start feeling better. She unwillingly rose, removed her gown, opened the wardrobe, and began selecting a dress. She was completely ready within 20 minutes. She locked the house around 7:00 p.m., placed the keys in her purse, and drove away. She didn't notice Mrs. Molly standing at her front door, staring at her.

The party was hosted at a ranch near Calabasas by the renowned production house 'Boseman Brothers.' Nobody asked them why they were throwing the party, and they also didn't tell anyone. Almost all of the prominent figures of the adult industry were present there. As soon as Dakota arrived, all of the cameramen raced over to her with flashlights. Many of her photographs were captured in a matter of seconds. Other guests at the party were ecstatic to have their photos taken with her. She was the focus of attention at the event. This gave her a great deal of relief.

Her mood had improved significantly as a result of the respect she was receiving there. She began to believe that she had made the right decision by arriving here. She took a glass of wine and began to walk away. She noticed Danny seated a little distance away. Alongside him sat a black porn star. He also turned away from her when he saw Dakota and moved in her direction. Dakota hugged Danny and then they sat in a less busy corner, away from the crowd. There was a tiny bit of darkness there, and the music was also muffled. Danny realized Dakota needed to talk to him about something important. After so many years of acquaintance, she had started trusting Danny a lot. She explained everything to Danny that happened that afternoon slowly and hesitantly. Danny was shocked to hear it as well.

He went on to say, "Dakota, You should have met his parents at that very moment and told them about his conduct."

"He's not from around here. He has arrived at his uncle's place. And how can I complain to his family about him? I, too, have been deceiving them."

"You've always done the right thing. We can't tell people about our work openly. What difference does it make whether they find out sooner or later? They will, at best, refrain from speaking to you."

"Maybe you are right, Danny. I'm curious where he got the nerve to blackmail someone."

"They are kids, Dakota. At this age, mistakes are common. Who knows, he could have fallen in love with you. Perhaps he is immersed in your thoughts all day and night," Danny remarked mockingly.

"If that was the case, Danny, he would not have asked me to do all that with his cousin. Danny, you had a desire for me as well. You worked to get me, didn't you? But how wicked it is to push someone into agreeing to your point of view."

Danny didn't say anything. Perhaps the things Dakota said were true.

She further said, "I feel that porn is the cause of developing such negative thoughts in young people of this age group. I started to feel somewhat guilty."

"If porn is the cause of all this, then those who allow them to watch porn are to blame. What we create is intended for an adult audience, not children. Don't hold it against yourself. Forget about what happened. I am confident he will never appear in front of you again."

"But Danny, what will I do if they come again at night?"

"Dakota, do one thing. Please stay at my house tonight. I'll drop you off at home tomorrow morning."

Dakota agreed with him.

***

On Monday, Danny dropped Dakota off at her house around 10:00 a.m. Dakota had calmed down somewhat by this moment. She had to go to a studio in the afternoon for an interview for a monthly video magazine. The following day, Tuesday, a lesbian movie was being shot. She had the rest of the week off. She left the house an hour before the shooting in the afternoon, and as soon as she began to sit in the car, she spotted Molly. She was standing at the front door of her house. When Dakota waved at her, she overlooked her and entered the house after turning her face away. It made Dakota feel really odd. She then reasoned that Molly might not have noticed her. On the way, she kept wondering about what would happen if the kids told Molly the truth about her. Her mind, however, was denying this. If they disclose the truth about her, their secret of watching porn may also be revealed.

She arrived at the studio entangled in these thoughts. Her interview got started. She couldn't deliver a proper interview because of her nervousness. Everyone who was around noticed this. As she was about to leave, the producer assured her not to worry. He said that this interview wouldn't be made public until it had been properly edited. She returned back to her house.

She had to leave early the next morning. The shooting location was around 80 miles away. She arrived at the set at 10:00 a.m. Because the shooting was going to last the whole day, the producer had arranged for lunch on the set. There were three more models in addition to her at the shooting location. The shoot proceeded smoothly. She arrived home at dusk and went to bed early because she was exhausted.

On Wednesday evening, when Dakota left the house for a walk, Molly was arriving from the front. As Dakota wished her 'good evening,' she turned her face to the other side. Dakota was likewise in the mood to clarify things today. For two to three days, she suspected that Molly was ignoring her even after seeing her. She felt a little suspicious that perhaps those kids had revealed her true identity to Molly. However, that was not going to make any difference to Dakota.

As soon as Molly passed by, Dakota grabbed her hand and asked, "Mrs. Molly, why are you treating me like a stranger?"

Molly jerked her hand away and murmured, "You are like a stranger to us. You've been residing in our neighborhood for such a long time, and we, being such naive people, have no idea what kind of work you do?"

"What's wrong with my work?" Dakota inquired, knowing that Molly was already aware of her profession. Perhaps she wished to hear it directly from her.

"Now don't be so innocent." Molly teased her, saying. "If selling your body for money is not evil then is it virtuous?"

Dakota's suspicions had been confirmed. She reverted to her genuine self and asked, "Are you considering me a prostitute?"

"You're even worse than that. I've often wondered what the secret to your affluent lifestyle is. Now I understand you gained all of this by selling your body."

Dakota was surprised. Is this the same woman who previously suggested that she should pursue modelling? She controlled herself and said in a low voice, "Look, Molly, I am a performer and nothing more. We are extremely professional individuals who never cross any boundaries while working."

"You can make any excuse but I will say that people like you are a danger to society," Molly's voice was rife with venom.

"What danger do people like me pose to your society? And what do people like us do that people in your society do not?"

"We live in a respectable society. There is no place in it for a lady like you."

Dakota mocked, "Are you talking about the same respectable society from which your kids hail? Do you know what demand did those two make to me?"

"Don't get the facts mixed up, Dakota. People like you are to blame for the decline of today's children."

"However, we never create anything for children. Whatever we create is intended strictly for adults only. If your children manage to watch porn, then it is an example of bad parenting. Molly, it's not our fault at all."

"Make whatever excuses you want, but you must accept that there is no forgiveness for your sins. You will perish in hell." Molly glanced at him with scorn and spat on the road. Then she quickly turned and continued on her way. Dakota remained motionless. She was astounded by how much people despised her profession.

Due to the positive response her movies had received from the people, until now she believed that society liked her profession highly. But that was just her delusion.

The ten days that followed were the most restless of her life. Everyone in the town began to stare at her uncomfortably. Women began to look at her with hatred, while most men began to stare at her with eyes full of lust. She was aware that her profession was now known to everyone in the town. She already knew that any news spread like wildfire in this area. All of this occurred because of Charlie, who was unconcerned about his own secret being disclosed. However, no one considered how inappropriate it was for a child to see an adult movie. Many porn stars were open about their work. They openly told people about their profession. Even the families of many openly supported them. But she had kept her identity a secret from the public. She was surprised how in a matter of days, her status in the eyes of others had changed. Now it appeared as though she was a sex object rather than a living individual. Whether she walked into the laundry shop or the grocery store, she began to feel as though every person she encountered was eyeing her body and waiting to fuck her. It didn't take long for her to realize that the tall Napier grass she had seen many times in the bizarre dream that had terrified her for so long was the people of this town.

During those ten days, she participated in shooting three times. One scene was shot with Danny and the other two were with other male models. She continued thinking of the same mysterious man every time she had sex. Perhaps the sex she had with him was incredible. She had never experienced such contentment while having sex with anyone before. Due to the changed attitude of the people of the town toward her and being extremely busy with the shootings, she did not even realize that she had missed her periods.

On Sunday morning, she had nausea. She also felt a metallic taste in her mouth. She got out of bed and went to take a bath. After breakfast, she had a hankering to visit the church. She arrived on time and sat on the last bench on the left side. Two women were already sitting on that bench. When they saw Dakota, they both got up and moved a bit further to sit on another bench. Another woman noticed her and exited the chapel. Dakota wasn't surprised. She kept a sweet smile on her face. People reacted as if she had a contagious disease. There was much whispering about her in the church hall, but she was unaffected. She sat quietly as she awaited Father Davis.

After a few moments, Father Davis arrived. He was dressed in a black cassock. He was holding a Bible. He reached behind the pulpit and placed the Bible there slowly. He then turned to face the corridor. He noticed Dakota sitting in the rear seat. Father Davis looked at her with a strange expression on his face. Maybe he didn't think it was suitable for her to come there. He was the same person who occasionally encouraged her to attend church.

He remained silent for a while before beginning his sermon. He started by thanking everyone who attended for coming and offering their time to God. Then he mentioned that during Jesus' final days, today, 29 March, 33 AD, was also a Sunday. He then shed some light on the happenings of the day.

Jesus triumphantly entered the city of Jerusalem and mounted humbly on a donkey in keeping with prophetic messianic prediction. He later predicted his impending death and taught at the Temple.

The following day, Jesus cursed a fig tree, symbolizing spiritually barren Israel, and cleansed the Jerusalem Temple, possibly for the second time, in a prophetic fashion. He thus acted as the one who was going to restore proper worship as the replacement and fulfilment of the Temple.

People were transfixed as they listened to the sermon. The Father then began explaining about Jesus' teachings. He explained, "Because money is the root of all evil. Because of their greed, many people have strayed from the path of religion and are now on the road to damnation. A person's necessities are obvious, but if he is possessed by greed, no amount of money he receives appears to be insufficient. Such people can be found all around us who succumb to greed and sell their faith. Even worse individuals trade their precious bodies and do not feel guilty about doing so."

Dakota's brow furrowed. She comprehended that Father was specifically targeting her. As soon as Father delivered those final words, several people's heads started to turn in her direction. She wished to get up and leave immediately, but she was stopped by some inner fortitude. She remained silently seated on her bench.

Father went on to say, "Evils are prevalent in the society of every era, but a man should develop his inner understanding so that he knows he has to avoid these evils and not get lured by their glitter and glamour and absorb them within himself. Over the past few decades, certain types of films have promoted dirt in American society. Sinful films are being produced, corrupting the entire civilization. Even governments have been unable to stop it. It is our obligation to boycott such films. Also, avoid those who make such films. Such people have no right to live in society since they cannot think of anything good for the society and, instead of trying to make the society better, they aim to drag it to hell."

The people in the hall applauded, indicating that they agreed with what Father said. Dakota couldn't take it any longer and stood up. She also began clapping with both hands and continued to do so even after everyone else had stopped. She was the only one clapping at the moment and everyone else was looking at her with curiosity. "Well done, Father," she said. "You said some lovely things. But please respond to my inquiries."

Father Davis glanced at her, surprised, and asked, "Ask whatever you want to ask."

She asked, "All those beautiful flowers that bloom in this world are to be seen or to be covered?"

"I don't comprehend anything," Father Davis admitted. "What do you want to say?"

Dakota asked, "If I have a beautiful body and I show it to others, what's the harm?"

"You not only expose your body, Dakota, but you also do very despicable and disgusting things with other men." Instead of saying 'my child', Father addressed her by her name.

"Father, when did sex become a despicable act? That is a holy act. At least, that's what I believe. If it was a heinous chore, I would perform it in private and never in front of others. We don't barter our bodies. It is an act of love and we present it elegantly. A pornographic scene skillfully shot is no less than a melodious song."

Father Davis continued to silently stare at her after hearing her comments. Maybe he couldn't find answers to Dakota's questions. She went on to say, "And, while you're urging people here that such films should be boycotted, did you know that your so-called religious people also watch these films? You could deny what I say today, but in the future, you will admit that I was speaking the truth."

Dakota went on speaking in a single breath. She had no idea that more than half of the people in the hall had left while she was speaking. The only reason for this may be that Dakota's statements shook their beliefs. Father Davis stood at his place and listened to her. Molly was sitting on the first row of the bench.

She whispered in the ear of the woman seated next to her, "We will only breathe a sigh of relief the day this bitch leaves our neighborhood."

Dakota further said, "Your people secretly watch porn, but we secretly pray to God. Your religious practice is just for demonstration. Your true self is revealed when you are all alone and no one is watching you. I can assure you that you have never prayed while you are alone. We make love in front of the camera but pray in private. God only recognizes those human activities that are performed in private. I made love to 29 men over my 11-year career, and I did it all openly. I have never done anything in my life that I have tried to hide from society. But you must have done something." Father Davis wiped the sweat off his forehead.

"As far as I know myself, I can confidently assert that neither dishonesty nor greed exist in my thoughts. Father, I am the lily flower that Jesus was referring to when He said, 'Consider the lilies how they grow, they toil not, they spin not, and yet I say unto you, that Solomon in all his glory was not arrayed like one of these'."

Father Davis and the others seated in the hallway were silently staring at Dakota. The courage with which she slapped everyone in the face was something only she could have done. She hurried out of the chapel, leaving them all frozen like statues.

Dakota thought that after unleashing her rage in church, she would be relieved of the discomfort of the previous few days and would be able to sleep easily tonight. This, however, was not possible. She got heartburn shortly after dinner. She tried to recall if she had eaten anything unhealthy. But it wasn't like that. She couldn't sleep because she was in so much pain. While bathing in the morning, she noticed that her breasts were sore. She became worried and, without wasting much time she made an appointment with the doctor over the telephone. She got an appointment at noon. She arrived at the clinic on time in her car. The doctor inquired about all of her symptoms before taking samples of her blood and urine for analysis. He asked Dakota to rest in his clinic for two hours. When all the reports arrived at around 2:30 p.m., the doctor informed Dakota that she was pregnant.

A Glimpse into the Life of Father Walter Davis

Walter Davis was born in the year 1935. His parents had moved from England to Arizona, an American state. He was his parents' only kid. They migrated to California after the outbreak of World War II. His father began working in the shipping industry there. When he was 12 years old, his father died of an illness. After his father left, he was raised by his mother. She worked in a factory and took him to church every Sunday. Walter's interest in religion stemmed from this. After high school, he earned his bachelor's degree. He studied theology and religion. He subsequently went to seminary for five years, was ordained by a bishop, and began living a religious life.

In December 1895, France invented the cinema. Following World War I, French filmmakers began producing pornographic films. After a while, America began to make naked movies as well. 'Stag films' were commercially available for private viewing by the 1920s. The majority of the people at the time despised these things. Walter Davis's viewpoint was no different.

Playboy caused quite a stir after 1953. Adult theatres had proliferated in America by the end of the 1960s. There were two groups of people in the overall population. There were supporters and opponents of adult films. There was no one who was impartial. Walter thought it was anti-religious. At the time, he was in California. He also visited the state governor and urged that this should be prohibited. The governor admitted that pornography will morally corrupt future generations. He assured him that he would do whatever he could. But it appeared impossible to put a halt to this storm. By the early 1980s, pornography had reached a large portion of the American population through video cassettes.

Although Walter was a highly truthful and honest person, he had a dark secret that no one knew about. He married covertly and had three children. Priests are not allowed to get married, but because he was in love with a girl, he married her by lying about his job. He claimed to be a factory manager. He kept his family in San Diego and paid them two visits per month. In Burbank, no one knew he was married, and no one in San Diego knew he was a priest.

***

On Tuesday afternoon, two days after the church incident, Father Walter Davis boarded a Greyhound bus to Irvine. He was secretly going to meet his family after taking four days off. The trip from Burbank to San Diego took roughly five hours. He used to go from Burbank to Irvine, then take off his cassock and put on a shirt before boarding a bus to San Diego. No one would doubt him this way. He arrived at Irvine about three o'clock in the afternoon. There he first changed his clothes and then took light refreshment.

That day, he noticed there was a lot of chaos around the bus station. A group of 10 to 12 people had gathered at a shop. He went there as well. They were all engrossed in listening to the radio. There were reports that the president had been shot. This news was very shocking for him also. He had once met him when he was a state governor before he was elected president. He appeared to be a genuinely pleasant person who cared deeply about America. He prayed for the president's life while he sat on the bus.

He arrived home at 5:30 p.m. His three children, two daughters and a son rushed up to him and hugged him. He lovingly caressed everyone's head. Then his lovely wife also came to him. Walter hugged her too. She whispered softly in his ear, "Darling, I have some great news for you."

***

Dakota was seated in front of the director, Tim.

"Did you find out anything about the newcomer who came to the shooting that day?"

Tim asked, "What's wrong, Dakota? That incident happened more than a month ago. Why do you still consider it? What exactly was so special about it?"

Dakota continued rather than responding to her query, "You told me that day that the agency people said they would soon tell you the whereabouts of that man."

"Dakota, please tell me the whole thing. Why are you looking for him so desperately?" Tim asked in surprise.

Dakota remained silent for a while. Then she told him, "Tim, I am pregnant. And I have no doubt that this was done by the same man."

Tim sprang out of his chair. "What exactly are you saying, Dakota? How is this even possible? Didn't you use protection that day?"

"I inserted a birth control pill into my vagina just before the shooting. I always follow the same method. But I'm unable to figure out why it didn't work that day."

"Dakota, this is quite unusual. It is also extremely harmful. Consider the damage that could be done to all of us if incidents like this become frequent. Sometimes I feel that condom use is the safest for sex. However, the public does not like it. We are compelled to do film scenes without condoms because of this. Well, all this happened just a short while ago. Still, the issue can be solved. I'll give the doctor a call right now. From here, you go directly to him. Nothing to worry about, everything will be all right."

"I have not come to you to arrange an abortion, Tim. That is my problem, and I can solve it on my own if I so desire. I've come to you to find the man who got me pregnant. My question is straightforward and I want an answer in simple words." Dakota's voice was vehement.

Tim had picked up on it. He sat on the chair and murmured quietly, "Listen, Dakota. That day, something strange happened."

Dakota asked Tim, looking him straight in the eyes, "Tell me what strange thing happened. I want to know, Tim."

Tim said, "The agency people told me that the name of the model they sent for the shooting that day was Xander."

"What's strange about it, Tim?" Dakota questioned.

"First, Dakota, listen to the whole thing. When this person Xander was driving to the shooting location in his car, he met with an accident and couldn't reach us."

A tremendous shock jolted Dakota. "Then who was that motherfucker who fucked me?" she screamed.

"No one knows anything about him, Dakota," Tim remarked. "He simply appeared at the shoot that day and then vanished. Since then, no one has seen him."

Dakota said, "You're scaring me now, Tim. If something like this happens, you are entirely responsible. The safety of all of us was in your hands and I always trusted you." Her voice was filled with rage. And only she knew whether the reason for her rage was the arrival of that anonymous man there or whether he had stayed anonymous till now.

"I know, Dakota," Tim admitted. "And I agree that I made a significant error on my part. However, if you use your intellect to reflect on the events of that day, you will see how this error occurred. I kept assuming that he was the man sent by the agency. The agency was unaware that their man had been admitted to the hospital otherwise they would have informed me about the situation. As soon as I found out about it, I went to see Xander in the hospital. His car had hit the divider and turned over, fracturing his shoulder. He told me that he was approaching the set at a rapid pace when suddenly darkness appeared in front of his eyes and he lost his vision. The car slammed into the divider before he could comprehend anything."

Dakota's face lost its radiance. Her whole body began to shake. "Tim, I should leave now," she remarked as she stood up. "I'm not sure what's going on with me these days."

"Look after yourself, Dakota. And kindly keep me updated on your situation." Tim's voice sounded worried.

***

At a private property in Pasadena County, a sex scene involving Danny and two female models was being filmed. The two girls were identical twin sisters. No one could believe that this was their debut film after watching their work. As soon as the shooting started, both of them lunged at Danny as a lion might at its prey. Danny's screams were louder than the two of them inside the room. The director had a broad smile on his face. He had a feeling that this scene would be unforgettable and that these two girls would earn him a lot of money. It was 11 in the morning when Dakota's car stopped outside the property. She got down of the car and went inside the house.

The entire crew was inside the room where the shooting was taking place, including the director and cameraman. Dakota did not think it was appropriate to enter the room since she knew it would cause distraction. Outside in the courtyard, there was a huge pear tree. She sat calmly on one of the two unoccupied chairs under the tree, waiting for the shooting to end. After roughly 20 minutes, the scene was completed and the director was the first to emerge. When he saw Dakota, he greeted hello to her, and she reciprocated the greeting with a smile. Then she revealed that she had come here to meet Danny. The director returned to the room and told Danny that Ms. Fawkes had arrived. Danny emerged from the room, cleaning his penis with a hand towel, while neither of the girls got out of bed and remained to play with each other's bodies long after the scene was over. Because the sun was too bright outside, Danny wore goggles on his eyes but no clothes on his body. He approached Dakota fully naked and shook her hand.

Then he sat on another vacant chair in front of her. He had bite marks all over his body, including his neck and shoulders. It was evident that he was very uncomfortable after performing this scene. Simultaneously, looks of confusion could be seen on his face. Perhaps Dakota's unexpected arrival here was the reason for this. "Dakota, are you all right?" he asked. "How did you come here unexpectedly?"

"First tell me what was going on inside," Dakota joked. "You've never been in such a terrible situation before."

"Problems strike without a warning, Dakota. After the scene started, I realized how violent both models are and how far they can go," Danny explained. "I would have refused to work in this movie if I had known earlier."

"Danny, you are a warrior. Are you afraid of those two young girls?"

"I simply don't know what to say, Dakota. You would have been shocked if you had witnessed what they did to me."

"So wasn't that all in the script, Danny?" Dakota asked.

"No. In reality, there was no script. All of this happened because of Tim. Due to the huge success of his movies, other filmmakers did not place any restrictions on models. They are allowed to do whatever they want."

A spot boy then brought two lemonade glasses on a serving tray for each of them. They both grasped the glasses in their hands.

"Now tell me, Dakota. You have never unexpectedly come by to see me before. Is everything all right?" Danny expressed concern.

Dakota said, "Nothing is fine, Danny. I'm not sure what's going on with me."

Danny asked, "Are you feeling well?"

Dakota replied, "I'm okay, Danny. I came to you because I needed to talk about some really important issue with you."

"Speak up, Dakota."

"Last week I found out that I'm pregnant."

Like Tim, Danny also jumped out of the chair. "What are you talking about? How is this even possible?"

"It's true, Danny," Dakota said. "My life has taken a turn I never expected. I had never considered even getting married, and now this child?"

"Do you know who is the father of the child?"

"I know and at the same time, I don't."

Danny was quiet for a few moments. "So what have you thought next, Dakota?" he asked.

"For a couple of days, I wasn't sure what to do. But then, after thinking it over all night, I made a significant decision. That's why I've come to you this morning. If I start hesitating even slightly in making this decision tomorrow, if I get weak, don't let me change my mind. Please don't let me flee from this."

"Do you want to keep this baby, Dakota?"

"Danny, that's what I want. However, I also want to permanently quit this industry at the same time."

"What is the need to do this, Dakota? You are getting an adequate income from the industry. This will enable you to care for your child properly. What will you gain by leaving this industry?" Danny asked, really confused by her decision.

While both of them were talking, sounds of sighs and moans were coming from the shooting room. Even after the camera was turned off, the bodies of both girls were still entangled with each other. Perhaps their thirst was not quenched even after squeezing Danny.

Dakota continued to say, "Many incidents have happened simultaneously in the last few days, Danny. Firstly, I got pregnant. Additionally, I have been exposed to my society. Now everyone is aware of my profession."

"But you are one of those people who don't give a shit about these things."

"I was like that, Danny. But I'm not like that any longer. Ever since I came to know that I am carrying a child inside me, I have started worrying about it. Danny, the way those people are looking at me, my child will not be able to endure such gazes when he grows up. He would not be able to live such a discriminating life." While speaking, her eyes welled up with tears.

"If you've already made up your mind, Dakota, that's fine. Please let me know if you need any support."

"Danny, I am going to leave this place forever and move to Miami as soon as possible. After I leave, you sell my house. I'll utilize that money to purchase a house there. But until then, I will need a place to stay there."

"Don't be worried about it, Dakota. I have my own house in Miami. You are welcome to stay there as long as you desire."

"All right, Danny. I am going to close my bank accounts and take all of my cash with me in a couple of days. If everything goes as planned, I'll leave this place by next week."

Danny was overcome with sadness on hearing this. Dakota noticed his sadness and cradled his face in her hands, saying, "It's hard for me to leave you, Danny. You are like my brother. I will continue to see you. Danny, please take care of yourself."

Then two completely naked girls emerged from the shooting room, holding each other's hands and laughing wickedly and proceeded to the nearby shower room. Even inside the shower, they couldn't stop giggling. Dakota, upon seeing them, exclaimed, "It's amazing, Danny, these two look exactly alike."

"Yes. Both are twins, Dakota, Lucy and Kitty." Danny pointed toward the shower room and said, "The kind of non-serious and non-artistic people are increasing in this profession, I think the golden period of this industry will end soon. From that perspective, your decision to leave the industry seems right, because good people will have no value in the future."

Dakota thought that Danny was worried about non-serious and non-artistic people joining the industry. But he was quite unaware that anonymous people had also entered the industry.

After two days, Danny introduced Dakota to a realtor he knew and Dakota showed him her house. The realtor asked Dakota to hand over the keys to him after vacating the house. As soon as a seller is found, he will sell the house to him and send the money to her address in Miami via demand draft. To avoid having to travel from Miami to sell the property, he made Dakota complete all the paperwork in advance.

Dakota said her final goodbyes to Burbank on the last day of that week. Even as she moved away, only one face lingered in her thoughts. Dakota's heart and intellect had been deeply affected by that mysterious man. She was desperate to find him but was helpless. She was thinking that she was leaving for the sake of her child's future, but she was also giving up the chance to meet that mysterious man again. If she hadn't quit the adult industry and instead kept working in the movies, he would have appeared in front of her again. But, in order to avoid any negative consequences for her child, she did not waver and kept to her decision.

The following week, Lucy and Kitty were sitting in front of the same realtor Danny knew. They wanted to buy a house in the San Fernando Valley. They traveled from Northern California to become a porn star. In their hometown, both of them had made a significant amount of money by doing odd jobs. They didn't face any problem in finding work after arriving here because of their unique talents. In the very first scene, the director was pleased with their performance and paid them far more than the set amount.

The two sisters visited Dakota's house with the dealer the following day. They both liked the house very much and the deal was finalized. On the third day of getting the property in their name, both the sisters moved to Dakota's house.

Mrs. Molly's family sat at the dining table late at night. Charlie's father brought him back to Utah a week ago. Jacob finished his meal and then walked to his room.

Mrs. Molly's husband said, "I noticed that someone has moved into the house next door to us. Have you met them? Who are they, exactly?"

Molly started speaking in a single breath, "Yes, I met them today when they were moving their stuff inside the house. They are both students with a nice attitude. Both have a similar appearance. They will be merely two or three years older than Jacob. They have been admitted to the university. They appeared to be really bright students. They inquired as to who had previously lived in this house. I mentioned that some salesgirl used to live there. I didn't tell them the truth. The poor girls have come to study. By knowing the truth their attention would go toward the wrong things. Did I do it right? It's a good thing the witch has left. We may now say that this is a society of decent and honorable people."

Dakota left Burbank permanently, but before we say farewell to that town, we want to share some of the events that occurred in that house after Dakota left. Lucy and Kitty moved into that house. Both of them began revealing their true colors after a few days. They appeared to be experiencing extreme discomfort while wearing the clothes. They only dressed up when they had to leave the house. They lived completely naked inside the house, with not a scrap of clothing covering them. They used to dress up before departing for the shoot and then return to their natural form as soon as they arrived on set. It would be fair to state that only the open sky had seen both of them in their clothes, not the house's roof and walls. The situation was such that if someday both of them sat fully clothed , the house would not have recognized that the owner was sitting. The house felt as if a visitor had arrived.

When the newspaperman entered inside their house to collect the monthly bill one day, the wealth of the entire world appeared insignificant in compared to what he saw inside. Both of them left no stone unturned in providing hospitality to the visitor. From then on, the guy started ringing their doorbell every morning before respectfully placing the newspaper in their hands. The plumber experienced almost the same thing. He first came to fix a pipe, and then he kept coming back on a regular basis. He purposefully kept a connection slack so that his services would be required again in a few days. And whenever he went to mend something, his own repairs would also be done at the same time.

Whether they both paid his wages or not, they never let him complain about his life.

When fortune was suddenly being so nice to so many people, how could Jacob stay unaffected? Whenever he left his house, they flashed their boobs through the window. That poor guy would have had a terrible time controlling his emotions. He had previously only been interested in video games, and upon viewing both of them, he lost control over himself. But he lacked the confidence to approach them.

It's said that nature works to unite true lovers, but in this case, the situation was different. The issue here was not one of true love but of pure lust. Nature continued to play its game. Molly told her husband one night at the dinner table, "Darling, I was thinking of asking the neighborhood girls to give Jacob some tuition in spare time. They seem to be pretty intelligent in my opinion. If they agree, Jacob's grades might increase. Throughout the day, he concentrates on video games. It's possible that as a result of their companionship, he will begin showing an interest in his studies." Her husband also liked Molly's suggestion and agreed. Jacob kept his head down, listening to both of them. He became aware of an erection in his penis. The next day, Molly approached Lucy and Kitty as they were heading out of the house for work and started talking to them about her son. Jacob was watching the three of them from the window inside the house. He couldn't hear their voices, but he knew they'd agreed to teach Jacob. Molly began walking back home after thanking them when one of them noticed Jacob in the window and pressed her left eye. Jacob got a significantly stronger erection than the night before.

That same evening, Molly sent Jacob to both of them. Molly was confident that her son would return having learned something new. And exactly the same thing happened but in a different field. Jacob gently scooped up his books and went outside to ring the neighboring house's doorbell. After that, whatever occurred to him inside the house was something he could never have imagined even in his wildest dreams. His cousin Charlie had undoubtedly seen many adult movies, so he was likely aware of all the things that could occur between a man and a woman. Although Jacob was innocent, both of them did not let him stay innocent for long. Whenever he had the opportunity throughout the day and both of them were at home, he would enter their house without hesitation, and he often began visiting there in the night after his parents had gone to bed. This went on for several days, although the neighbors were unaware of the situation. Lucy and

Kitty, like the rest of the neighbors, remained good and respectable in Molly's eyes. Molly always thought they were both bright and promising students. Dakota, on the other hand, had done nothing wrong yet had become infamous despite this.

One night Jacob made a telephone call to Charlie's house and gave him a detailed account of all the incidents happening to him. Charlie was thrilled when he heard his words. He insisted on his parents visiting Jacob. They did not, however, agree. They reasoned that Charlie had returned recently after staying with Jacob. They said that they would invite Jacob here on the next vacation. But Charlie insisted on going to Jacob's house. His parents said that now they would not send him anywhere. He needed to focus on his studies.

Charlie was left heartbroken. Every week, Jacob updated him on his recent experiences over the phone, leaving Charlie with no choice but to bash his head against the wall. Molly found herself in a similar scenario, slamming her head against the wall, when she noticed Jacob's grades had already dropped. She had no idea why this was happening. Jacob had changed significantly. His interest in video games had disappeared as well. However, his grades were not improving.

***

We now say goodbye to the town of Burbank and return to our main story. Dakota spent around two months at Danny's house in Key Biscayne, Miami. The mansion was gorgeous. Dakota knew Danny came from a wealthy family and had plenty of money. He merely got into the industry as a hobby. He still had several connections in Miami from his school time. One of them provided Dakota with a lot of assistance. Her bank account was also opened. After receiving the demand draft for the sale price of the house in Burbank, Dakota began looking for a house for her. She purchased a small house in Little Havana downtown with the help of the same person in a matter of days. She was delighted. The place had a lively vibe. She intended to open a flower shop there, entirely burying her past. But this was her long-term strategy. She was only thinking about her unborn child at the time. People around her were also showing her a lot of love and respect. Time seemed to be flying by. Now, just by looking at her belly, anyone could tell that she was expecting.

One night, the couple next door told her that their car had broken down and that they both needed to attend a bonfire party on South Beach. If she was free tonight, could she lend them her car? Dakota agreed. Then he suggested to her that she might accompany them if she wanted to. Dakota liked his suggestion and agreed. She felt that on this pretext she too would have some outings. Dakota started the car and headed for South Beach as soon as they were both seated inside. They arrived at the location in about 30 minutes. As soon as Dakota and her two companions exited the car, a brand-new pink Cadillac Eldorado pulled up next to them, and two people, a 25-26-year-old six-foot tall man and a stunning young woman stepped out.

"How are you, Alonso?" Dakota's neighbor asked upon seeing him. "Congratulations and best wishes for your marriage and new car." The man thanked him and smiled before shaking hands. Dakota's neighbor then introduced him, saying, "This is Alonso Barros. He was my junior in high school. He just got married last month." Dakota shook hands with both of them as well. Then they all moved together toward the bonfire. There was a large bonfire pit, and many people were hanging around and drinking nearby. They were enthusiastically welcomed there. The music was blaring at full volume.

Dakota avoided drinking because she had a child growing inside her. The couple who had accompanied her was busy meeting other people, while she sat alone on a chair, staring at the bonfire pit. Nobody knew what was going through her mind. The newlywed couple that arrived in the pink car vanished without a trace. Maybe they came merely to show their faces. Dakota understood that newlyweds were more interested in each other than in anything else. They can't stay long without loving one another. And perhaps this was the reason why they left the party early.

After the dinner, the party wrapped up about midnight, and the guests began to say goodbye to each other. Dakota, too, sat in her car with her neighbors and drove away. The beach was deserted, but the bonfire was still burning. They arrived in Little Havana in 20 minutes because there was little traffic on the roads. Her neighbors thanked her and returned to their house. Dakota also went inside her house after leaving her car parked on the road.

She emerged after ten minutes. She was holding two hefty bags in each hand. The doctor had prevented her from lifting heavy objects, but no one knew what was going on in her mind at the time and she didn't think it was important to be cautious. She put both bags in the trunk of her car and drove back to South Beach.

It was already 1:00 a.m. After 20 minutes, she returned to the same location where the bonfire was still burning. She stopped her car beside the pit. Then she emerged and fetched the bags from the trunk. She unzipped one of the bags. Inside, there were several video cassettes. She took out the video cassettes one by one and began to toss them into the flaming pit. The fire began to burn more quickly. The bonfire in the pit began to emit black smoke. Standing motionless, she threw the cassettes into the fire one by one, like a machine. The black smoke billowing from the burning pit did not rise to the sky, but instead spread all around and encircled Dakota.

Dakota's eyes became inflamed as a result of the smoke, and some of the smoke entered her lungs. She coughed and moved away from the spot. In the second bag, there were still some cassettes left. She bravely stepped back into the swirl of smoke and ignited the remaining cassettes. When she began to throw the last cassette, her gaze was drawn to its title. Her hand abruptly came to a halt, and tears streamed from her eyes. She remained like a statue for a few moments and then put the cassette back in the bag, put the bags back in the trunk and then drove away.

That same year, on November's full moon, she gave birth to a moon-like daughter. The beauty of that infant captivated everyone in the room. Dakota named her daughter 'Luna'.

***

In the summer of 1994, a 50-year-old man in a black robe sat on the carpeted floor of a wooden cabin on a private ranch outside Houston, Texas. His face was obscured beneath the hood, but his Egyptian goatee beard and lips were apparent. A large number of candles were lit on a table to his left. The same candles provided lighting in the room. There was no light bulb inside the cabin. Some incense sticks were burning alongside the candles. The cabin was filled with an enticing aroma. Two girls in their early twenties sat on the ground in front of the hooded man. The man appeared to be giving a sermon, and they were both paying close attention to him. "There is nothing sacred about sex," the man said. "It is the filthiest act. Sex can be considered sacred only when it occurs between two strangers. Strangers, who have never met before and don't even know each other's name, and even after that act, they say goodbye to each other without revealing their identities to each other. That is the only way to maintain the purity of sex."

The entrance of the cabin suddenly opened, and a muscular man with a scar on his forehead above his left eye entered, bowed his head, greeted the hooded man and stood next to a wall. He was holding a large brown paper envelope. For a while, the man in the hood stopped speaking and beckoned the man with the scar to come closer. The man approached him, delivered the envelope to the hooded man and said, "Mission completed, Master." He then returned to his initial spot and stood silently. When the hooded man opened the envelope, a magazine emerged from it. The sound of 'hmm' came out of his mouth as soon as he saw the cover of the magazine, and he turned to face the man with a scar and said, "Good job."

"Thank you very much, Master," the man with the scar responded.

The hooded man then fell silent for some time, as if he was sending or receiving a signal. After a few moments, he remarked, "This magazine's idea was born in the mind of its founder at the same time this woman was born. These two were incomplete without each other. The purpose of both of their existences has now been fulfilled."

The man in the hood continued speaking, "Man is not even allowed to pick up a pebble lying on the seashore and put it somewhere else. And he continues to try to eliminate the presence of some things from this world in which he will never be successful. In the process, he simply wastes his time and energy. And when nature backfires to maintain the balance, he blames his fate since he doesn't grasp the procedure. Whatever occurs in this world serves a purpose. That thing will vanish on its own once its purpose has been completed." The three persons in the room were silently listening to him.

Then he asked, "Are you looking after that family?"

"Yes, Master."

"Good. Keep an eye on them and safeguard them until the job is over. That mission, like this one, is critical." The hooded man stated as he put the magazine back into the envelope. "You will need to monitor the situation closely at all times. You will need to take prompt action to correct any deviations in this story and keep it on track until it reaches its intended goal. We can prevent a major natural disaster from striking that small town in this way."

"Indeed, Master."

"Because of my ability to see into the future, I was able to detect the imbalance caused by that priest's hurting a sacred heart and began working on it in due time."

"Yes, Master," the man with a scar gently nodded his head and left the cabin.

***

On 31 December 1999, a New Year's Eve celebration was taking place on Miami's South Beach. The gathering had a really hot vibe. The song 'Baby One More Time' by Britney Spears was playing on the DJ, and many teenage boys and girls were dancing. A stunning young lady in a purple sleeveless outfit was also dancing with her friends. A man who appeared to be in his mid-40s with a French-cut beard and a bucket cap on his head was seated a short distance away and was closely observing that girl. He was holding a Bourbon Limoncello Cocktail in his hand which he was sipping very slowly. Even though there were other attractive girls dancing around, his attention was solely on that one. It didn't appear like he was giving her a seductive glance. Rather, he was lost in contemplation as he looked at her. The DJ continued to play hit music one after the other. The girl kept dancing intoxicated, while the man sat like a statue and stared at her. This went on for approximately half an hour. The girl then stopped dancing and sat on an empty chair. Either her intoxication had worn off or she was tired and fatigued. Her other friends continued to dance. Perhaps none of them noticed she had split up with them and moved away.

The man with the French beard rose from his seat and started moving toward her. He picked up an espresso martini while strolling and approached the girl, saying hello. The girl looked at him, puzzled, and replied, "Hello." He extended the glass to her. The girl thanked him while receiving the drink from him.

Once the girl received the drink from him, he gained confidence and sat down in the other chair close to her. With great casualness, the girl asked, "Excuse me, do I know you?"

He replied, "No. But maybe I know you."

The girl's look showed a hint of surprise. Then she said, "I didn't understand anything. Who are you? Could you please clarify?"

The man sipped from the glass in his hand, took a long breath, and asked, "Can you tell me your name?"

"My name is Luna, sir," the girl said. "But why do you ask?"

"If I'm not mistaken, you're the daughter of Dakota Fawkes. Am I correct?"

With a smile, the girl asked, "Do you know my mother?"

With the girl's question, everything became clear to the man. He took a frigid breath and glanced up into the sky before saying, "Yes, I know very well. But it's been a long time since I've seen her."

The young girl remained silent. The man went on to say, "Did you know you look exactly like your mother? My last interaction with her was in 1981. Do you live with her?

"Yes," the girl nodded.

The man inquired, "How is she now?"

"She is good."

"Does she have a friendly relationship with you? I'm wondering whether she's told you anything about her past life."

That girl chuckled. Then she added, "My mother has never withheld anything from me. I've never kept anything from her, either."

"I was aware of it. She is a fearless and powerful woman. I hold a high regard for her. By the way, my name is Tim Blue and I am a filmmaker. And I've come to Miami for some very essential business. I would like to speak to you about something important if you could spare me a little time."

"Please carry on."

Suddenly one of her friends shouted out her name, "Luna, Come here, baby."

"It's not the appropriate time to talk," Tim said. "Keep my business card and call me tomorrow."

"It was nice to meet you, Tim," she added after accepting the card. She placed the espresso martini glass, from which she had barely taken two sips, on a nearby table. She then rose from her chair and went to dance with her friends. The DJ was playing Christina Aguilera's 'Genie in a Bottle' at the moment. Tim sat there smiling as he looked at her.

This was the exact same location on South Beach where Dakota had attended a bonfire party just before Luna's birth and subsequently returned to burn the video cassettes of her movies to ashes.

***

After an exhausting Friday night, Luna stayed in bed on the first day of the New Year. She slept the entire day, and not even Dakota felt it was appropriate to wake her. On Sunday morning, she got up early. She had breakfast with her mom. In the afternoon, she felt like going out. When she reached inside her bag for the car keys, she found Tim's visiting card. She had almost forgotten about the meeting that evening. She opened her mouth to tell her mother about her meeting with Tim but then became silent after a moment of thought. She decided to meet Tim first and see what important matter he wanted to discuss with her. She will then inform her mother about it. She reached inside her bag for her Nokia 3210 handset and dialed Tim's number. Tim was delighted to speak with her. He extended an invitation to Luna to dinner, which she gladly accepted.

That night, Luna went to the restaurant chosen by director Tim Blue for dinner. While they were eating, Tim asked Luna, "Have you reached the age of eighteen?"

Luna revealed that she had only turned 18 a month ago. When Tim inquired about Luna's future intentions, she replied that she had completed high school and intended to pursue law in the future. However, it was extremely expensive, so her mother had urged her to reconsider.

Tim stated, "She is correct. Alternatively, you might also work a part-time job to help pay for your education."

Luna said that she was also considering it.

They both continued to eat. After a pause of a few moments, Tim said, "Luna, now I will get to the point. I've invited you here to discuss a very important issue with you."

"Please continue, sir."

Tim said, "I'm in Miami looking for talent. I'm looking for a stunning model for my upcoming film. I met some girls, but none of them appealed to me. And when I saw you the night before yesterday, it appeared like I was looking for you. Dakota used to be my first choice in the past. She used to set the screen on fire with her performance. I see her reflection in you."

Luna was stunned. She remained speechless as she stared into Tim's face. The fork in her left hand came to a halt in the air before reaching her mouth. Tim said, "I'd like to make you this offer. If you don't mind, I'd like to cast you in my next film. You will also receive a substantial sum of money."

Luna placed the fork on the dish and sat silently for a bit. Tim's statements elicited no response from her. There was no doubt that there was a lot of conflict going on inside her head.

"Do you get upset about what I said?" Tim asked. "If that's the case, then I apologize."

"No, it's not like that," Luna responded calmly. "Your offer seemed weird to me. But I can't tell you my decision right away. I'll need some time to think about it." She appeared to have regained her stability. She resumed eating.

"Look, Luna, I'm not in a hurry," Tim responded. "Think about it thoroughly and then let me know. You'll undoubtedly speak with your mother as well. It must also be done. She has made many sacrifices for you. She left this profession at the height of her career just for you. The industry's golden period ended with her departure. I don't know why, but after seeing you, I have a strong feeling that you will carry out the task she left unfinished."

Luna remained seated silently. Tim went on to say, "Usually, when we're looking for a new model, we visit strip clubs and meet the strippers and present our offer to them. The majority of strippers accept our offers. Making this offer to anyone other than them is extremely risky. This may aggravate the condition. That's why I first confirmed if you were Dakota's daughter. I understand that having sex in front of a camera is awkward for everyone. You, too, will have weird feelings at first. But, like everyone else, you will quickly feel at ease."

Luna smiled and replied, "This will not be the first time I'll perform sexual activity in front of the camera, sir."

Tim was shocked by what she said. He inquired, "I don't understand anything, Luna. Have you previously shot sexual content?"

Luna said, "Sir, my boyfriend likes videography. He frequently films his sex sessions with me. He later watched those videos with great curiosity. So I will never have an issue with cameras."

Tim laughed and said, "That's good, Luna. I was concerned that you, like other girls, could feel a little awkward for the first time. Was your boyfriend with you at the beach party that night?"

Luna replied, "No, he's in Mexico for a few days for family business. He will return in two weeks."

Tim asked, "Will you need his permission also if you feel like working on my film?"

Luna replied, "I can't say anything right now. First, I will discuss this with Mom. Now I should leave. I will call you in two to three days and let you know about my decision."

Both had finished dinner. Tim smiled and said good night to her and then Luna left, leaving Tim sitting there.

The next day in the afternoon, Luna was seated at the dining table in her house, reading her boyfriend's SMS on her mobile phone. After a while, Dakota, who was in her late forties, emerged from the kitchen. Her beauty had not at all faded, even at this stage of life. Her hair had obviously turned grey in some places. She was holding two platters of tuna salad. She approached Luna's chair slowly and placed a dish on the table in front of her. Then she sat down on the other chair in front of her. Luna set her phone aside and the two of them began eating lunch. Dakota asked after a brief pause, "Have you discussed this with Matthew?"

"No, Mom," Luna said. "I've only spoken to you. I didn't feel comfortable calling him in Mexico and discussing this."

Dakota asked, "But what if he had an objection?"

Luna said, "I don't think he'll mind. When he returns, I will have a thorough discussion with him about this. Right now, all I need is your permission."

"I don't want to influence any of your decisions, my child," Dakota expressed concern. "You are my life. I sacrificed my career to provide you with a better life. You have the freedom to live your life in any way you wish. You do not need my permission. I shudder when I recall the events that occurred to me back then, and I worry about what would happen if you find yourself in the same situation in the future. I somehow dealt with the circumstances. However, you are really innocent, Luna."

Luna said, "But, Mom, I have no plans to get married or have children."

Dakota replied, "Nothing in this world happens because of our planning, my child. You're fully aware that I had no plans for you either. Whatever is meant to occur will occur."

Luna said, "Mom, times have changed significantly and people have become more modern. I doubt I will ever have to deal with the issues you did at that point in your life."

Dakota sighed, "I too hope that this won't happen."

Luna added, "And your daughter isn't so innocent that she can't fight the wolves in the industry. I, too, am a strong lady like you."

Dakota smiled, "Wolves aren't in the industry, Luna. Wolves are part of outer society. You'll find many good-hearted and honest people in the industry. Whenever I needed support, someone in the industry was there to help me. On the contrary, many in the outside world who label themselves as religious and civil attempted to exploit me. You will be able to detect the difference in a few years."

Luna remained listening to her quietly.

Then Dakota asked, "Tell me the truth. Did you decide to choose this profession just because of your meeting with Tim Blue, or did you previously have a latent yearning within you, and you're now talking to me after receiving an offer?"

Luna replied, "No, Mom, I had never even considered this. My main ambition is to study law. I merely want to pursue this career so that financial constraints won't prevent me from continuing my education."

Dakota's face lit up with a smile. She explained, "Once you've entered this dazzling world, my child, you'll forget you have to do any kind of study in the future."

Luna stayed silent. It appeared that a dilemma had developed in her mind. Dakota had apparently read her mind. With the purpose of rescuing her from her predicament, she said, "If you have decided that you want to join the industry then I have no objection. It's your life, live it anyway you want. My happiness depends on your happiness."

Luna knew her mother well therefore she expected a similar response from her. She stood up, walked over to Dakota, and hugged her from behind. "Thank you, Mama," she said. Dakota laughed and added, "This Tim is a devil. He found me again after all these years, in the guise of you."

Luna wasted no time after receiving consent from her mother and quickly called Tim and said yes to his offer. Tim already knew she would not turn him down at any cost. Within two days, he called his crew to Miami, and production for Luna's debut movie began. The shoot was scheduled to last two days. After that, two days would be set aside for editing and other tasks.

***

Luna appeared to be in a good mood on the day of the shooting. She was also quite enthusiastic about this project. She had never imagined herself as an adult model before this. Her passion was to study law. Her decision to accept this offer was solely influenced by the expensive legal education. Tim had assured her that she would be paid well for her work. Luna reasoned that if she made decent money, she would not have any trouble pursuing her academic goals. But now, as soon as she stepped into this movie set, she began to feel as if this was her ultimate destination. Everyone on the crew gave Luna a hearty welcome. When the makeup artist was applying makeup to her body just before the shoot, she told Luna, "Dear, by applying makeup to your body, I have reduced the beauty of your body a little. You look even more amazing without makeup."

Within a few minutes, the shooting began. Tim had to shoot three parts in that movie. Each scene lasted 20 minutes. Luna's solo scene was the first. She removes her clothes one by one before playing with her private parts and then inserted her fingers into her vagina. After that, she played with a dildo. Everyone present at the shoot had their eyes wide open after seeing Luna's beauty. No one dared to blink for fear of missing something important.

After some time, the scene was completed. The second scene was a lesbian scene in which Luna would be joined by two more female models. The three girls began to caress each other's bodies. They then began licking each other's vagina and used their fingers to appease their partners. That dildo made another cameo in this scenario, but the girls' fingers and tongues played a major part. Because of their enticing groans, the atmosphere on the set grew quite heated. Luna performed that scene with ease too. Anyone who has met Luna's mother could tell that she inherited all of her skills from her mother. After that, the director called for everyone to pack up, and they all got to work. The other two models' roles were completed, so the director gave them a pay check and let them go. Then he instructed Luna to arrive at the set the next day at precisely 11:00 a.m.

Dakota noticed her daughter seemed quite cheerful today while eating dinner. She remembered when she came back from the first day of shooting, she was extremely thrilled, too.

On set the next day, Tim introduced Ricardo to Luna. This was the boy with whom Luna had to shoot her first boy-girl scene. He lived in Houston. He, too, was Luna's age. He joined the industry a few months ago. He'd previously worked in a movie under Tim's direction.

The makeup artist reluctantly applied Luna's makeup just before the shooting. In the shooting room, a smoke machine was mounted. When Luna and Ricardo finally faced each other, they were both naked. Ricardo was nearly as tall as Luna. Luna kissed his nude shoulders before moving on to his lips. After that, she accomplished all of the other jobs with elegance. It was a soft-core scene, and Tim, like in his earlier projects, let the models go free. The crew members, who, the day before, had watched the shooting of Luna with lust in their eyes and drool running down their mouths, were filled with jealousy today. Everyone was mentally abusing Ricardo. Tim applauded when the scene was finished in 20 minutes. Both models left the room wearing their clothes.

When Tim handed Luna her pay check, she jumped with joy. The amount written on the check was way bigger than she expected. Tim assured her that his film would be ready for distribution in only two days. Then he'll come to her house and deliver her the film's CD, as well as meet her mother.

Before saying goodbye to Luna, Ricardo requested her phone number, and she happily gave it to him. He said he would call her. He was obviously quite impressed with Luna.

***

Luna's first film under Tim Blue's direction turned out to be so spectacular that everyone who saw it was stunned. The reason was that Tim's working approach had been enhanced by years of expertise, making him even more experienced. Also, Luna reminded of Dakota to everyone. Dakota herself seemed to have performed in that picture, appearing even younger than before. With their respective talents, the two of them created havoc in that one-hour film.

Tim delivered the film CD to Luna's house. Dakota embraced him, and tears welled up in her eyes. They all ate dinner together.

After that, all three of them talked till late at night. Dakota said to Tim, "Tim, I have full confidence that you will take care of my sweet daughter."

"Dakota, your daughter is equally strong as you. She is capable of looking after herself. And now let me tell you that I'm leaving the industry forever."

Both were shocked to hear his words.

Dakota inquired, surprised, "What are you saying, Tim? What is the reason for leaving your favorite work?"

Tim was silent for a few moments. Then he said, "In the last few years, there have been many ups and downs in my life. I developed depression as a result of failed relationships. I couldn't focus on my work at all. My last three films failed to do any special charisma. I used to visit a spiritual person for many years. He told me something strange when I informed him about my constant failures. I was deeply impacted by his words. He informed me that I had already completed all of the work required in this industry. After that, no matter how hard I work, I will never be satisfied. He advised me to give up my profession and move to the Himalayas in order to find mental peace."

Both were speechless as they looked at his face. Tim continued, "But I didn't want to leave this industry by getting labelled as a flop director. I thought I'd come into the adult industry with a bang and would retire with a bang. Then I decided to make a film with a fresh face. Then I set out to find that face. I met a lot of girls, but I wasn't satisfied."

Then he turned to face Luna and said, "That night, my eyes fell on you. When I saw you, I realized that the film I wanted to make would be impossible without you. That's why I approached you, and you did me a huge favor by accepting my proposal. I want to express my heartfelt gratitude to you for this."

He took Luna's hand in his. Then he said, "Now it's up to you whether you want to continue or not after this. If you wish to continue working in movies, it would be fantastic. Your prospects in the industry are promising."

Luna nodded and added, "I think I should pursue this as a career. Just need to get one more person's permission."

Tim smiled and stood up to leave. Dakota hugged him once more and added, "Tim, take care of yourself." Tim said goodnight to both of them and moved out. Luna carefully placed the CD in her handbag after he left. Matthew, her lover, was supposed to return to Miami in a few days. Luna wanted to surprise him. Meanwhile, Ricardo began calling Luna every night, and the two of them would talk for hours. By the time Matthew returned, Luna and Ricardo had become close friends.

After a few days, Matthew returned. During his three weeks in Mexico, he only called Luna twice. He called Luna in the taxi on his way home from the airport and informed her about his arrival. He added that he would like to meet Luna tonight if possible. Luna was also eagerly waiting for his arrival. She wanted to give him a grand surprise. Matthew liked viewing porn a lot. He had an obsession with many female porn stars. Luna was aware of his passion. Prior to engaging in sexual activity with Luna, he would always turn on an adult film on TV. And he used to have sex with Luna in the same way that the models did in that film. He was also interested in videography. He usually carried a camcorder with him wherever he went. He had recorded CDs of his sex scenes with Luna, which he watched in his spare time. Luna also supported him in this. She never objected to Matthew filming their sex interactions. Perhaps the hidden porn star inside Luna, whom she was unaware of, found solace in having her sessions recorded.

Luna arrived at Matthew's house around 8:00 p.m. She pressed the doorbell. Matthew opened the door and took Luna into his arms. They kissed each other on the lips and entered the house. Matthew pushed Luna onto the couch, and the two of them began exchanging intense kisses. They were finally meeting after three weeks of separation. Then the doorbell rang again. There was a pause in their romantic endeavors. Luna asked Matthew, with a gesture, "Who could be outside?" Matthew asked her to wait with a gesture and got up to open the door. The pizza delivery boy was standing outside. Matthew had ordered pizza for both of them some time ago. Matthew collected the pizza and Coke bottle from him and headed to the kitchen. Luna also got up from the couch and followed him, where she poured the Coke into two glasses. Then they both came out and sat down. While eating pizza, Matthew continued to tell Luna about his trip to Mexico, to which Luna listened attentively.

After they finished their meal, they realized it was time to continue the episode they had started before the pizza arrived. Matthew took Luna's left boob with his right hand and began pressing it. Luna gently pushed with her hand away from her chest and urged him to wait a moment. Then she got up and proceeded to turn on the TV and the VCD player that was mounted above it. Matthew understood Luna's desire to watch an explicit film while having sex. He likewise stood up and began walking toward his bedroom, where he stored his CD collection in a cupboard. But then he noticed Luna taking out a CD from her handbag. He was a little surprised. Luna had never brought a CD with her before. Then why did she bring it today? He returned to his seat without asking anything.

Luna inserted the disc into the player and then grabbed the remote placed on the top of the TV. She then took a seat close to Matthew. The menu of the film directed by Tim appeared on TV. Luna put her left hand between Matthew's legs and started massaging his penis, and with her right hand selected the third scene from the menu displayed on the TV screen. When Matthew's penis became absolutely stiff, Luna grabbed it in her fist over his trousers. Meanwhile, Ricardo's sex scene with Luna started playing on TV. After watching that scene, Matthew's face turned pale. He broke down as he stared at the television. Luna became aware of his plight as his penis shrunk in her grasp. Then Luna stared at him. Matthew's face has lost its luster. He yelled, "Luna, what have you done?"

Luna was terrified when she saw his rage. In a shaky voice, she asked Matthew, "Darling, what's wrong with it? I wanted to give you a surprise. I've chosen my career. I expected you to be delighted as you're a huge fan of porn stars."

"You bitch." Matthew's rage had reached a boiling point. He grabbed an empty Coke glass from the table in front of him and hurled it at the TV. The screen shattered. "I loved you with all my heart and in return, you have done this to me."

Luna stood up right away. "Please calm down, Matthew," she murmured tremblingly. "I made a mistake. I would not have accepted this offer if I had realized how horrible you would feel. Please accept my apologies."

Matthew became absorbed in thought as he rested his left hand on his forehead. Luna sat at his feet, pleading for him to forgive her.

After a few moments, Matthew calmly said, "Luna, get out of my house right now and never try to meet me again." Luna walked out in tears, sat in her car, and drove back to her house.

Dakota was surprised to see her daughter return home early. Luna usually returned from Matthew's house after midnight or the next morning. She had a feeling something was awry. She entered Luna's room and asked, "Is everything all right, Luna?" Luna raced to embrace her mother, crying, and told her the entire story. Dakota gently stroked her hair and whispered, "Look child, there will be many times in your life when you have to make a choice between two options. You have to choose what you require more. If you need Matthew's love, you'll have to give up your favorite profession. If you do not wish to leave this profession, you must leave your boyfriend. There are times in life where you must make sacrifices. You must make a decision. Matthew will certainly forgive you if you promise not to work in the adult industry again. But if you want to make a career in the industry, you should forget about him."

Dakota then laid her down on the bed and said, "Now sleep comfortably. Think about it once you wake up in the morning."

Luna lay peacefully on the bed. But her eyes were wide awake. In her mind, there was a lot of turmoil. She tossed and turned for quite long before finally falling asleep after midnight.

She awoke just after 10:00 a.m. She checked her phone while lying in bed. There were four missed calls from Ricardo. She remembered that she had put her phone on silent mode before heading to Matthew's house so that no one could bother them both. As a result, she couldn't know Ricardo had been calling her repeatedly. Ricardo had called her three times during the night, the most recent only a few minutes ago.

Luna dialed Ricardo's number. Ricardo picked up the phone and asked her, "Luna, are you okay?" Reluctantly, Luna told him everything that had happened the night before. When Ricardo heard all of this, he became extremely sad.

Then Luna said to him, "Ricardo, I'm not sure what to do. I never imagined that one of my decisions would lead me to face this incident. I am very confused. Please tell me what's best for me."

After a brief pause, Ricardo replied, "In my opinion, you should prioritize your career, Luna. No relationship is going to last forever. If your break-up with Matthew had not occurred today, it undoubtedly would have occurred at some point in the future. The person who wants to leave you will eventually come up with a justification. It is not appropriate to jeopardize a career over these kinds of relationships."

Luna began to think that when her mother faced similar circumstances, she prioritized her relationship over her career. But she did it for the sake of her child. For a mother, the most essential thing is her child. She is willing to go to any length for the betterment of her child. Can a woman's lover, however, be so vital to her that she must give up her career? There are several instances of this happening.

Her mind was still in a state of confusion. She felt incapable of making a choice. There was a long pause before Ricardo asked her again, "Luna, you still there?"

"Yes, Ricardo," Luna said in a quiet voice.

Ricardo continued, saying, "Luna, pay close attention to what I'm saying. Making decisions in life should come from within, not from the perspective of anyone else. There should be no room for compromise. The person who genuinely loves you will accept you in your originality."

Ricardo was only eighteen at the time. Even he was surprised at how such a profound idea came to his mind. His words, however, touched Luna's heart. She found it easy to make her choice. Ricardo had provided the solution to the question she had been searching for since last night. She thanked him and disconnected the phone. She felt much more relaxed now because the weight in her mind had dissipated. After conversing with Ricardo, her ability to think coherently returned. She made the decision to stay in the industry. She also informed her mother about her decision in the afternoon. Dakota was happy to see that her daughter was strong from within.

***

Luna's debut film, as expected, was a huge success and caused quite a stir in the adult industry. Luna received several new offers. She also received the adult industry's most prestigious award in the best newbie category that year. Although there were several porn production offices in Miami, she frequently had to go to other states for shooting. Her schedule got really hectic. She began to make a lot of money from movies. Dakota was overjoyed to see her achievement. Luna bought a large house on Star Island in three years. Dakota didn't move with her there. She said she was happy in that little old house. Luna would spend the weekends with her mother. Luna was so content with her life that she had entirely forgotten about her ambition of becoming a lawyer.

She once expressed her desire to her mother to change her surname slightly. She said that she prefers the surname Fawx over Fawkes because the letter X is very significant in her life. Dakota liked her suggestion as well, and she agreed.

Her bond with Ricardo grew stronger over time. That bond had become as strong as it had ever been between her mother and Danny. In Dakota's life, there was only Danny whom she trusted more than herself whereas in Luna's life, there were two persons—her mother and Ricardo. Despite living 1,200 miles apart, they used to speak on the phone every day and continued hours-long video chats at night. Whenever Luna faced an uphill battle in her life, she would only consult Ricardo.

Ricardo was everything to Luna, a father, brother, mentor, screen partner, and friend but not a lover. That void in her heart that only a lover could fill stayed unfilled for a long time. Her eyes filled with tears every time she thought of Matthew. She wondered if Matthew had remembered her as well. He liked viewing adult movies. Luna had been in so many adult films throughout the years. It was impossible for Matthew to have never seen her in any film. It was also conceivable that he was now regretting his decision. But if that was the case, he would have sought to meet her or call her at some point over the years. She once suggested to her producer that he must shoot a sex scene where a boy and a girl engage in sexual activity while watching porn on TV. She simply wanted this because if Matthew saw it, he'd recall the wonderful time he spent with

Luna. Despite this, Matthew never attempted to contact her. He appeared to have forgotten about her and was happy with someone else. Luna's recollections gradually vanished from her heart as time passed. She no longer cried when she thought about him.

Ricardo, on the other hand, used to talk with someone else on the internet in addition to Luna. That boy was from San Diego and his name was Karl. Both Karl and Ricardo were passionate about the bikes. Additionally, they both met through Yahoo Messenger in a biker's group. They grew close and frequently talked about their experiences together. Ricardo kept his status as a porn star a secret from Karl. Karl considered him to be a motorcyclist. When Ricardo inquired about Karl, he replied that he worked as a sales associate for a company. His family included his parents, two sisters, and a brother. He was the youngest of his siblings and his father's most beloved. His siblings were no longer residing with them. His father was a factory manager who had now retired. His father's health was also deteriorating. Karl was a quiet, reserved young man with very few friends. He was mostly content in his own company. He enjoyed reading books and was interested in various religions. He detested narcotics as well. He was more mature than his age. He believed in traditional values. He believed that as the world became more modern, it was also heading toward disaster. It was quite obvious that he inherited such beliefs from his father.

***

In the early days of 2003, a transgender woman established herself as a successful producer/director in the porn industry. Her name was Rita Montenegro. After working on the first film with Luna, she became a close friend of her. They were approximately the same age. In the previous year, she directed five mega-hits, three of which starred Luna.

They were both sitting in a coffee shop that evening. Rita took out her laptop and began to check the reviews of her most recent movie. Her film had received a lot of mixed reviews. However, the majority of people were complaining about how similar her films were. Noticing her friend's facial expressions, Luna asked, "What happened, Rita?"

Rita asked, "Luna, can we try something different in our next film? Something no one has ever done before?"

In response to her question, Luna asked, "Do you want to work on some new genre, Rita?"

"Luna, I'm thinking something similar. However, I'm not sure what to do."

"We can shoot outdoor sex," Luna swiftly responded.

Rita was surprised by her suggestion and said, "This is a very good suggestion. Where did you get this idea so quickly, Luna? You are a genius."

"I have inherited all of this from my mother, Rita," Luna remarked with a smile. "She began working in adult movies when 70% of the American population had no idea that when two people have sex, the third can also have fun." They both laughed. Then Luna asked, "Will you cast me in your next film?"

"Do you still doubt it, sweetheart? You know very well that my first and last option is only you," replied Rita. "Just pick your on-screen partners."

"You can do that better, Rita," Luna remarked.

Rita selected four male models within fifteen minutes, with whom Luna had to shoot sex scenes in public places. Luna expressed her approval as well. Then, while they sat there together, they decided where they needed to shoot the scenes. A secluded road was chosen for the opening scene, which would feature roadside sex. The second scene was to be filmed on the small mountain range near Miami. The third scene was planned to take place on a moving bus. In addition to the models, director, and cameraman, only the driver would be present on that bus. That bus would continue to traverse the streets of Miami, and the film would continue to be shot inside it. The riskiest scene was the final one, which resulted from Luna's wicked thinking. She suggested filming a scene in the stadium during a soccer match the next week. Rita was initially hesitant, claiming that it was extremely risky and that if the secret was disclosed, she may face a huge penalty. But Luna assured her that they would shoot very carefully and that no one would know about it until the film was released. Rita consented after some deliberation.

The soccer match was still seven days away. Luna asked Rita to reserve 15 seats in the back row. She then began working on the first three scenes. The first sex scene was scheduled to be filmed on an open road. For this, a less-traveled route was selected. Rita was behind the wheel of her own Lincoln Navigator. Luna occupied the seat across from her. The male model and the assistant sat in the back seats. At one point on the route, they came across a massive rock lying on the roadside. That was, everyone agreed, the ideal location for the shoot. They reasoned that if anyone happened to pass by, they would immediately hide behind that boulder for a while to avoid being discovered. They were completely prepared for filming. Rita retrieved her handycam from her bag and turned it on. Since this movie had to be shot outdoors, all of the shooting had to be done with a handycam. Everyone was wearing sunglasses over their eyes. The scene began with Luna sucking her screen partner's penis. Then he stripped Luna, made her lie on the car's bonnet, spread her legs, and began licking her vagina. Both models became absorbed in each other, but Rita and her assistant maintained a close eye on both sides of the road so that if a vehicle approached, they could hide behind the massive rock.

Luna then laid a sheet on the ground and made her partner lie on his back on it. Then she sat on him, took his penis in her hand, and pulled it into her vagina. Within a short period of time, they both switched three positions. Luna eventually stood up. She also lifted him up by holding his hand. Then she grabbed his hand in hers and proceeded toward the huge rock. Rita trailed after them, holding the camera. Luna approached the stone, placed both hands on it, and stood with her legs open. Her partner acknowledged her signal and approached her, holding his erect penis in his hand. Then he gently put his penis into Luna's vagina from behind. Then he began fucking her rapidly. The hotness of the moment was at its peak at the time. Rita and her assistant were equally absorbed in the scene. At the moment, all of them were completely unaware of their surroundings. Luna's partner was rapidly inserting and pulling out his penis from her vagina. Luna was sighing with delight. Luna's partner took out his penis after two minutes and poured his cum on Luna's buttocks.

Just then, everyone's attention was drawn to the screeching sound of a vehicle applying its brakes. A black BMW car had pulled over to the side of the road. The windows had darkened glass. It was impossible to determine who was inside the car. All four of them became terrified. Rita tried hard to keep the camera from dropping out of her hands as a result of the abrupt shock. Luna covered her boobs with both hands, while her partner nearby covered his penis with his hands. Rita and her assistant stood in front of both models, covering them. They were so engaged in the scene that they failed to notice the approaching vehicle. That car remained there for 15 seconds. They were all as still as statues. The driver then pressed the accelerator, and the car sped away from there. They all just stood there staring at the car as it drove away. Everyone breathed a sigh of relief when it vanished from view and then returned to Rita's car.

Rita had to film the second scene for her movie on the third day of this incident. Except for one person, every passenger in Rita's car was the same. Luna's co-star on that day was a different model. A black model was selected to perform the sexual act with Luna. At about 11:30, they headed out for the shoot. They were supposed to arrive at the shooting location in two hours. Rita's car was speeding through the roads of Miami. A black BMW was tailing the vehicle. Nobody had taken notice of this. The weather was not clear that day, and a strong wind was blowing.

They left the city after about an hour and began moving toward the mountain range. The BMW was also chasing them. At one point, instead of following Rita's car, the BMW took an alternate route and headed toward another hill. After some time, Rita and her team arrived at their intended location. The time was 1:30 p.m. They got out of the car and looked around. The strong wind that had been blowing suddenly calmed down. Everything appeared to be in order to them, so they decided to get to work.

The two models stripped off their clothes and put them on the roof of Rita's car. Then Luna put the black model's penis into her mouth and began sucking it, which was around one and a half times longer than her partner's on the first day. Following that, all of the remaining tasks were carried out in the correct order. That forty-minute scene was jam-packed with fun-filled pranks. Rita recorded the entire hotness of the scene, sitting and standing at moments. She appeared to be content. The scene was finished. Suddenly, out of nowhere, there was a tremendous wind gust that blew Luna's and her partner's clothes off the roof of Rita's car.

They all stood helpless as they witnessed this. They had no notion that this would happen to them as well. It seemed impossible to discover their clothes in this location. By then, it was nearly three o'clock. Rita noticed Luna's worries and told her, "Luna dear, you don't need to worry. We'll all stay here until it gets dark, and then we'll leave. Nobody will notice that you're both naked in the car at night. Everyone must be hungry at this point. First, let's have lunch."

Rita and her assistant then took four foldable chairs and a table from the trunk of the car. Luna and her black partner sat naked on chairs. Rita extracted a bottle of wine and two boxes of food from the car. Then she set the package down on the table. The boxes contained spinach hummus wraps and a spicy pineapple slaw. After pouring the drink into glasses, they began to eat while conversing.

They had nothing to do after finishing lunch. They had to sit idle for almost four hours, which they found quite tough. They all sat and spoke for a while.

Luna abruptly rose from her chair and said to her friends that she was going for a walk alone for a bit. Everyone thought her decision was weird. How can one stroll around in an unknown location without clothes? But they were well aware that there was no population in the area. Luna left them seated and turned to move in a direction. She spent a long period walking naked on those mountain routes. She experienced intense pleasure every time the breeze brushed her bare skin.

No one knows what occurred to her as she was walking, she took off her sandals, threw them away, and began walking barefoot. She had the sensation of being unusually inebriated. Maybe she'd never felt so close to nature before. She wandered aimlessly like this for an hour before returning to her group. Her companions were seated together and conversing. She, too, sat on her chair and became absorbed in their conversation. They were totally unaware that a black BMW car was parked on another hill nearby, and that someone standing alongside had been monitoring all four of them through binoculars for a long time.

As darkness fell, the four of them made their way back to the city. Rita's assistant sat in the front seat, while Luna and her partner sat naked in the backseat. They were still a long way from the city, and the road was deserted. Rita turned on the dome light and stated to both of them, "If you guys agree, we can shoot a new scene in the moving car."

Luna and her partner looked at each other as if they were seeking each other's opinion on Rita's idea. Rita added, pointing to Luna's screen partner's penis, "If this gentleman has no objection to doing double labor in a single day."

The male model laughed and replied, "It won't be a problem at all, ma'am. All of this is pure pleasure for this gentleman rather than hard work."

Everyone burst out laughing. Everyone agreed on the concept. Rita handed the camera over to her assistant and continued driving. Luna and her partner continued to have sex in the back seat while the assistant recorded everything.

Rita booked a bus and started shooting her third scene a few days later. All four of the models who were picked for the project had to film a gangbang scene with Luna. In contrast to the previous two days of shooting, this day was problem-free. Luna was the only one who faced the problem. To deal with four powerful penises alone was no small task. She stood in the field like a brave person despite not losing courage. Then, one by one, she vanquished the quartet.

The day finally arrived for them to shoot the final and most dangerous scene of this film. They arrived with their crew before the game began. Luna was dressed in a skirt and a T-shirt. Rita was anxious, but Luna seemed entirely at ease. They had reserved 15 tickets in total. Luna and her partner sat in the middle, and Rita joined them. Members of their crew who had no business there sat on both sides of them. Those people were just brought in to provide cover for the two models. For the first forty-five minutes of the game, they all watched in silence. During the second half, when the match had become highly intriguing and the entire audience was engrossed in it, Luna signaled to Rita. Rita retrieved her camera from her bag and turned it on. Luna slowly unzipped her partner's pants and extracted his penis. Rita continued to film everything. Luna continued to caress the penis diligently. After a while, its size grew. Luna then rose from her seat and took a seat at her partner's feet. She put his penis in her mouth and began to suck. Subsequently, she got to her feet and removed her underwear from beneath her skirt. She then inserted her partner's penis into her vagina while she was sitting over him. Rita lowered her camera hand and began to take a low-angle shot. The audience was intensely engrossed in the game. Luna was performing quietly without making a sound. Then she removed her T-shirt. Her partner grabbed her boobs and began licking her nipples.

After a while, Rita handed over the camera to her assistant, who was sitting on the other side, and he started capturing the scene from there. After ten minutes, Rita signaled Luna, who slid down from her partner's lap and sat in her seat. She then slipped into her T-shirt and panties. The camera was switched off, and the assistant raised his thumb and said, "Well done." Everyone except the crew was unaware of what had happened. However, the second half of this scene was yet to be shot.

The match was gradually approaching its conclusion. The audience's interest was likewise at an all-time high. However, some of the spectators in that stadium were totally uninterested in the game. Their purpose for being here was different. Rita stood up, grabbed Luna's hand, and hauled her up as well. Luna motioned her partner with her finger to get up and headed toward the ladies' restroom. That model also started to follow them quietly. They locked the door of the restroom from inside.

Rita turned on the camera, and both of them removed all of their clothes in one fell swoop. They enjoyed fantastic sex without fear for the next 15 minutes. By the time they finished all of this work and emerged from the restroom, the match was over. The crowd was cheering as they exited the stadium. Rita, too, wanted to cheer, but for different reasons. She had no idea which team had won the match. She came back with the winning team of her own.

When this movie was released after the completion of editing work, it caused quite a stir. All the scenes of the film were superior to one another. Rita was elated this time after reading the audience's reviews and tears of joy welled up in her eyes. The owners of the Soccer Stadium, on the other hand, had voiced their vehement opposition to this course of action.

A month after the release of her new film, Rita and Luna were sitting in the same coffee shop. Rita was staring at her laptop screen while Luna sipped her coffee. Luna realized she was witnessing something really interesting when she looked at her face. After a while, Rita moved the laptop toward Luna and asked, "Luna, would you please read this email?"

Luna moved the laptop closer to her and noticed that Rita's mailbox contained an email from Madame X. She began to read the email whose content was like this:

Dear Rita,
Congratulations on a wonderful career. I admire your work greatly.

I am a highly wealthy and distinguished woman. In my life, I've made a lot of money and gained a lot of fame. My name appears on the list of America's wealthiest people. My fans come from all across the world. At the age of 28, I have accomplished all of my goals. I just have one wish left in my heart that I want to fulfil. But that would be the end of my respect. And that is something that I would never want.

Meanwhile, I shortlisted several extremely talented individuals who can assist me in achieving my dream while maintaining its secrecy. Then I began to keep an eye on them. Finally, I decided to put my trust in you. A black BMW pulled up next to you during an outdoor shooting last month. I was sitting inside it.

Now, allow me to tell you about my wish. I'd like to appear in an adult movie directed by some highly talented person. I have a fantastic body. I want everyone to notice and admire my body. They should observe my lovemaking abilities as well. But I don't want to reveal my face at the same time. I'll wear a rubber mask to conceal my face. The rest of the body will be naked. Will you film a scene for me under my conditions?

If you can fulfil this wish of mine, please respond to this email. I will cover all of the costs associated with filming this entire scene along with your fee. Just don't try to figure out who I am. I can be anyone—a political figure, a Hollywood celebrity, a business mogul, etc. My heart tells me that I can trust you.

Your friend
Madame X

After reading the email, Luna sat bewildered for a while. Then Rita broke the silence by asking, "What do you think, Luna? Should I accept or decline the offer?"

Luna said, "She trusted you, Rita, so you should help her."

Rita was quiet for a while. Then she added, "Luna, I have a concern. According to a study, while watching porn, viewers focus more on the model's face than on her private parts. And her face, according to this lady, might be covered beneath a mask. In that case, this scene will not spark the audience's interest."

Luna stated, "That should not be our concern, Rita. She is bearing the entire cost for this project. It won't matter whether or not someone enjoys the scene."

Rita agreed to Luna. "Should I respond to her email?" She asked.

Luna said, "Yes, respond right away. And ask her which model she prefers to have her sex scene filmed as well."

Rita drew the laptop close to her and typed the email quickly. "I accept your offer," she wrote. "You can rely on me. I will never strive to figure out who you are. And if you have a preference for your screen partner, please mention his name."

Rita sent the email. Five minutes later, her response arrived, with only one word scrawled—Ricardo.

Even though it was almost dark outside, those two friends were sitting in the same coffee shop. Luna thought for a long time before saying, "My mother used to tell me that many times people have a crush on a porn star. And when they don't see any other way to get intimate with them, they enter the adult industry to satisfy their craving. This allows them to spend quality time with their crush.

Someone by the name of Danny joined the industry just because of my mother. Eventually, their friendship became stronger over time. And during hard times, he provided my mother a lot of support. He and Mom are still in contact. He frequently talks to her over the phone. He has also made a few visits to see her. Rita, my heart whispers that this mysterious woman is likewise in love with Ricardo. She has created so much drama just because of him."

Rita kept listening to her very attentively. Then she said, "This world is really weird. Isn't it, Luna?" Then they both chuckle. Rita then said to Luna, "Please call Ricardo and ask him to give me the date for my next scene. I'll contact that mysterious lady once I know the date."

Luna took out her phone and dialed Ricardo's number. According to the message from the other end, that number was out of network range. Then she remembered something and told Rita that Ricardo had gone on a long bike ride with a friend of his from San Diego. She was not sure when he would return.

Rita emailed Madame X once more, informing her that she would notify her via email as soon as the shooting date was finalized. She insisted her to arrive on the shooting spot on time.

Ricardo returned from his bike trip at the end of the same month. He called Luna as soon as he arrived. Luna informed him that Rita would be casting him in her upcoming film. Rita and Ricardo spoke over the phone, and a date for the shoot was scheduled. Madame X was also briefed by Rita. She advised Rita to have as few crew members as possible present throughout the entire shooting process. Rita assured her that there would only be one or two additional persons in addition to the three of them. The shooting day had arrived. Luna was also invited by Rita. When the assistants finished setting up the lighting, etc., they were ordered to depart. Ricardo had arrived earlier than expected. He gave Luna an embrace the moment he spotted her. It had been a while since he had seen her.

After a while, a black BMW pulled up outside the studio. A six-foot tall lady came out of the car as the door opened. She had covered her face with a latex hood full face mask with a ponytail hole, as she had indicated. She was likewise dressed in black. Through the mask, only her eyes and lips were visible. Her golden hair hung down from the top of her head and touched her waist. Her figure was amazing. Rita greeted her as she entered. Rita sat in her office for 20 minutes and chatted with her. In another room, Luna and Ricardo were seated together. Rita eventually called Luna to her office. As soon as Luna emerged from the other room, she saw the lady wearing the mask. The moment their eyes met,

Luna sensed jealousy in the lady's eyes. She began to find her theory to be completely correct. That lady was undoubtedly in love with Ricardo, and in most cases, Luna was Ricardo's screen partner. So that lady's jealousy of Luna was completely justified. She, too, wished to be Luna in some manner, and today she got the chance.

Luna sat next to Rita on the chair, and the lady entered the room where Ricardo was sitting. Then she locked the door from inside. Luna had a puzzled expression on her face but said nothing. Rita read her expression and told her that she wanted to discuss something with her screen partner, which is why she called Luna out of the room. Luna only smiled.

After about half an hour, the shooting began. Luna chose to remain at Rita's office. There were only three people in the shooting room. In the absence of her assistant, Rita was operating the camera herself. Luna continued hearing both models moaning. She waited for the shooting to conclude patiently while sitting there. This entire process took around ninety minutes. The door then opened, and Rita emerged. Luna asked, "How was your experience shooting with Madame X?" Rita described her as 'a very passionate lady'. However, some retakes were required due to her lack of experience.

After five minutes, both of them came out of the shooting room. They had put on their clothes now. Madame X handed Rita a sealed envelope and said, "It contains the amount agreed between us for this work. From the bottom of my heart, I appreciate your help." She promptly exited the studio and drove away in her car.

Rita ordered some snacks after she left and the three of them sat in her office, chatting. They both noticed Ricardo appeared to be quite joyful.

Luna asked Ricardo, "When are you returning to Houston?"

Ricardo replied, "I have a flight tomorrow morning."

"You've met after such a long time," Luna objected. "You should have stayed with me for a minimum of two days."

"There is a lot of work in Houston," replied Ricardo. "After returning from my bike trip, I flew straight to Miami."

Luna quipped, "Did you have a good time with your lover?"

Ricardo said, "Hey, I was with my friend. Not with any of my lovers."

Luna said, "I'm talking about that black cat you just fucked."

Ricardo's eyes widened, "I don't even know who she is. How can you term her as my lover?"

Luna asked, "What did you both whisper when she shut the door from inside just before the shooting?"

Ricardo chuckled, "Luna, I never hide anything from you. She merely disclosed to me that she intended to use cocaine prior to the shooting in order to enhance her performance even more. Along with her, she gave me some cocaine."

Luna and Rita both realized why Ricardo appeared overjoyed. Luna was well aware of Ricardo's sporadic cocaine use.

"So she didn't tell you anything about herself?" Luna asked.

Ricardo replied, "No, she didn't tell me anything."

In the meantime, Rita connected her camera to her computer and transferred the video files. The three of them then continued to watch it play. After seeing Madame X's performance, Luna was likewise impressed. She was perplexed as to how someone could provide such a flawless performance in her very first shoot. It is unquestionably due to the effects of cocaine.

She turned to Ricardo and asked, "What do you think, Ricardo? Should I also try that drug?"

Ricardo said, "As you wish, Luna. If you need, just let me know and I'll make the arrangements."

Rita turned to Luna and said, "I have captured more than eighty minutes of their intimate moments on camera. After editing, the film will run longer than seventy minutes. In this video, they had given the maximum amount of time for foreplay. Luna, according to you what should be the movie's title?"

Luna thought for a while and said, "The Dark Side of Madame X."

***

2006 was an important year in her career. She received the Best Female Performer award this year. This was her career's second award. She won the best newcomer award in her initial year. After receiving the award, when she emerged from the auditorium at the conclusion of the event, the throng of admirers waiting outside greeted her warmly. She had witnessed a nearly identical scene when she received this honor for the first time. That day, as she walked out of the auditorium following the award ceremony, only a few individuals were taking photographs with cameras, while the rest of the audience applauded. But she soon discovered that today there was less applause and more photographs being taken because everyone had a camera phone in their hands. Friends and industry colleagues suggested throwing a party that night, which she gladly accepted. The celebration lasted the whole night, and she arrived at her hotel room at 7:00 a.m. Her flight from Los Angeles to Miami was scheduled for 3:30 p.m. She decided it would be best to sleep for a while. She awoke about 1:00 p.m. She had a bath and then caught a taxi to the airport after lunch. She arrived in Miami about 8:30 p.m. Her car was parked in the airport parking.

She then drove to downtown and rang the doorbell of her old house. Dakota opened the door and was delighted to see her. Dakota felt proud when Luna told her that she had won the award for Best Female Performer tonight. Tears of joy began to fall from her eyes. They sat in the living room for a long time, holding each other's hands. Dakota reflected on the past, and said, "No such awards existed in our times. Such honors raise the artist's spirit and inspire them to perform better. Additionally, the degree of joy parents experience when witnessing their child's accomplishment."

Luna became sorrowful and said, "You are both my mother and father to me. I've never met my father. I have no idea what he looks like. And I'm not even sure whether he's aware of my existence."

Dakota remained silent. Luna asked again, "Do you really have no photo of Papa?"

Dakota cupped Luna's face in her hands and murmured, "My child, I've already told you that I've only met your father once. The man never showed me his face again after that."

"So you never tried to find him again after that?"

"I tried for a while. But then things changed quickly, and I had to leave that town. After that, the chance of ever seeing him again was lost. The main reason I never witnessed him again was due to the fact that I left the industry forever. Perhaps he worked in many more films that I am unaware of." Then she snapped out of her emotional trance and remarked, "Leave it here, Luna, don't get busy discussing old things. Today is a day to celebrate."

Luna reached inside her bag for a bottle of champagne, which she opened, and the two of them began to chat while drinking it. Dakota said, "My child, I pray that you continue to progress like this day and night. However, never compromise your ideals. The performers of our time had a personality that is not evident in today's celebrities. Yes, they have more squeaky clean and gleaming bodies than we have. You are a part of this dazzling world, but you should never become lost in it. If you stay on the proper track, you will be able to obtain a lot of essential experience."

Luna asked, slightly surprised, "What kind of experience are you talking about, Mother?"

Dakota explained, "When you're having sex with your partner in front of the camera, there comes a moment where you reach the heights of intimacy and completely forget that everything is being recorded. That moment is so delightful that it is beyond description. You become one with existence at that point. I want my daughter to have that experience as well as enormous fortune and fame."

Luna felt confused by what her mother had said. She might not have been mature enough to comprehend such a profound notion yet, but she chose not to ask Dakota to elaborate.

Dakota went on, "I have lived my entire life sticking to my principles. I have never compromised on my principles. Maintaining success in life requires a great deal of discipline. Throughout my ten-year career, I performed sex in front of the camera only. With the exception of filming, I have never had intercourse with anyone. I never found a partner and never felt the need for anyone."

It was the first time Luna had ever heard this from Dakota's mouth. This surprised her immensely. Then all of a sudden, a thought went across her head. "Mom, if this is true, then there must have been a camera recording that moment of your meeting with Papa," she said to Dakota. "As a result, Papa's face would almost certainly have been captured on video."

From the expressions on her face, Dakota appeared to be trapped by her own words. She had no choice but to accept the truth. She then confessed to her daughter the reality that she had kept secret up until that moment.

That day was packed with surprises for Luna. She said, "I am certain, Mom, that you must have that videotape."

Dakota didn't respond and remained silent for a while. She then got up from her chair and proceeded to her bedroom. After five minutes, she returned with a video cassette in her hand. It was the same cassette that she had not tossed into the fire years ago. She placed the cassette in Luna's palm quietly. There was excitement in Luna's face. She couldn't wait any longer and turned on the TV and VCR that were lying nearby. She then inserted the cassette into the VCR and returned to sit next to her mother.

The movie began to play on the TV screen. As soon as the first scene started, Luna commented, "This appears to be Tim Blue's direction."

Dakota smiled and added, "Your keen sight must be appreciated. This is, of course, Tim's work." The movie continued, and they both continued to watch it silently. That film included three sequences in total. The first two scenes were shot with other models. Dakota's gangbang scene came at the very end. Tim's fantastic direction and the models' outstanding performance kept them both from realizing an hour had passed. The gangbang scene, which was shot in two parts, then started. The first part took place in the pool, while the second took place in the bedroom. Dakota stepped into the pool naked at the start of the action. Luna was completely engrossed in the scene. Perhaps the reason she began watching that movie had faded from her memory.

The fourth anonymous model played a minor role in the pool action therefore the camera did not focus on him much. In that scene, there was not even a close-up of anyone's face. Luna continued to watch that part of the scene silently. When the second part began and the fourth man's face was revealed, Luna's jaw remained open. Her eyes widened. Even if she tried, no sound came out of her mouth. Dakota noticed her face's lost radiance and shook her, asking, "Is everything okay, my child?"

Luna asked, pointing at the television screen, "Is this the man, Mama?"

Dakota said, "You got it exactly right. That man is your father. But why are you so nervous?"

"But how is this possible, Mama?" Luna spoke in a shaky tone. "I've seen this dude so many times on film locations. And he still looks the same today."

Dakota felt dumbfounded by what she had just heard. "How can this happen, Luna?" she said. "You must have some kind of misunderstanding. Many people have faces that are identical to one another."

"Mom, I am not a child who can be mistaken in recognizing someone," Luna said. "I'm quite sure this is him. And he's still quite young." For a while, she became silent. After some deliberation, she said, "According to my birth date, this video should be from the early months of 1981. How is it possible for a man's appearance to remain unchanged for so long? Even now, it appears precisely the same. I only remember him because his face is so distinct and appealing. I'm not sure why he comes to the set, but he definitely does and is never inside while shooting."

Dakota still couldn't believe what Luna was saying. Luna's nervousness was obvious to her. She put her hand on her thigh and said, "My child, as you look exactly like me, the guy you saw could be your father's son, that is, your brother from another mother."

"I agree that it is possible that the father and son's appearances are identical in many cases. But is it possible that they both have a scar on their forehead?"

Dakota was at a loss for words.

"From now on, whenever I see that man, I'll secretly click his picture with my phone and show it to you. Only then you would trust whatever I have said."

Dakota said nothing. She continued to believe that her daughter had some misunderstanding. Her mind was not prepared to comprehend that the unknown man she had worked so hard to find but was unable to locate would pay a visit to the set of her daughter's films. It was weird that after receiving the news, which should have made Dakota overjoyed, there was no wave in her mind and she stayed sitting in her seat in the same calm manner. Nobody knows what the cause of this was. Perhaps she had lost her zeal after reaching a certain point in her life and all the hope was lost. That is why despite her daughter being so confident, she refused to believe her. Luna's entire existence, on the other hand, experienced panic and fear. Her focus had been completely diverted from her accomplishment of the day, and an unfamiliar worry had taken place in her head. She couldn't figure out why that person appeared on the set. Was he aware of Luna's connection with himself? She had made up her mind that from now onwards, whenever he appeared in front of her, she would quickly take his picture. But, following that episode, he was never seen by Luna again.

One night at the end of that year, Luna received a phone call from her mother informing her that her longtime friend Danny had moved in with her. Danny had also bid adieu to the adult industry a few years ago. He had an unbreakable bond with Dakota. Luna was really relieved to hear this news. She had expressed her worry about her mother living alone on several occasions. However, she knew deep down that someone would eventually come to fill the void created by her separation from her mother one day.

***

After receiving the prestigious award for Best Female Performer, Luna began to be recognized among the prominent celebs. Her fan base has also grown significantly. She began receiving modelling offers from a variety of agencies. But she accepted such proposals only after much consideration. This was also due to her being excessively busy. She once received an invitation from a nonprofit organization asking her to throw a fundraising event for their animal shelters. Luna thought this was a noble thing and immediately agreed.

That event had been arranged in a club on Ocean Drive. The program was divided into two sections. The first activity was called 'interaction with a star,' and it required participants to strike up a discussion informally with Luna Fawx. The second activity was a fundraiser supper. It was eight in the evening. However, hall's donor count was quite low. This caught even the event organizers off guard, in addition to Luna. Neither Luna nor her mother had ever donated anything to charity. She believed that the belief in charity was limited to the elite.

There were just about 20–25 individuals in the hall. The three men seated in the first row did not appear wealthy from any perspective. One of them, who sat in the middle and had a moustache, was staring at Luna. The way he looked bothered her. A short man was seated on his right side, while the man on his left side had no hair on his head.

The interaction began.

A forty-year-old woman posed the first question. She asked Luna, "Could you please tell us whether girls are physically exploited in the adult industry? Do you have to sleep with the producer in order to get a role?"

Luna replied calmly, "Madam, no such incident has occurred in my six years of career. They select you on the basis of your talent. Such corruption does not exist in the industry at all. Yes, if the film's producer is also doing a role in the film, we need to have sex with him."

After hearing Luna's response, the audience burst out laughing. People continued to ask Luna a variety of questions for the following 20 minutes, which she answered confidently. Most of those people were older, and they were asking questions about the adult industry as if they were quite interested in it. Despite this, it did not appear that they knew her mother based on their statements because no one told her that there was an adult actress in their times who looked exactly like her.

A man in the second row, perhaps 50 years old, asked Luna, "Ma'am, I often wonder why watching porn is solely a male pastime. Why aren't the females interested in this?"

Luna replied with a smile, "I can't say anything about this, sir. Only a psychologist can provide an answer to your question."

Another man sitting nearby took the microphone from him and said, "I know the answer to this. Women are solely interested in attractive apparel, which are regrettably not seen in pornographic films."

The entire hall resounded with laughter. Luna couldn't stop laughing as well.

A young girl in the last row took the mic and questioned Luna, "Ma'am, tell us why, despite being so beautiful, you chose this profession when you could be a supermodel or a Hollywood actress?"

Luna smiled as she heard the question. Then she said, "Sometimes you don't choose a profession, it chooses you. The same thing happened to me. I was dancing at a beach party when a director approached me and offered me the opportunity to work on his film, which I couldn't reject. And, interestingly, he didn't inform me at the time that it was his last film. After that, he planned to leave the industry forever. After his film was completed, he divulged this secret to me and said that I could pursue this field as a career if I wanted to. Because of the fantastic experience I had working in that film, I chose to continue in the future."

"Would you like to tell us about your experience?" The girl probed further.

"Sure," Luna responded. "It was an extremely satisfying experience for me. A person searches for enjoyment in simple things throughout his life. But, many times, even after living his entire life, he is unable to find contentment. When I was 18, I shot my first adult film, and it brought me such joy and calm that I couldn't put it into words. I felt like I was born to do this sort of work."

Subsequently, the man with a moustache seated in the front row raised his hand, and the controllers transferred the mic to him. The man asked, "Madam, please tell me what kind of work you did before entering this profession?"

Luna responded, "No, sir, I've never done any other work. After finishing high school, I entered into the adult industry."

"Then how can you say that after working in your first film, you knew you were made for this? That can only be said if the person has previously tried multiple professions and been dissatisfied with them. But you've never tried anything else, according to you."

"Sir, I didn't comprehend anything," Luna said, perplexed.

"Allow me to explain. Do you agree that it is possible that tomorrow you might do something else that will bring you more happiness than your current profession?"

Luna said nothing. He went on, "Happiness and peace of mind are just tricks to fool the people. The point is that the industry satisfies your needs. Spreading your legs brings in money. No hard work is required. You get to have sex with new men every day. Other people work hard, earn money, and then have fun. But you guys make money along with having fun. Many ladies find that they are not satisfied with only one partner. They require several partners. Did this line of work provide you that kind of fulfilment?"

Luna's face turned red with rage. She replied fiercely, "I'm talking about the fulfilment of creative instinct. Please, sir, don't put words in my mouth."

"I'm not going to put words in your mouth." Looking at his companions on either side of him, he laughed and remarked, "We've got better things to put in there."

"Sir, Will you please shut up?" Luna's rage had reached a boiling point. She lost control and said to the man, "It is not your fault, sir. It is your upbringing that is to blame. A man learns how to treat women from his father. You most likely learned these things from your mother's clients."

That man became enraged as well. He stood up from his seat, and his two companions followed him. He appeared to be preparing to attack Luna. Two security guards hurried toward them, sensing the danger. The man motioned with his hand to the guards to stop and declared, "I'm leaving." Both of the guards came to a halt. He turned to go, and then turned to Luna and asked, "Which animal shelter are you fundraising for when the biggest animal shelter is between your legs?"

Furious, Luna remained seated in her spot while he and his companions stormed out of the hall.

About a half-hour later, the same three men were drinking beer and conversing in an Irish pub on Ocean Drive. "Whatever happened, Charlie, you were not nice to that sweet girl?" remarked the short man to the man with the moustache.

"Indeed," Charlie remarked, "It was nothing. I had intended to reveal the true faces of the event organizers."

"Why do you hold a grudge against them?" The third person inquired.

"Hey, these shameless people have destroyed all decorum," Charlie muttered as he took a sip from his glass of beer. "They've invited a prostitute to a charity event. Since charity is a holy endeavor, who is promoting it for them?"

"You feel bad about something very quickly, Charlie. That poor girl also considers herself an artist," the short person remarked. His remarks included sarcasm.

"Artist, my foot." Charlie responded angrily, "What kind of art is required in making porn? All that is needed is one camera and a shameless bitch. A porn star is someone who wants to be in show business but lacks talent."

"No, Charlie, there's an awful lot of talent." The third person added, "You remain restless after watching them perform until you do something."

The trio laughed. They had no idea that a hooded man with a scar on his forehead was seated at a nearby table. He was secretly listening to their conversation.

Charlie went on, "I say that whoever comes across these bitches should immediately show them a mirror. That is exactly what I do. These people are the scum of civilization. They are not entitled to a dignified life. We in Utah believe so."

The small individual inquired, "Have you ever met anyone else who is involved in the same business, Charlie?"

Charlie admitted, "Yes, I met someone else when I was quite young. She resembled her as well. By sucking the penises of several guys throughout their lives, they all get identical looks."

Everybody fell silent for a while. Suddenly Charlie remembered something and his cheeks flushed red with rage. "That bitch has abused my mother," he began to say. "She won't be spared by me."

The short man asked, "Charlie, what are you going to do?"

"I'm going to rape that bitch tonight."

"Charlie, this won't end well. When she abused you, you responded appropriately. And, as a result of that episode, everyone present there noticed all three of us. There's no use in pursuing this any further."

Charlie grew angrier. "I don't care whether you guys support me or not," he said. "Tonight, I'm going to teach that bitch a lesson."

"Don't say that, Charlie. We'll be there for you. Tell us what to do?"

"The event will conclude at 11:00 p.m. There are 15 minutes remaining. We'll follow her as soon as she exits the hall. Once she gets home, we will teach her a lesson."

"Okay, Charlie. As you say. Shall we now leave?"

"Yes, everyone, get up." Charlie stood up, and the other two followed. The man with the scar who was listening to them stood up fast and followed them. The trio emerged from the pub's rear entrance and arrived at a tiny street. The club where the fundraising event was being hosted was nearby.

At 11:30 p.m., a dancer from a strip club located a short distance away from that Irish pub was giving the club owner a blowjob in his office. The dancer suddenly felt lightheaded, and a few seconds later, she puked on the carpet. When the owner asked, she said she wasn't feeling well. The owner advised her to go home and take some rest. She hastily adjusted her clothes, grabbed her bag, and left through the staff-only back entrance. As she noticed something in the street, she screamed. Three dead bodies were sprawled on the ground in front of her. She puked for the second time right away. She then dashed back into the club and told the owner everything. After discovering the dead bodies, the club owner called the local police station from the club's landline telephone. After ten minutes, the police arrived. They were all slain by slicing their throats with a sharp object. There was no cell phone or ID in their pockets through which the police could find out anything about them. The dead bodies were removed from the scene after a preliminary examination.

The next day the authorities appealed to the public through newspapers and television that if there were any eyewitnesses to the murders on Ocean Drive the night before they should come forward to help the police. On the same evening, a 30-year-old guy arrived at the police station and stated a wish to meet with the officer investigating the murders. After a few moments, he was sitting in the cabin of the investigating officer. In addition to those two, an FBI agent was present in the cabin. When the officer questioned the man why he arrived, he explained that the three killings had occurred right in front of his eyes.

The officer inquired about his name and other information, which he provided. The officer then requested him to show his identification, which he did. After validating everything, the officer asked him, "Now tell me the entire story from beginning to end. Where were you when the murders happened?"

The man started speaking, "Officer, I was having sex with my girlfriend in my car, 200 feet away from that location. It's a deserted street with few people passing through. When I saw three men approaching, I got the feeling that they were likely to harm us if they spotted us like this. My girlfriend and I crouched. After a while, I raised my head and noticed a hooded figure approaching fast behind them. The man approaching them did not even speak to them before pulling a knife from his pocket and quickly slit the throats of all three of them."

Both the police officer and the FBI agent were staring at him with wide eyes as if they were unwilling to believe a word he was saying.

Subsequently, the man continued, "When all three of them died, the hooded man snatched everything from their pockets and took it with him."

They still couldn't believe what he said. The FBI agent questioned him, saying, "So you're trying to say that a single man murdered three people and they couldn't defend themselves against him? Could you perhaps explain how this is possible? Who was he, a fucking superhero?"

"I'm not sure who he was, officer. However, the three guys who perished while fighting him were punching in the air as if they had lost their vision. Perhaps this is why he was able to murder three people so effortlessly on his own."

"How could they have lost their sight in such a way? Did he spray something in their eyes?" the officer asked.

"I don't think he would have done anything like that, Officer. I didn't notice him doing it."

"When did you get out of the car, then?"

"We were both terrified, officer. We hid in the car for quite a long time. We came out after you removed the dead bodies."

"However, there was no reason to be scared once the police arrived at the scene. It was the perfect time for you to come out and tell the whole story."

"Officer, there was a greater reason to be scared."

"I do not get it. What exactly do you want to say?"

"The owner of the club outside whose backdoor the murders occurred was also present there the entire time."

"So?"

"Actually, the woman in the car with me was his wife."

***

In month of April in 2010, Karl, Ricardo's biker friend, who was in his late twenties, was quite depressed. Many unsavory events had occurred in his family. Both of his elder sisters' marriages had failed, which was a matter of greatest concern to him. His father was likewise suffering from a number of terrible ailments as he grew older. He couldn't get out of bed. In addition, he had a lot of difficulties speaking. Nobody else in the house could comprehend what he was saying. Only Karl understood what he was saying. Karl was a philosophical type of person by nature. He'd studied a lot of books on philosophy and religion. He studied these books for the answers to his life's questions, but he did not succeed. Many religious and philosophical thinkers believe that suffering is a part of life. He agreed wholeheartedly with this. However, he hasn't been able to figure out the reason behind it. He knew his father had worked hard throughout his life and wondered what had caused his current state of illness in his old age. Both of his sisters were completely loyal to their spouses, so why did their marriages end? These things bothered him a lot. He pondered where he would obtain the answers.

He was sitting in a library one evening, reading a book when he noticed two young couples conversing over at the table next to him. Two days prior, one couple had returned from Houston. One was telling the other that Ulisses, a charismatic cult leader, was the person they had spent a month with. That leader made a big impression on both of them. Karl put down his book and focused on paying close attention to what they were saying. They both told their friends about the unexpected transformation in their lives after meeting that cult leader. It appeared as though their life of sorrow had ended and extremely fortunate things had begun to occur. Their remarks struck a chord with the other couple, who began to tell them that they too wanted to meet that man. The librarian approached them at that very moment and requested them to stop talking loudly. After apologizing to him, the four began whispering to each other about the rest of the story. Karl didn't hear anything else from them after that. He had memorized the terms from all the talks he had overheard with those people—Houston—Cult Leader—Ulisses.

Karl searched for a Houston-based cult on Google the same night, but no results were returned. Then he typed Ulisses, but no results were displayed. He grew dissatisfied. He began to realize his mistake. He believed he should have approached those people and informed them of his desire to meet with the leader. He was confident at the time that he would be able to discover that leader using whatever information he obtained from what those folks mentioned. However, the situation had changed drastically.

He was worried the entire night. The next day, it dawned on him that he might seek assistance from his friend Ricardo, who resides in Houston, in this matter. He texted Ricardo and urged him to call him whenever he was free. Ricardo called later that evening. Karl requested his help in locating the Cult Leader Ulisses. Ricardo informed him that he had heard of it but didn't know much about it. He would contact Karl as soon as he found something.

Then, a week later, Ricardo called again and said he had discovered everything. 'The Cult of the Lost' is a well-known cult in Houston. Famous people, including film stars, politicians and top businessmen, visit its leader. He doesn't meet with anyone directly. A reference from a cult member is required to meet with him.

Karl asked, "So, where will we get this reference from now?"

"A few years ago, someone I knew belonged to their cult," Ricardo revealed. "But he's now moved from this place. I'll make an attempt to contact him. If I find him, your job is done."

Carl went on to say, "Hopefully, you'll be able to contact that cult member soon."

Ricardo disconnected the call and then dialed director Tim Blue's number. However, Tim's phone was switched off. Tim was a member of the cult years ago when he worked in the adult industry. Three or four times a year, he would travel from Los Angeles to Houston and spend a few days with that cult leader. Tim quit the industry on the same leader's recommendation, and it was uncertain where he was at the moment. Then Ricardo got an idea. He emailed Tim, saying that one of his friends wanted to meet the cult leader and that they needed his support. Tim's reply arrived about a month later, in which he sent a code to Ricardo and indicated that after providing this code, they would be able to see the leader.

Soon later, Ricardo gave Karl a call and shared the wonderful news. Karl had given any hope of getting this done by this point. He was ecstatic to get this news from Ricardo after waiting so many days. In addition, Ricardo texted Karl with all the information about that cult. The cult's leader's name was Eulisses. Karl did not add an E in front of Ulisses when searching for that name on Google, which is why no results were displayed.

Karl took a four-day leave from work on Tuesday, the next week and flew directly to Houston. Later that evening, they arrived at the ranch outside of the city, along with Ricardo, where the leader of Cult of the Lost resided. They were asked for the code at the entry, and once they provided it, they were allowed to enter. After roughly fifteen minutes, they were seated on the ground in front of Eulisses, their leader. Eulisses was dressed in his normal black robe, with a hood covering the upper half of his face. Ricardo was bothered by the atmosphere in the room, but Karl appeared fully normal and confident. Eulisses examined each of them attentively before turning to Karl and saying, "You seem to have come a long way. Please explain why you wanted to meet with me."

Karl inhaled deeply and began to speak, "I've heard that you've changed the lives of some people. I also have a lot of issues and concerns in my life. I have no idea why they exist. I also can't come up with a solution. I tried to find the solution by reading books but it didn't work. That is why I have come to you, hoping that you will help me in some way."

"Worries and troubles are part of human life. However, relatively few individuals make an effort to fix it," Eulisses said. "You possess such bravery. Most people find that turning away and closing their eyes works better in these situations. They use drugs to aid in this work."

"However, I hate drugs excessively," Karl said.

"I can definitely see that," Eulisses said. "Tell me now what issue or query prompted you to travel so far to see me."

Karl began saying solemnly, "My question to you is why a person's old age is so painful."

Eulisses remarked, "Old age is not at all painful. Growing old is a rewarding time. It is the outcome of an individual's lifetime labor. It becomes painful in that situation if someone has lived a falsehood his entire life. An honest person who has worked hard throughout his life would never be troubled by old age. Throughout his life, he remains as simple as a child."

Karl was dissatisfied with his remarks. He couldn't believe his father would ever lie to anybody. He opened his mouth to raise an objection, but Eulisses gestured with his hand and requested him to remain silent, adding, "Humans make mistakes all the time. They have no idea how to live an ethical life. Suffering is sometimes caused by our lifestyle rather than our acts. Our hearts always guide us toward what is right and wrong. It also explains the cause or reason behind the pain. Therefore, when someone gets into problems at any age, he instinctively understands why this is happening to him. It is up to him whether he shares this with anyone or not. Now tell me what you would like to say."

Karl's confusion was exacerbated by his statements. Then he gathered the confidence to say, "The cause of my problem is my father's health. Can he find a remedy to his suffering?"

Eulisses remarked with a smile, "I can see that you love your father a lot. And you're quite concerned about him. He has lived a very prolonged life. Additionally, he is currently facing a lot of suffering. He can get relief from his suffering. However, it is only possible if you get married."

Karl was shocked, "I didn't get this. What does his health have to do with my upcoming marriage?"

Eulisses responded calmly, "Everything in this life is connected to each other in some way or another. Therefore, a human being can slow down any process by performing a specific action. You asked if there was any way for your father to find relief from his pain, so I have told you that your marriage will be the catalyst for his suffering to come to an end."

After listening to him, Karl fell into deep thought. Eulisses continued to examine his face, attempting to decipher his thoughts by his expressions. Then he said to Karl, "I'm not the type of person who instructs people what to do and I never give them advice. I solely inform them that if they do this, this will happen. If they don't want it to happen just don't do it."

After some time, Karl said, "Whatever I have witnessed in the last few days has completely destroyed my faith in marriage. The marriages of both of my sisters have failed. That is why I doubt I will have the courage to get married."

Eulisses said, "Anything lacking a solid foundation will not last long. Most marriages are based on money or sex."

Karl inquired, "Then which marriage will last until the end? What kind of foundation is required to make it last longer."

"That's what I am going to tell you," Eulisses said. "A person can fall in love with anyone. Nobody can prevent him from doing so. Furthermore, a person is free to have sex with anyone he desires. If it happens between two strangers then it is much appreciated by nature. However, marriage is an entirely different matter. It is ridiculous to associate these things with marriage. It is important that you select the ideal mate for marriage, who has been created specifically for you. You will not succeed in marriage unless you are with that person. This assurance will not be available to anyone else. I can say with certainty that even while a lot of marriages end in success, the fulfilment that comes from being with the perfect partner is not always achieved. And I must tell you that not everyone is made for marriage, only a select few are, and if they are wise enough, they will find the appropriate companion."

Karl asked, "So how can anyone find that perfect mate? It looks like an unachievable task."

Eulisses looked him in the eyes and said, "Listen carefully. If you follow the path shown by me, whatever you have seen happening around you that has upset your mind will never happen to you. Your life will be full of delight. Perhaps you heard about this from someone before coming to me."

Karl bowed and replied, "You are absolutely correct, sir. Tell me what you'd like to say."

Eulisses took a deep breath and said, "So listen, kid, two people who are made for each other are born on this planet on the same day and at the same time. So, if you're considering getting married, try to find a girl whose birthday and birth time are exactly the same as yours. She might be anywhere in the world. You can't quite comprehend what marriage entails unless you wed that girl."

Karl remained stunned as he stared at him. He'd never read or heard something so profound and perilous before. His subconscious was attesting to the fact that it was accurate.

He appeared to be utterly mesmerized. He was staring at Eulisses without saying anything.

Eulisses continued, "The enigmas of nature are limitless. It contains numerous deep secrets. Some people divulge these secrets through their amazing intelligence. Nature rewards them for their work. However, it forbids them from disclosing the secret to anybody else. Considering your circumstances, I have exposed a grave secret to you. Keep in mind the outcome that is going to occur. You have to understand that nature will do everything it can to prevent you from making the right decision. You may have to face a situation that shocks your mind, and you may not be able to dare to continue on this right path. Keeping everything in mind, continuing forward on that path will require a great deal of courage. Therefore, I urge that you begin this task only if you have the strength to finish it. Nothing will be accomplished if you abandon it halfway through. Let me also assure you that whoever nature created for you has the most pure intellect. She possesses celestial attributes and is a marvel of nature."

Karl was lost in thought. He sat still for a long period of time, like a statue. Ricardo sensed that the cult leader had finished speaking and that it was time for them to stand up and leave. He tapped the hand of Karl sitting next to him and

Karl glanced at him. Ricardo indicated that they should both leave now. Karl gave a nod in approval and turned to Eulisses, saying, "If we want to meet you again, can we come here?"

Eulisses smiled and said, "Visitors are not permitted to see me twice. You will have to join the cult in order to do so. If the visitor sees me for the second time, he does not recognize me."

Karl's thinking became muddled once more after hearing his remarks. He lacked the fortitude to take any more shocks at this point.

Then they both stood up. After greeting the cult leader, they both left the cabin.

They were discussing late at night after dinner at Ricardo's house. "Buddy, the man's remarks have shaken my entire existence," Karl said to Ricardo. "I've never seen a more dangerous man."

Ricardo laughed and asked, "Did you find the answer to the questions for which you have traveled so far?"

Karl remarked, "I got it to a large extent, bro. However, there is also a task. I've just begun to sense that I ought to find a life partner. I should find the right partner and watch how my life unfolds."

"I believe that leader's words have had a profound effect on your hearts and minds," Ricardo remarked.

Karl said, "You're right, buddy. Tell me now will you help me with this other task as well? These days, aren't you incredibly busy?"

Ricardo stated, "Don't be concerned about me. I am free throughout the entire week. How many days of leave have you taken?"

"It's Tuesday today. After four days off, the weekend comes. I have the entire week as well."

Ricardo asked, "So, tell me, what do you want to do, buddy?"

Karl said, "Bro, in order to locate the girl whose birthday and birth time match with mine, we must first gather the birth data of the United States."

Ricardo considered for a while. Then he asked, "But that girl could have been born in any country in the world," he then questioned. "The data of the entire world cannot be arranged by us."

Karl answered, "Yes, this is definitely possible. However, we can begin from the United States. If we can't locate that girl here, we'll think about the next move later. Is there someone in your network who can organize and furnish us with that information?"

Ricardo paused for a moment and then responded, "I don't know anyone in the Bureau of Vital Statistics. Indeed, I do know a detective. He can certainly use some sort of method to extract this info. I'll speak to him early tomorrow morning."

The next morning, Ricardo called his detective friend and urged him to use his influence to collect the birth statistics of every state of the United States for a particular day from 'Vital Statistics.' The man readily agreed to complete his task. The Bureau only had statistics for the state of Texas. They downloaded the remaining states' data from the intranet and copied it onto the detective's thumb drive and that thumb drive arrived at Ricardo's place before dark. Ricardo saved the information on his computer. A list of all the state-by-state children born on that day across the nation was stored on that thumb drive. In the United States, 9986 babies were born on the day Karl was born. Following each child's name, the list included information on the baby's gender, parents' names, address, and birth time. Ricardo first accessed the state of California's statistics. He used a filter on the birth time column and then sorted it in ascending order. It was easy for him to find Karl's name. Following that, Ricardo continued to access the files of other states one by one, inputting the time according to the time zone of that state. However, the computer continued displaying 'No Results Found.' Both of them so far have seen data from around twenty states. Next, the Florida State file number appeared. Ricardo added three hours in Karl's birth time, typed the input into the search bar, and hit enter.

"One Result Found," flashed on the monitor. Their curiosity grew stronger. The moment he hit the enter key and saw the name appear on the monitor, Ricardo experienced a 440-volt electric jolt. He leapt from his seat and stood up. That name was—Luna Fawkes—Miami.

Karl had no idea about what had happened to Ricardo all of a sudden. "What's the matter, bro?" he asked. "Why did you become so upset after reading this girl's name? Do you know who is she?"

Ricardo attempted to respond to his question, but his throat went dry and his voice was unable to come out. He simply nodded yes.

Karl exclaimed joyfully, "This is a good thing, bro. We will no longer have any difficulty getting in touch with her."

Ricardo whispered tremblingly, "Bro. I don't think you'll be likely to marry her."

Karl inquired, "Why do you think so? Is she married already?"

"No dude. That isn't like that."

"So, what is the problem, dear? Tell me clearly."

Ricardo mustered the guts to say, "Actually, this girl is a porn star."

"What are you saying, Ricardo?" It seemed as if Karl had likewise received a powerful electric jolt. "How are you so sure of yourself? You may be surprised to learn that these porn stars never divulge their real names. They all enter the adult industry under pseudonyms. The actual name of Luna, whose films you may have seen, must be something different."

Ricardo took a deep breath and placed both hands on Karl's shoulders, saying, "Just try to understand what I'm saying, bro. Not only I've watched this girl's films, but I have worked with her in several films. I never told you I am also a porn star."

Karl was shocked even more this time. He smacked his right hand on his forehead and exclaimed, "Oh God, what else is yet to be heard?"

Ricardo took Karl's hand in his and pressed it, saying, "I'm sorry, brother, I kept my truth from you. But I had no idea fate would bring us to this juncture. If you have any negative thoughts about me, please eliminate them. We shall continue to be friends as before. I will attempt to collect as much birth data from different nations as possible. Then we'll find you the ideal match."

It was as if Karl hadn't heard him. He asked Ricardo, "Do you have any photographs of this girl?"

Ricardo's face revealed an astonished reaction. Then he said, "Yes, friend. On my computer, I have images of her. Would you like to see it?"

Ricardo showed Karl a picture of Luna after he nodded yes. Karl's eyes were charmed by Luna's exquisite beauty in that photograph. He asked, "Why did she need to choose this profession? She could have become a movie star or a supermodel if she wanted to."

"That's exactly what everyone says about her, buddy," Ricardo responded.

"So you're claiming she's your co-star? You've collaborated on a number of films together."

"That is correct, dude. I was also cast in her debut film alongside her. You met this cult leader just because of the director who cast us together."

"Dude, this is all really puzzling. I'm feeling dizzy now. Tell me, when the first sex scene was shot between you, was she a virgin at that time?"

"No, dude. She had a lover at the time, but I can't recall his name. He broke up with her immediately when he learned that she had worked in a pornographic film. She became extremely upset as a result. She used to cry while having a phone conversation with me. But with time, she forgot about him as she got engrossed with her career. However, it took her a long time to recover from that shock. She never let another man into her life after that."

Karl remained attentive to what he said. After that, he remarked, "Do you remember what that cult leader had said that nature will make every effort to keep me from making the right decision? I might have to face a situation that will completely shake my confidence, and I might not be able to continue on this path. Is this not the circumstance he forewarned us about?"

Ricardo was surprised by what he said. He'd never considered it before. He paused briefly before saying softly, "If you have no objections to her profession, then I can guarantee you one thing, dude. You won't find a more sincere girl than her anywhere in the world."

Karl was lost in thought. He sat motionless for ten minutes. Then he informed Ricardo, "I've made up my mind, bro. I shall continue on this path. I can't go back now. Let's see what impact this marriage will have on my life. Even if I do not receive anything else, I will gain experience."

Ricardo patted him on the back as if admiring him on his courageous decision.

Then Karl said, "But I'm not sure if that girl will accept my proposal or not."

Ricardo laughed and said, "Don't worry about it, friend. I have already laid the foundations for this task over ten years ago. You consider your work accomplished. We shall go to bed now. We'll make further plans in the morning."

***

On Thursday morning, Karl approached Ricardo with the request to watch some videos of Luna. Ricardo brought six DVDs of Luna from a video parlor on the corner of the street. Karl maintained a close eye on her performance. His expression showed that he was awestruck by Luna's beauty and talent.

Ricardo explained his plan to Karl over lunch in the afternoon. This went something like this, Karl would first return to San Diego and resign from his job. After that, he would enroll in a one-month course on photography and videography. Ricardo would then utilize his connections to find Karl a job as a cameraman in a Miami-based production company. For this purpose, they chose the company that used to cast Luna in the majority of her films. When they had gotten to know each other well, Karl would propose to Luna for marriage. Ricardo informed Karl that they were not going to disclose to Luna that they both knew each other. When Karl proposed to her, Luna would consult with only two people. One was her mother, and the other was Ricardo. They couldn't tell her mother's opinion but Ricardo would definitely ask her to accept the marriage proposal. And there's a better chance she would agree. Finally, Ricardo advised Karl that when proposing to Luna, he needed to say exactly what Ricardo would tell him.

Karl then went to San Diego the next day, on Friday, to work on the plan. He went to the office on Monday morning and tendered his resignation, and the next day, he enrolled in a photography course. For a month, he worked hard to learn the job. In the meantime, he kept calling Ricardo. A month after completing the training, Ricardo informed him that his new job had been confirmed. He should arrive in Miami in three days with his stuff. Ricardo will be waiting for him there. Karl informed his elder brother that his parents would need to move in with him since he would have to move to Miami for a new job. Karl's brother agreed and two days later, he sent his parents to his brother's place and boarded a flight to Miami the next day.

When he got out of the airport at midday, he called Ricardo instantly. Ricardo's cell phone was busy. After a while, he gave it another go, but it was once again busy. Five minutes later, he received an SMS from Ricardo in which he provided an address and stated that he was now engaged in some extremely important business and would meet him in the evening. Additionally, he instructed Karl to hail a cab as soon as possible, get to the location he had given, and give them Ricardo's reference. Those people are expecting him. Karl sat in the taxi and arrived at the address provided by Ricardo. It was an apartment, and there were filming preparations underway. There were about 9–10 crew members present. No one paid attention to him because everyone was too busy arranging things quickly. Karl approached the overweight man seated in the director's chair and introduced himself along with Ricardo's reference.

With a smile, the man greeted him and informed him that the shooting would begin in thirty minutes. They anticipated greater work from him. Karl promised not to disappoint them. A boy then offered him a mug of coffee. Karl sat on an empty chair, wondering whether Luna would show up for today's shooting. He had noted that the entire crew consisted of guys. There was no woman present.

It would have been quite uncomfortable for a female model to perform in front of so many males on such an occasion. It should be extremely difficult for her to manage. While he was sipping his coffee engrossed in this confusion, two boys, in their early twenties walked into the room. The director greeted them warmly. Karl knew they were both performers the moment he laid eyes on them. He began to wonder if today these two were going to have sex with Luna or some other model. His mind was racing with questions, but he sat perfectly still. When the set was ready after ten minutes, the director asked Karl to take his position behind the camera.

Till now no girl had arrived on the set. Both male models were sitting on the bed in their underwear. Karl was excited with anticipation to see which girl would walk into the room. He switched on the camera and as soon as the director called 'Action' and was shocked to witness what happened there. Both of those models began kissing one another. Karl's jaw dropped open. Both models put their hands into each other's underwear. Karl realized that gay porn was being filmed there. In his thoughts, he began abusing Ricardo. When he took his phone from his pocket to call him, he heard the director say, "Cut." The director then turned to him and stated, "You have to shoot this scene with a camera, you motherfucker, not with your phone." Karl was humiliated and apologized to the director. He subsequently put the phone in his pocket. The scene resumed, and Karl continued to record it all. He sighed with relief as the scene was finished in half an hour. The director then asked him to return to the same location at 11:00 a.m. the next day so that the remaining shooting could be completed. Karl said her goodbye and left. In a rage, he clenched his fists. Upon encountering Ricardo, the first thing he was going to do was punch him hard in the face.

He spent the entire day wandering here and there. He thoroughly liked that city. He'd arrived here for the first time in his life. Everyone appeared to be in a good mood. The atmosphere was upbeat and enjoyable. Perhaps this was why, after wandering around for a few hours, his rage at Ricardo had subsided a little. He thought that when he met Ricardo, he would not punch him but would definitely abuse him. However, Ricardo was not answering the phone. Around 5:30, he received a call on his cell phone from Ricardo. When Karl answered the phone, Ricardo explained that he had been shooting all day and was only now free. He texted Karl the location of a coffee shop and asked him to come there right now. As soon as Karl got there, Ricardo was already waiting for him at a table. As soon as Karl sat on the chair in front of him, he poured out all the foul language he could muster on Ricardo. Ricardo kept on smiling.

Then Karl asked, "Motherfucker, where have you sent me? Do you have any idea what those people were up to? And you were absent for the whole day."

Ricardo burst out laughing and exclaimed, "Buddy, I told you I was shooting all day. That is why I was unable to answer your phone."

"You were having fun, and you were aware of what was going on with me," Karl was yelling in rage.

"Calm down, bro," said Ricardo. "Allow me to explain everything. Do you recall that it was part of our plan not to let Luna know that we knew each other?"

"So?" Karl asked.

"So, if I had gotten you a job immediately in that production house, Luna would have learned about our friendship because she has a deep friendship with the producer-director of that house. She would undoubtedly inform her that the new cameraman was hired on the recommendation of Ricardo. And our secret would have been revealed."

Karl agreed with what he explained. Ricardo continued, "That's why I got you a job in another production house. Those people only make gay movies. You collaborate with them for a few weeks. After that, you should independently run into the producer, and she will hire you."

"What makes you so certain of this?" Karl inquired.

"She has discussed it with me. At present, a cameraman in their team wishes to leave his job, and they have somehow persuaded him to stay on until they find a replacement. She has asked me to find her an experienced cameraman. But I'll not do it for her. You will go to her on your own."

Karl's rage had subsided totally. He had grasped Ricardo's strategy. "Let's spend the night in my hotel room," Ricardo offered. "Tomorrow, we'll locate an accommodation for you. After that, I'll head back to Houston. I need to go to bed early today. I'm exhausted. Your future wife has squeezed me badly today."

Karl's rage flared up once more. He shouted, "You were having a good time with Luna, motherfucker. I was waiting for her on the set of those fags, and she was having fun with you."

Ricardo burst into laughter. Then he said, "Now get used to it, brother. There will be several occasions when you will shoot my videos with your wife."

The next day, Ricardo found an apartment for Karl to rent and returned to Houston. As he was leaving, he promised Karl that he would contact him to let him know when it would be appropriate to apply for a job at the new production company.

***

The next five weeks were the most challenging of Karl's life. The man, who had never seen boy-girl porn before, was compelled to shoot gay porn. That production house's crew also acted suspiciously. He had a strong impression that the crew was glancing at her hips the entire time. As a result, he frequently became irritated. He had to shoot that content three or four days a week. Many models approached him and asked for his phone number, but he always declined. He was aware of their intentions. It became too much one day. The producer asked him to sit close to him and said, "Look, young man, your work is wonderful. You do your job with complete dedication. However, a cameraman is paid less than others. You can earn four times more if you want to. You have a nice appearance. It is beneficial for you to pursue a career in modelling. Our videos are in high demand in a large community. If you opt for it, you can achieve fame."

Karl wanted to punch that producer in the face. But he kept his cool and responded quietly, "Okay, sir, I'll think about it."

The producer patted his shoulder and said, "Please inform me of your decision as soon as possible." Karl stood up and walked away. It was now difficult for him to devote even a single day to this job. Then, on the same night, he received a phone call from Ricardo, for which he had been waiting for two weeks.

Ricardo instructed him to see Rita Montenegro at the 'Heat n Lust' studio in South Miami tomorrow morning to discuss his job. That is his final destination. Karl breathed a sigh of relief at hearing this. He appeared to be writhing in some prison for the last six weeks. However, he knew deep inside that nature would do everything it could to keep him from achieving his destination. He realized it was nature's conspiracy to have him spend six months performing such work in order to destroy his morale and cause him to flee, leaving the work unfinished. His perspective on life changed significantly after meeting that cult leader. He was no longer readily distracted.

Rita was also intrigued by his calm demeanor. He was sitting in front of her in her office around 11:00 a.m. Karl noticed posters of Luna Fawx's movies on the walls of Rita's office. Rita interviewed him for a few minutes. Karl honestly answered most of her questions. He only lied in response to one question. When Rita questioned why he quit his previous job, Karl explained that the pay was inadequate. Then Rita explained, "Today we are not shooting any scenes. Tomorrow, you must arrive at the studio at this hour. The next three days will be spent shooting continuously."

Karl shook her hand and walked out. He called his producer in the evening and informed him he was unable to continue with them. When the producer inquired about the reason, he replied, "I had accepted the advice you had given me. I want to be a model, but I have signed a contract with another studio." Karl then hung up before hearing his response.

He arrived at Rita's studio on schedule the next day. In the studio, there was a black model. As soon as Karl saw her, he knew that Luna would not be coming today. A bondage scene involving a white male was to be shot with that model for roughly 80 minutes. Karl performed an excellent job. Rita was quite pleased with his work.

Karl's second day was likewise filled with disappointment. On this day, a sex scene featuring an Asian female and an African man was scheduled, and it was also a bondage scene along the lines of the first day.

Following the completion of the scene, Karl recorded an interview of both models at Rita's request. The final scene of that film was to be shot on the third day. Karl was hoping that he would get to see Luna today. He was cleaning his camera lens on the set. Then a 25-year-old guy entered. Karl was surprised. He was a gay model, and Karl had recently shot three scenes of him. Karl was unable to figure out why he had come there. The guy said hello to everyone and shook hands with Karl. Then he questioned Karl, "Do you work here now?"

Karl informed him that he had recently joined this production company. The guy then turned to Rita and pointed toward Karl, saying, "We've both worked together before." Rita smiled. The guy then said, "Has Miss Fawx arrived?"

Rita said, "Not yet. She'll be here in ten minutes." After hearing these words, Karl's happiness knew no bounds. It seemed as though he was intoxicated. After ten minutes, the intoxication was amplified when Luna appeared on the set with a gleaming figure in a black dress and a radiant smile on her face. Everyone greeted her warmly. Karl continued to stare at her with wide eyes. But Luna had missed the fact that there was a new face present that day. That basic question which was even more surprising had slipped Karl's mind from the moment he heard her name until she arrived. The question was what was a gay model doing there that day? But, as time passed, Karl figured out the answer on his own. The final scene of that movie, which was supposed to be filmed on Luna and that model, Luna had to fuck that gay model wearing a strap-on dildo.

Karl continued to take very precise shots once the scene started. Luna wore a leather outfit that covered most of her upper body. The bottom half was uncovered. Her hands were gloved with latex. That gay model laid out naked on a wooden table. Luna had used a rope to tie up his hands and feet. She then sat on his face. The model writhed restlessly or pretended to writhe. After a while, Luna moved away from his face and began to suck his genitals. In addition, she spat on his genitals. Karl was quite thrilled with her performance. She truly was an extremely bold lady.

When she put that strap-on dildo and slid it inside the model's ass, Karl began to think seriously. He assumed that this was his first encounter with Luna and that if he witnessed something like this it just meant that nature wanted to convey him a message that after marriage, Luna was going to fuck him like this for the rest of his life. He reasoned in his mind that even if something worse happened, he wouldn't change his decision. The scene was finished after an hour of tormenting that model. After removing the outfit, Luna changed into her regular clothes and hurriedly said goodbye to everyone before leaving. Perhaps she needed to go to another place. Karl was shocked to find that Luna had ignored him. Karl became nervous. He had hoped to meet and get to know that lovely woman further today, but he was never given the chance to do so. Luna didn't even give him a glance. He was well aware that Luna was a very popular adult star with a busy schedule. She'd have to do more than one shoot in a single day. And how will he find the time in her hectic schedule to express his feelings to her? He consoled himself by reminding him that there would be plenty more opportunities in the future. Ricardo also told him that he had nothing to be concerned about as he had a flawless plan in place to complete the task. If everything had gone according to plan till now, it would undoubtedly continue to do so in the future.

***

Rita had planned a small evening party at her place on the same weekend. She had invited her friends, as well as some special guests from the adult industry and members of her crew. Karl was also among the guests, and Luna was also present there. She looked stunning in a purple backless dress. She was sitting on the couch with Rita, the party's hostess. When Rita noticed Karl, she called him to sit alongside her. As soon as he approached her, Rita introduced Karl to Luna and informed her that he had recently joined them. Luna shook Karl's hand and said, "Nice to meet you." As soon as their gazes locked, it was as if time stood still. Luna also felt that Karl's personality had a certain allure that she couldn't resist. The party went on till midnight. Both of them kept drinking and meeting new people while discreetly staring at each other.

The next morning, Karl called Ricardo and told him that Rita had introduced him to Luna the night before. Ricardo expressed his happiness and informed her that he needed to propose to her as soon as possible. And at that point, note down what you need to say to her. Karl took up a pen and paper and jotted down what Ricardo said.

Rita left for a ten-day trip to Europe the next week. Karl flew to San Diego to see his family as he was free these days as well. Rita had returned by the time he got back. Rita used to produce and direct movies under her own banner, but back then, the owners of an adult website sent her a proposal. They wanted Rita to direct a black gangbang scene for their website. In the scene, Luna was signed against three black models. Rita accepted their proposal.

The shooting was scheduled four days later. The founders of that website were extremely wealthy and had multiple properties throughout America. The shooting was to take place in one of their South Miami villas. Rita had brought only Karl along with her. As soon as they arrived, they noticed Luna was already there. When Karl's gaze met Luna's, her eyes sparkled and a naughty smile appeared on her face. Karl knew that the girl had started liking him.

The three black models had arrived on site as well. As soon as everyone exited the makeup room, Rita sat in the director's chair and Karl set up his camera. Following that, the game of love began. Luna appeared to be brimming with vitality. She was expertly having sex with all three of them. Karl began to assume that, despite the fact that he has watched only this woman's porn videos he can confidently state that no one else in the entire world will have such incredible skills. In that 70-minute action, Luna never let those black dicks feel the slightest sense of loneliness for a single second. Those three dicks stayed in her mouth, in her hands, in her pussy, or in her asshole the entire time.

Luna eventually got down on her knees and all three of them poured sperm on her face. Luna then licked each of the three dicks one by one. She rose up from her seat as soon as the director said, "Cut," and began seeking the towel by twisting her head here and there. But everyone in the room at the moment was engrossed and immersed in the spectacle, and no one thought of handing the towel to Luna.

When Luna moved toward the makeup room, Karl quickly shifted the camera to the side and practically sprinted after her. As soon as he stepped inside, he asked the makeup artist to move out for a while. Since the makeup artist didn't recognize him, she asked, "Who are you?" Karl replied that he would tell everything later. Then he grabbed her arm and pushed her out of the room, closing the door from the inside. The makeup artist stared at the closed door, stunned.

Luna stood there entirely naked, watching everything. Her face was in a weird state. Her hair and face were splattered with sperm. One of her eyelash extensions was dangling halfway down. In a surprised tone, she asked Karl, "What's the matter? Is there anything else to shoot?"

Karl ignored her question and knelt on his knee. Then he took Luna's left hand in both of his and murmured, "I fell in love with you at first sight. Will you marry me?"

Luna's mouth opened wide when she heard his remarks. She yanked his hand away and asked, "Do you even know what you're saying? Why do you want to marry me when I had just fucked three males in front of you?"

Karl stood up and held Luna's hand once more. Looking her in the eyes, he continued, "No one knows what his partner is up to behind his back. At the very least, I am aware of what you do. Your body can be shared with anyone, but your heart will always belong to me. My love is sincere, and I want you in your originality. I accept you exactly as you are. You are perfect the way you are."

His words appeared to cast a spell on Luna. She instantly said yes to Karl. She also hugged him at the same time. Karl felt as if he had entered a different universe after receiving her embrace. Then he fled the makeup room and returned to sit next to Rita. Rita indicated the sperm marks on his T-shirt. Karl smiled and winked in response.

Karl called Ricardo late at night and said, "Dude, your words did magic. She agreed."

Ricardo couldn't believe what he had heard. The girl who sought Ricardo's advice on every minor issue made such an important decision on her own. He said, "Dude, you must have had some sort of misunderstanding."

"No, it's not the case, bro. I asked her straight, and she immediately said yes," Karl replied.

Ricardo was overwhelmed with happiness as well as jealousy for his friend. He congratulated Karl and promised to meet him shortly.

Ricardo didn't sleep through the night. He continued to walk here and there. He had a feeling that even though Luna had not consulted him beforehand, she would call him and tell him about this. But the night passed without receiving any call from her. He called Rita in the morning and inquired about her well-being. Rita informed him that Luna was getting married.

Ricardo became even more bewildered. What could have happened if Luna had spoken to Rita about her decision but not him? He was agitated throughout the day. In the evening, he called Luna. Luna was at home at that time. Hearing Ricardo's voice, she said, "I have some good news for you."

Ricardo said, "Luna, the news that I should have received from you first, I have got it from other people. You've changed drastically."

Luna said, "It's not like that, Ricardo, everything happened really fast. I was high on cocaine at the time. I need drugs to perform better when I shoot stuff with multiple dudes. The same thing happened yesterday. Karl proposed to me just after the shoot when I was flooded with emotions. I couldn't say no to him. I realize I should have asked for some time to consult with you. This, however, skipped from my mind. I sincerely apologize. I should have informed you. He's a really wonderful guy. You reach here as soon as possible. I would like to introduce you to him. Also, we're getting married soon."

After listening to her, Ricardo's rage eased slightly. He stated, "I'll be in Miami tomorrow, Luna."

He then disconnected the phone.

When Luna told Dakota about her decision, she burst into tears. She embraced her daughter. Luna did not inform anyone in the industry about this except her closest friends. They made the decision to keep the wedding ceremony small.

***

The same year, on 29 September 2010, Wednesday was selected for Luna and Karl's wedding. Because there was very little time left for the wedding, everyone began preparing for it with full enthusiasm. Luna, along with her mother and Rita, compiled the guest list. There was a thorough discussion about the budget. Karl called his brother to inform him that he was getting married and asked him to come to Miami to attend the wedding, but his brother expressed his inability to come due to his tight schedule. As a result, the only person Karl knew who was going to attend his wedding was Ricardo. In the view of others, he, too, was a stranger to him. When Karl asked about where they should go for their honeymoon, Luna recommended that they should go to Spain.

Then the day arrived for them to tie the knot at Miami's Trinity Church. Luna looked like an angel in her white satin wedding gown. Everyone who saw them believed that they were made for each other. A week after their wedding, they went to Spain for three weeks on honeymoon.

For the first time, Luna had ventured out on a journey with someone. She had always traveled alone until now. And Karl has only done bike tours till the moment.

On the fourth day of their honeymoon, at the entrance to Carrero de les Bruixes, commonly known as the Alley of Witches, in Cervera, 60 miles from Barcelona, a photographer approached them and asked if he may click their picture. Luna refused, claiming she had her own digital camera. The printed photo is of no use to them. However, Karl said that he would mail that photograph to his house because he does not have a computer at home. His family will be pleased to see their photograph. The photographer clicked their picture, handed them his business card and added that they may pick up their photograph from his studio after three hours.

Both of them got the photograph from the studio in the evening. The photograph was stunning. Behind them, the entrance board of that place was clearly apparent. Before leaving the place the next morning, Karl posted that picture to his home address.

Luna and Karl made the most of their three-week honeymoon. They traveled throughout Spain. They traveled via Barcelona to view the colorful shores of Costa Galicia and the white sand beaches of Ibiza. Luna's outspoken personality left a lasting impression on Karl. All of the people he met in the adult industry after joining Rita's company as a cameraman appeared very alive and honest to him. The world he came from was full of malice and deception. He was confident about Luna that she would never have lied in her entire life and would never be unfaithful to him. But there was still a doubt growing in his mind. That night, he mustered the courage to ask Luna if she was addicted to anal sex. Luna replied with a smile that there was no such thing. She indulges in anal sex only during the shooting. Since Matthew ended their relationship, she had only had on-screen relationships. Karl trusted her words wholeheartedly. Ricardo had given him the same information about her.

They were both wandering the streets of Madrid on the final days of their honeymoon. It was 6:30 in the evening. Luna, unlike other ladies, was not fascinated with indiscriminate shopping. Throughout the trip, she did virtually little shopping. This attribute of hers impressed Karl deeply. While they were walking, Luna's gaze was drawn to a Cartomancy Shop, where cards were used to tell people's fortune. Luna insisted that she wanted to go inside the shop. Karl agreed, and the two of them entered the shop. At the same time, 6,000 miles away, the doorbell rang at Karl's brother Luke's house. It was 9:30 in the morning. Luke was getting ready to leave for work. As he opened the door, the postman handed Luke a white envelope.

The illumination in that spiritual shop was exceedingly weak. A pleasant aroma was also present across the shop. Because there was carpet on the floor, they had both removed their shoes outside the shop. They noticed an elderly woman dressed in traditional attire sitting on the ground. In front of her was a six-inch-high wooden table on which tarot cards were placed. The woman smiled at them both, and they smiled in return. The woman then gestured for them both to take a seat in front of her.

They sat down silently. The woman took up the cards in front of her and asked Luna to choose three of them. Luna silently picked three cards from the deck and handed them to the woman. The woman placed the three cards on the table with face down.

Luke entered the house after receiving the envelope from the postman and opened it while sitting on the couch. An 8×10-inch color photo of his brother and his newlywed bride emerged from within. His face lit up with a smile the moment he saw that picture. He called his mother. When his mother arrived, he informed her that Karl had sent a photo of himself with his wife. Her mother saw the photo and remarked, "She's so gorgeous! Let us show this to your father."

The Cartomancer took the first among the three cards kept face down in front of her and while looking at it said to Luna, "You are the owner of a very balanced existence. There is absolutely no straying in your life. You are on the right path. Seldom does this happen to humans. Nature also aids you in your task. Your married life is full of joy."

Then she picked up the second card and informed Luna, "You will encounter a spirit in your life." Luna became tense after hearing her remarks. The woman noticed her horrified expression and remarked, "You don't have to be afraid. She'll come to you looking for a solution to her wanderings. She will have no intention of hurting you in any way."

Luna breathed a sigh of relief when she heard this.

After picking up the third card and studying it, she continued, "You have the most pure intellect. You are a natural wonder. You are an earthly angel. You will receive whatever you desire in your life. Some divine power is guarding you. There is no force that can damage you. The sheer thought of causing you damage will destroy your enemy. You were born on this planet for a specific purpose, which is now almost completed. Your arrival on this planet has saved many innocent lives." They both began to glance at one other in amazement after hearing that.

The woman then put her left palm in front of Luna's face and murmured, "Always be happy."

Luke and his mother cautiously opened his father's bedroom door. On the bed in front of them, supported by a pillow, sat Father Walter Davis. They both approached him and showed him the photo. Luke's mother pointed to Luna's photo and said to Walter Davis, "This is Karl's wife." Walter Davis suffered from a variety of health issues. He also had trouble speaking. Nobody could understand much of what he said. But his vision was intact. He grasped the photo with shaky hands and examined it closely. His eyes widened as he gazed at Luna's face. Then his focus was drawn to the board behind the picture, where 'Carrero de les Bruixes' was written. When he saw that board, he felt another great jolt and his entire body began to tremble with fear. That photograph slipped from his grasp.

His wife and son were terrified when they saw his condition. His wife shook his shoulder and asked, "What happened to you? Are you all right?"

But it appeared that Walter Davis did not pay attention to her. He began murmuring, "This woman is a witch. I encountered her a long time ago. Even today, she looks exactly the same. She has remained youthful throughout all these years."

It was completely beyond their comprehension what Walter was talking about. Luke put his ear closer to his father's mouth in an attempt to listen. Walter began shedding tears from his eyes. He continued to murmur, "She had uttered the name of Jesus with her unholy mouth. She's got my son in her grasp. She's taken him to her house. One day, she will devour him. Dear Lord, please save my son from this witch."

Subsequently, his eyes closed and his neck tilted to one side. His life had vanished.

***

Epilogue

Spring had finally arrived in Houston. The days had become quite clear. Each day, the temperature rose slightly. There were occasionally two or three white clouds drifting in the glass-clear sky. The constant flow of traffic on the congested highways started to act like a drunken elephant. One afternoon, in the renowned Lake Club of the city, there was a lot of activity. There were people with smiling faces. It appeared that the weather had an effect on them as well. The sound of cheers and laughter could be heard from all directions.

A stunning blue-eyed lady in her late twenties dressed in a yellow corset dress walked into the club. Her face bore a look of profound grief. Even spring was unable to have an effect on her. She used to come here frequently to eat. It was one of her favorite spots in town. She was well-known among the staff here. She had never seen such a large throng here before. Her preferred table had already been occupied. She would have made reservations earlier if she had known there would be such a large crowd here today. While she was standing still and contemplating all of this, a waiter abruptly approached her and said, "Good afternoon, madam. You will have to wait for a while. Right now, the hall is full."

She responded with a smile. The waiter moved forward. She was undecided as to whether it would be better to wait or move to a different place to eat. However, the dish she wanted to have today was the most delectable prepared here. She chose to hold off.

Suddenly, her gaze was drawn to a different-looking man seated in a corner. He was seated alone at the table intended for two. He was dressed in a sky-blue shirt with glasses on his eyes. He had a laptop on the table in front of him and was obliviously typing something. The lady approached the man slowly, who was in his mid-thirties.

"Excuse me, sir," the lady turned to the man and asked, "are you waiting for someone?"

Raising his head, he smiled at the lady and added, "No, ma'am. I came here by myself."

"If you don't mind, can I share the table with you?" The lady hesitantly questioned.

"I'm fine with it. You are welcome to sit here," he said.

"What I intended to ask was whether you were working, will my sitting here create any hindrance in your work?"

"This won't happen at all. You can sit here comfortably."

After thanking him, the lady took a seat in front of him. The man started working on his laptop again.

"Have you ordered any food?" The lady inquired.

"No, not yet. I was stumped as to what to order. Could you please aid me in this?"

"I would be delighted to. By the way, Pollo Asado is a specialty of the house. That's what I'm going to order."

"If I'm not mistaken, it's the Spanish word for roast chicken."

"You are absolutely correct."

"So let's eat the food of your choice today."

The lady beckoned the waiter to her and placed her order for Pollo Asado, Pico De Gallo (fresh salsa) and Sauvignon Blanc.

The lady then began sipping water from the glass and the man got busy typing something in his laptop. After about two minutes of silence, the woman attempted to start a conversation by saying, "By the way, my name is…"

Before she could complete her sentence, the man gestured with his hand and stopped her from speaking. The lady thought that she might have disturbed him. She started feeling guilty and kept silent for some time. After continuing to type for ten minutes, he shut down his laptop and placed it in the bag that was resting on the side of the chair. The waiter served their order during this time. Seeing wine and food, their eyes sparkled. The lady opened the bottle of wine and poured it into both the glasses. Both got busy eating food without delay. While eating, the lady questioned, "Were you doing office work?"

"No. I was working on my upcoming book."

"So, you're a writer?" the surprised lady enquired.

"Yes, of course."

"So, may I get your name? Maybe I've read one of your works."

He expressed his helplessness and apologized, "Sorry, but that will not be possible for me."

"But why is this so?"

"I mean that I don't publish my books under my own name. I prefer to remain anonymous."

"Have you kept a pen name of your own? But why do you do that? Don't you like being famous?"

"You've asked three questions all at once." He chuckled.

"You are not required to answer these questions if you find them challenging."

"There is nothing challenging for a writer. I attempt to respond to each one separately."

The lady smiled and sipped her wine.

"But promise me that you won't be sad after hearing the answers to your questions."

"Mister, at this point in my life, I have reached the pinnacle of sadness. There is nothing beyond that."

"Is that so? So pay attention. Your initial query was, 'Have you kept a pen name of your own?' So, the answer is 'Yes.' I use a pen name. However, the book I'm currently writing does not go by that name. It will be published under the actual name of someone. I intend to have my book published in the name of the woman I loved. She left this world ten years ago only as a result of an incurable illness. She passed away at the age of 24."

That lady was genuinely shocked. She became speechless as she looked at that man. Listening to him, it appeared like she had lost the sense of taste in the food.

"I'm really sorry," she added in a hushed voice. "What happened to her?"

"When we are not naming anything here, it would not be appropriate to name the disease."

"I resurrected your bad memories," she said, "I apologize."

"It's not a memory I'll ever forget. I've always lived with it. Please don't blame yourself. I was madly in love with her. She was stunningly attractive and extremely intelligent. She was also a wild woman. I lacked any redeeming qualities. Still, she chose me. If she had been alive, she would have been famous all over the world. But now no one knows her. And here comes the answer to your second question, Why am I doing this? My talent is because of her. I was absolutely broken after she departed. Then a writer emerged from within me. I've made a lot of money writing books over the years. But no one knows who she was who awakened the writer in me. That's why I made the decision to publish a book under her name. This will serve as my sincere ode to her. For this task, it is crucial for me to maintain my anonymity. I hope you don't feel bad."

"This is not fair," the lady muttered in a resentful tone. "How would it be feasible to continue the conversation with you in this manner?"

"It is certainly feasible," he remarked with a smile. "Even I'm not going to ask you your name. Let it be a meeting of two total strangers."

With a pretty smile, she blinked her eyes and agreed to play the game. Then she asked him, "Has there never been another woman in your life in all these years?"

"Numerous ladies entered my life after she left. But I couldn't plunge into such depths of love with anyone. That's why no relationship ever lasted."

Hearing this, that lady also got lost in some thoughts. Perhaps this had refreshed some old memory for her too. The man drew her attention toward the food and said that they should not get entangled in things and let the food cool down. She smiled and started eating again. That man again said, "Your third question was whether I do not like to become famous?"

The lady smiled and asked, "Do you really dislike being famous? People are obsessed with fame."

"Being famous isn't all awful. However, it is extremely detrimental to my profession."

"But why?"

"Consider it this way. A writer is an artist. He has a flame inside of it. He has to maintain this spark. That light is extinguished by fame. The only way to keep that flame alive is to maintain your anonymity. There isn't another option. I can think of scores of authors whose debut works were masterpieces because no one had ever heard of them before. They were unidentified. But once their fame peaked, the flame inside them died. After that, every book they wrote was a rehash. There was nothing new to say. All of the other artists like singers, dancers, actors and musicians have no option to work in anonymity. Only a writer is able to accomplish his work while remaining anonymous. In summary, we may say that fame is to an artist what light is to a vampire."

The lady was taken astonished by his words. "I never thought like this," she remarked. "Does this really happen?"

"Yes, of course. This is what happens."

"Could you tell me how you found out about this?"

"An English poet has talked about this. Man acquires the art of living only in solitude." He drank a sip of wine and then said, "And, in my opinion, the goal of everyone on this planet is to create something. When you want to create something, that thing needs complete privacy. Writing a story is like giving birth. Just as a child grows in a mother's womb, so does an idea grow in the mind of a writer. And he will feel uneasy until he puts that concept on paper in the shape of a story. He feels the same enormous satisfaction after writing a narrative that a mother does after giving birth to a child."

"You seem to be quite uneasy, too. Is the cause of this likewise what you just explained?

"That's right. But I believe the time is approaching when I, too, will be joyous."

They both laughed.

The man was suddenly silent for a little while and his focus was diverted from the lady's face sitting in front of him to someone else in the restaurant hall. A young couple had just walked into the hall and was looking for a seat. The man's gaze was drawn to the couple. That lady didn't believe it was appropriate to turn around. She continued to sit where she had been. She received the impression that someone who knew the man seated in front of him might have arrived. Then, after a little while, he turned to gaze at that lady once more, and she continued speaking.

"I have met many eminent artists in my life, the majority of whom are film actors or singers," the lady told him. "I'd never met a writer before. I found writers to be really peculiar. I learned today that they are also quite fascinating. In this crowd, your face seemed to be looking different. Is it typical for the writers to maintain this level of anonymity and withhold their identities from the public?"

"Yes, of course. There have been innumerable such writers. There are several such publications whose writers are only known by their pen names. Nothing else is known about them. Their real names are not used in these publications. These writers' thinking is of the highest caliber. Ordinary folks will never think like them."

The man replenished the lady's empty wine glass and received a 'thanks' from her. He continued, saying, "I've opened a chapter of my life in front of you.

You can now choose to open your heart as well. Why did you claim to have achieved the pinnacle of sadness?"

That lady's face exhibited some hesitation. He became aware of his predicament. "There is no compulsion," he declared. "It is not a problem if you choose not to disclose."

"Actually, there isn't anything like that. It is all about the relationship. You have a profound love for someone. However, for whatever reason once that relationship ends, you are unable to get to that point with a new partner. You are constantly looking for the same happiness, but you are unable to find it. Then you continue to suffocate on the inside. In any case, a woman cannot speak candidly. She wishes for her lover to comprehend her emotions. However, most men prioritize their own enjoyment."

"Are you saying that your partner prioritizes his own enjoyment?"

"No. It's not like that. He is fantastic; never goes against anything I want. He, however, never understood me."

"Look, a woman's personality is quite complex. She is not as transparent as a man. I realize that it is pointless to expect anything from men in many fields. If a solution can be found simply by speaking from the heart, it should be expressed."

"You know how hard it is for a woman."

"I've spent a lot of time with women. I understand that a lady rarely speaks her feelings. She wishes her lover to read her mind. Just tell me one thing, if there was ever a situation that was passing in front of you and was about to vanish in a matter of seconds, in which you could speak up and obtain what you wanted in life, would you still prefer to be quiet?"

"I'm afraid I can't say anything about it right now. It would be much easier to speak if you are drunk."

"However, when you're drunk, you can't recognize the situation."

They both laughed again.

"It was a joy speaking with you. I can tell your books must be incredibly excellent."

"One should only pick up a pen and start writing when they have solved life's mystery. Not prior to that."

Both of them had nearly finished their lunch. The lady looked around the hall. The hall was still full. There was a lot of bustle around. "At times, I have the impression that everyone in the world is seeking something. Every soul here is parched. Additionally, we're all stumbling around looking for something. It seems that this planet was only created for us humans to wander. When a person solves the mystery of life, does their wandering come to an end?" The lady questioned while gazing into his eyes.

He paused for a moment. The couple who had entered the hall some time ago spotted a vacant table, and they both proceeded in its direction. The man's gaze followed both of them until they took a seat. Then, glancing at them, he began to remark, "Certainly, a man's wandering cannot end until he finds his right destination. Some people believe they have arrived at their destination at some point in their lives, but this is not always the case. They consider a beautiful stop on the way as their destination. But their final destination still lies further ahead. Very few people are so fortunate that their wandering comes to an end," he smiled "everyone else's wanderings end with their life. There are many such unfortunate people whose wandering does not end even after the end of their life."

"This implies that the person will just keep wandering helplessly throughout his life. It's not feasible that his thirst will ever be quenched, right?"

"That is entirely feasible. The pious are cared for by nature. Nature makes fixing everything in their lives a top concern. You'd be shocked to learn that a person's non-living possessions might sometimes assist him in this work."

"What function can non-living entities fulfil?"

"Non-living entities are capable of doing things that we cannot even imagine. They have feelings as well as deep understanding. Sometimes their feelings get hurt unintentionally. The pride of that old piece of furniture lying in the house gets shattered when it thinks that being ancient, it is the most sturdy and resilient and would last a long time, but due to the new trend, it is replaced."

The lady sat silently listening to him. Her expression indicated that she was quite impressed to hear this. The man asked her, "Tell me, what is the one thing you have that you love the most?"

"There are so many things I love. I can't think of a single one."

"Still, something must have become a part of your personality. You can't imagine living without it."

"I do have such a thing. My father owned a vintage car. Since I was young, I have adored it. I also loved the color of it. My father was also aware of how much I cherished that vehicle. He didn't sell it for a long time. On my 25th birthday, I received it as a gift from my father. I own three more cars, all the latest models. But the same vintage car remains my preferred pick even today."

"If you're as attached to that car as you claim, let me tell you that the car must understand your emotions."

"I find this idea kind of weird."

"Yes, it's weird, but it's also true. You drive that car, and you take excellent care of it. As a result, it understands your emotions. Whether you believe it or not, it is aware of your thirst. And if nature so desires, the car will assist you in reaching your target. Take heed of what I've said. It will undoubtedly happen someday."

The lady appeared mesmerized as she listened to him. She was completely unaware of her surroundings. Suddenly, the voice of the waiter interrupted her trance. He was asking if they wanted to order something else. They both refused and asked for the check. The waiter picked up the plates from the table and took them away.

Then he came back after a little while with the check in his hands. The lady opened her purse but the man stopped her and paid the amount himself. The lady thanked him and stated that she would remember this meeting forever. He smiled and said that anything that happened between two strangers was always memorable. He too would never forget this meeting.

Their focus was abruptly diverted by the sound of cracking glass. They both turned their attention to the sound's source. A glass of wine had dropped from the hand of a young man seated at a table some distance away, which was the lady's favorite table at this restaurant and where she frequently sat. The young man was speaking with someone on the phone. He had an anxious expression on his face and was extremely tense. Perhaps he had received some bad news on the phone. Then a waiter rushed over and started picking up the shattered pieces of glass on the floor and placing them in a tray.

The lady then rose from her seat. She wished the author success with his book and walked away. She slowly exited the club. As soon as she arrived at the parking spot, a surprised expression spread across her face. She cast a bewildered glance around and shouted, "Oh my God. Where is my car?"

***